PRAISE FOR JEFF

"*The Contest* sports a fun story that does what my favorite crime novels do – transport me to an unfamiliar world and weave in a page-turning mystery. Jeff Macfee does not disappoint with this crackling debut."

Alex Segura, bestselling author of
Secret Identity *and* Alter Ego

"Jeff Macfee drops the reader into a hall of mirrors with no way out. A singular book."

Adam Oyebanji, author of A Quiet Teacher

"A brilliant page-turner about obsession, compromise, child prodigies, and second chances, all set in a world where Willy Wonka made escape rooms rather than chocolate bars, *The Contest* is my favorite thing I've read this year."

Peter Clines, New York Times Bestselling author of
The Broken Room *and* Paradox Bound

"Like Willy Wonka if it was written by Hitchcock... LOVE THE BOOK. Seriously, it is SO GOOD. "

Stephen Blackmoore, author of Dead Things

"A mystery wrapped inside a riddle inside an enigma, *The Contest* is a clever puzzle box of a book. An intrigue-filled, cerebral theme park provides the setting for an affecting tale about finding one's worth after defeat, and Macfee's storytelling instantly drew me in from the first page."

Victor Manibo, author of The Sleepless *and* Escape Velocity

Jeff Macfee

THE CONTEST

DATURA

DATURA BOOKS
An imprint of Watkins Media Ltd

Unit 11, Shepperton House
89-93 Shepperton Road
London N1 3DF
UK

daturabooks.com
twitter.com/daturabooks
What happens when you get everything you want?

A Datura Books paperback original, 2025

Edited by Gemma Creffield and Steve O'Gorman
Cover by Sneha Alexander
Set in Meridien

ISBN 978 1 91552 345 7
Ebook ISBN 978 1 91552 346 4

Printed and bound in the United Kingdom by CPI Group (UK) Ltd, Croydon CR0 4YY

9 8 7 6 5 4 3 2 1

MIX
Paper | Supporting
responsible forestry
FSC
www.fsc.org   FSC® C171272

For Karen

One
September 9, 2000
Gillian Charles, Age 12

A long white panel snapped into place, blocking the hall. From above, an image projected against the surface.

> *Four Contestants occupy a room.*
> *Tommy solves a maze.*
> *Ellsberg plays chess.*
> *Leah bedazzles a pair of jeans.*
> *What is Gillian doing?*

Gillian Charles read the riddle three times. The intricate braids her mother painstakingly constructed frayed and dangling in her face. Her green-and-black flannel full of holes, her bell-bottom jeans torn open at her bloodied knees. And she was barefoot, her Keds lost somewhere in the maze behind. Today appearances didn't matter. Not hers, anyway.

What is Gillian doing?

A moment of panic. The question asked more of her than she expected. Every decision she'd made in the Contest up to now – each riddle solved and puzzle cracked. Maybe she'd misinterpreted the answers? Mom always said she acted too fast, didn't think things through. Maybe she'd jumped down a rabbit hole to a dead end.

No. This was the Puzzle Man at his best. Sebastian, testing if Gillian would doubt herself. The answer was obvious.

"Playing chess with Ellsberg," she said.

The panel raised and she advanced.

Another panel blocked her way.

> *What goes through your neighborhood and past the airport and brought you here, yet never moves?*

"The road," she said.

> *Gillian faces south.*
> *Leah faces north.*
> *They can see each other without mirrors.*
> *How?*

"They're face to face."

More obstacles. Sign after sign.

"The letter M."

"The door with the lion."

"Pull out the plug."

The assault continued. Each question making Gillian stronger. Sharper.

More likely to win the Contest Extraordinaire.

The hallway became a scummy cast-iron pipe, the top a good six feet above Gillian's head. Water streamed from grated downspouts, rising almost to ankle height. She found herself not alone. Ahead sloshed a tow-headed spindly white boy, clad in a blazer, polo, and shorts, a purplish birthmark splotch visible through his thin hair. Mr Peanut brought to life.

Martin Ellsberg lived in a trailer park outside Mobile, Alabama, where his fussy appearance had earned him his fair share of bruises. But he was tough – despite the Contest's rigors, he'd managed to retain his leather Oxfords, the most ridiculous footwear Gillian could have imagined. He'd decoded his last puzzle a full three seconds before her. Underestimate Ells and his affected hint of a German accent and you'd find yourself wheeled out of the Contest on a gurney.

Still, with no sign of the other Contestants, Gillian relaxed. She was comfortably ahead, and could easily beat Ellsberg in a foot race. He startled as she ran up, but quickly regained his composure. They exchanged the secret handshake – Slap. Backslap. Elbows. Fistbump – then walked side-by-side down the tunnel.

"On that last puzzle," he said. "You should have been quicker up the ladder."

"You took the ladder? Interesting."

He frowned. "What did you do?"

Gillian didn't answer. She pulled loose peanut M&Ms from her pocket. She'd never eaten the peanut ones until the Contest. Until Tommy. She popped a few into her mouth.

"What happened to Leah?" Ellsberg asked.

"She blew it on the Drink Me challenge. I saw her barfing everywhere."

Ellsberg nodded. *Of course.* "Food poisoning, I'll bet." He rubbed his birthmark. "Have you seen Tomas?"

The sudden memory of Tommy's stare: Gillian and he alone in the room. "Not since the beginning. He got stuck on the deduction puzzle."

"Probably out of it, then." Ellsberg's gaze lingered on her bare feet, maybe wondering how close she'd come to *out of it.* "Where do you think they go? When they lose?"

"Nobody gets hurt, remember? That's what Sebastian said."

Sebastian Luna had created the Contest Extraordinaire. He was an entertainer, a mogul, and a savant. His Bazaar – the puzzle palace above and the tunnels below – was a winner-takes-all opportunity for the first to escape. The prize gargantuan – a house, a new car, more money than their families had ever dreamed. But for Gillian, the Contest offered more. A chance for a life spent at Sebastian's side.

Ellsberg made a dubious noise. Looking at him, so full of himself, Gillian couldn't help but like him. She offered him the rest of her candy. He eyed the gift suspiciously.

"Are those the M&Ms Tomas gave you on the first day?"

"His mom sent him with a huge bag. She gets donations at the dentist where she works."

"I know. But you shouldn't accept gifts. You already spend too much time together."

She shrugged. *Do you want them, or not?* Ellsberg turned up his nose.

"Peanut are the best ones," she insisted.

"They stick to your teeth."

She smiled at him, her teeth nasty brown from chocolate and peanut fragments. Ellsberg grimaced but couldn't maintain his disgust. He burst out laughing, which got Gillian going, the pair in giggles when a new voice echoed down the tunnel.

"Hurry up. You guys are missing it."

All the humor drained from Gillian's body. She'd let friendship lull competition, and assumed she couldn't be beat. She was losing right now.

They ran up the tunnel.

* * *

He stood at the lip of the pipe, water cascading around him and plummeting over a thirty-foot drop. Tommy Kundojjala was cocky. Short and solid and no reason to be cool, yet somehow cool nonetheless. His voice was high-pitched and cringey. His right eye lazy. His Hannah Montana T-shirt practically spotless, even now. But he made friends with ease. Shook hands like the president, or someone famous. And he was smart – his Contest qualifying time the fastest among them. Motivation ran in the family. His parents had chased opportunity from Odisha to London, then finally to the US. They and Tommy lived with his six siblings and two aunts in a crappy apartment outside Chicago. He needed to win the Contest as badly as Gillian. But she meant to win, nonetheless.

Gillian approached and performed the handshake dance with Tommy. Then she stood as close to the edge as possible, as still as she could with the arctic cascade frothing at her naked ankles. The pipe was one of many in a vast cavern, each dumping water into the dark blue lake far below. Across the water, at the foot of a sheer cliff, she saw a sliver of beach. Above that, the sinister mouth of a cave. No ladder, no bridge, only one way down. This was the finish line, or close to it. She could feel it. But Tommy hadn't jumped yet, which made her nervous. His actions in the Contest so far were a mystery she couldn't solve.

On her left, the boy himself grinned, his teeth blinding white. "You ready for this, Gil?" His voice suggested she wasn't. "Long way down."

"I'm ready."

They stood side by side. Ellsberg shuffled nervously behind. Tommy cast a sidelong look at her bare feet.

"Won't your mom be pissed about the shoes?"

"Those were lost and found from the rec center. My real shoes are at home."

"Lucky you."

"Are you kidding? They're used. Mom lost her mind when I bought them – not enough ankle support." Gillian adopted her Mom voice. *"I would have bought you new shoes."* She sighed. "And she would have. So, no way."

"I like your mom. I'll apologize to her after I beat you."

He thought he was cute. And he was, kind of, but Gillian wasn't about to tell him. Instead, she pulled another M&M from her pocket and chewed obnoxiously. A slow smile crept over Tommy's face as he recognized his candy.

"A lot of talk," Ellsberg piped up from the back, "for someone who hasn't jumped."

"You in a hurry to get rid of me, Ells?"

"No." Ellsberg was strangely intense. "I'm suggesting you're frightened."

The boys had butted heads at the start – more Ellsberg's doing than Tommy's – but they'd grown friendly throughout the qualifiers, as had Gillian and Leah. Having survived the same puzzles, and come from similar struggling backgrounds, they'd found friends as much as competitors. The handshakes, the matching jelly bracelets. Fun, so long as no one mentioned what would happen on the last day. When only one of them would remain.

Tommy played it cool. "Am not."

"Yes, you are, you're scared to death. I can tell. You'll never jump."

"I can jump any time I want. Just give me a second."

"Ridiculous. You'll still be standing right here when I win."

Tommy got louder, "I'm not scared."

Neither of them moved. As Gillian reconsidered Tommy's behavior, she understood. The drift in his right eye. His terrible depth perception, his fear of heights. But Ellsberg she couldn't figure. His voice wavered. He breathed quicker. It wasn't Tommy stopping him – Ellsberg was also afraid. Afraid of whatever waited for them down below.

Their fears held them back. They hesitated, with everything on the line.

Gillian threw herself over the edge.

Frigid water raked her skin, the cold claws of a witch. The shock almost sent her to the bottom, a dark gloom she couldn't see. She kicked toward the light, her lungs straining, and quickly broke through. Once she got her bearings she stroked toward shore, eventually clawing her way onto the small sandy peninsula. She rolled over to see what she'd left behind. A world of water. PVC of various widths sucked water from the lake and routed it throughout the vascular system feeding the sprawling complex, only to dump it back here again via the many open drainpipes. Gillian wondered where the pipes went, but figured she'd have an eternity to explore when she won.

She stood and faced front. Before her lay the only visible exit. Stakes pinned a large cargo net to the sand, the rope rising toward the dark cave fifteen feet above. The mesh course resembled a giant's hammock, the cave a hungry, gaping mouth. Over the entrance a message had been engraved in plate steel: VICTORY.

This was it. This was the last challenge. Gillian looked around quickly, but the boys had yet to appear.

She ran for the rope course.

The braided coils scraped her skin. Each rope square just large enough that her knees plunged through the gaps, the course ensnaring her like some feral animal. But she learned to spread her stance, aiming for the thick knots where the ropes met. She was going to leave the beach behind.

A desperate choking cry, from over her shoulder. Every fiber in her being cried out to continue, to scale the path ahead and blaze down the yellow brick road, but despite herself, she turned. Ellsberg flailed in the dark lake. His chin frantically jerked above the surface. He couldn't swim.

From somewhere in her head, her mother's soft yet firm tone reached her. Mom towering, despite her short stature. *Gillian Charles, you intend to leave that boy? What kind of person does that make you?*

She froze. Her hands locked around the rope coils. Ahead lay everything. The way out of hand-me-downs. Prize money to afford treatment for Mom's lupus. The unfettered life she was owed, and not the trap she lived in. She pictured the couch she shared with her sister, their dumpy apartment so close to I45 you could hear the 18-wheelers running day and night. Winning promised access and money and everything she'd ever want.

Ellsberg gurgled. He disappeared under the water.

She wanted Ellsberg to be OK.

Throwing caution to the wind, she turned around. Crawled headfirst back to the sand. She hit the beach, keeping her head on a swivel. She stretched her peripheral as far as possible. There was no sign of Tommy.

She could do this. She could pull Ellsberg to safety and still win the Contest. Be cutthroat yet kind.

Into the water she went, bracing herself for the skin-stripping cold. With strong strokes she lanced toward the spot where Ells had vanished. The water thundered in her ears, and she realized only gradually it was the sound of her own heart. Every beat a ticking clock. The sound of Tommy drawing closer.

Looking down, she opened her eyes. She couldn't see the bottom, but she identified the dark thrashing form of a boy in leather dress shoes. Futilely scraping at the water as if trapped in amber.

Ellsberg, you dummy, you should have known. Sebastian knew everything about the Contestants. Their strengths, their fears, their weaknesses. *He'd have known you couldn't swim.*

Down she plunged.

She kicked hard. Water sluiced around her body. With arms extended, she torpedoed toward Ellsberg. Her fingers locked around his heavy blazer, the boy a sagging dead weight. She angled back, but drew no closer to the surface. Her lungs heated up. The water became a presence, a monster indifferent to her Contest victory, indifferent to her life in every way. She pulled. Her muscles stretched, her bones separating from the sockets. Ellsberg squirmed in her grasp, his every movement conspiring to send them deeper.

This idiot. This dumb kid with no chance. He was going to kill them both.

Ellsberg popped free of the jacket.

He hovered there, strangely weightless for a moment, buoyant with enthusiasm. Gillian grabbed his waving arm and again reached for the light above. Pressure drove her toward the surface, the urge for air and the urge to win. She'd seized this chance and spent months training and proving herself smarter than every genius in the room. Ellsberg wasn't going to stop her. Nothing was.

They broke the surface, gasping for air. Ellsberg clung to her, a torpid seal needing to be beached. With her muscles burning, Gillian tugged him to the sand. Together they stumbled ashore. Ellsberg collapsed immediately, coughing and spitting, but Gillian stayed on her feet, something more powerful than exhaustion driving her back to the rope course.

"I'm sorry," Ellsberg gurgled.

His words were cold comfort. She told herself she'd done the right thing. Told herself that now Ellsberg was safe, she could stop thinking about him. He wasn't the problem. The problem was someone she couldn't see.

Up the course she went. Her previous experience prepared her for another go. In no time she crested the rise and left the tenuous footing of the rope course behind. Without hesitation, she ran into the cave. Multicolored lights strobed in deep wall sockets, the tunnel a psychedelic whirlwind. The wind howled. Shapes twisted in the dark. Nevertheless, she ran. Her muscles burning, her feet bruised, she ran.

And then she stopped.

Ahead, the tunnel forked. At the end of each path stood a door, smooth and unmarked, the choices identical. No tracks to tell if anyone had passed, the tunnel floor swept clean. On the ground at the split, three somethings glimmered. Three boxes, labelled with nonsense phrases.

GOTH REF
FILTHIEST CULT LET
GEARHEAD TENT

Word scrambles. They weren't difficult, almost to Gillian's

chagrin. The answers overly reliant on the word *the*. Gillian carved answers from the muddle, and her expression soured. Sebastian thought he was being clever when he bestowed terms of endearment on each of the Contestants. Ellsberg, The Frog. Tommy, The Great Dane. As for Gillian, Sebastian sometimes called her his *little cuttlefish*. The fish a chameleon. A creature that saw everything, some scientists thought from before birth. Gillian hated the term.

She knelt and opened her box. Inside were two fox-eared skeleton keys. The bits of the left key enclosed, creating a square with the shaft. The right key bits hooked over that square, the bits open, but the gap not sufficient to pull the keys apart without manipulation. Devil's Keys. A chill went through her body, and not from the dampness seeping into her bones.

Sebastian knew their weaknesses. Gillian had never tested well on disentanglement puzzles. Mechanical frustrations with pieces that were difficult to both take apart and reassemble. But she spotted the two keyholes in the false bottom of the box. Quick experimentation revealed she couldn't turn one key at a time, but only both simultaneously. Behind these locks would lie the answer she needed. Which tunnel should she take?

She straightened and cocked her head toward a sound from behind her. She couldn't make out the words, but she thought she heard conversation.

Tommy would have hit the beach by now. She didn't have a lot of time.

She returned her attention to the puzzle. The left key – the left fox – had a groove toward the end of the shaft, narrow enough the gap in the right key bits would slide over. But that narrowed section lay outside the left key's square, the square the right key was trapped within. She'd have to move one around the other. But move which key, and which way? Given the right one held the gap, she started there. Turning the key toward the end of the left key's shaft, toward the groove. But the enclosed bits of the left key prevented her from reaching her destination. She tried going around the other direction, away from the groove, but fared no better. The square of the left key was enclosed with thick metal. How could she ever separate them?

Her hands trembled. She knew she relied too much on gut instinct. Twisting and turning and bullheading her way, finding answers through constant trial and error. Eventually she'd solve the puzzle, but through such a convoluted process entire nations could rise and fall. She didn't have that kind of time. It killed her to just sit here, but she needed to think. To plan.

A laugh sounded out on the beach. The noise of rope tendons stretching as someone threw themselves at the web leading to where Gillian stood with her thumb up her butt.

Hold the puzzle in your mind, Gillian. You can do this. Show him.

She could always guess which tunnel, but maybe neither tunnel was correct.

Slowly, she rotated the entanglement. Her brown eyes darted over the length of the keys. *Think in three dimensions, not two. Absorb every detail. Imagine the end state.* And then she smiled. There. The groove at the end of the left key wasn't the endpoint, it was only a stop along the solution path. On the loop of the same key, at the fox's cheek, another groove that she'd missed. Guide the right one there and the foxes could detach. The keys could then be inserted into the false bottom.

Again she brought the right key toward the end groove, but kept the length at a ninety-degree angle, on a z-axis relative to the left key. In this arrangement the gap in the right swung over the groove, putting the onetime right key on the left. Then she flipped it such that the bow was on top. Breathing slow, she moved the key down the length of its mate, toward her chest, toward the left fox's head. The bits of the right key passed over the cheek groove and put it inside the fox's head, inside the bow. She moved the right one clockwise, around the circumference. The right key again reached the groove, and she slid it out. The fox-eared keys separated in her hands.

Bare footsteps scuffed against the rock behind her.

Gillian jammed the keys into their respective locks. She turned, the bottom unlocked and popped open, and she found a tiny slip of paper lying underneath. She read the words without retrieving the paper.

TWO WRONGS.

Don't make a right.

The left tunnel.

She abandoned the box. Ran full tilt down the left tunnel, her arms pumping, her braids slapping against her face. When she hit the door, it opened without resistance. Ahead lay only darkness. She didn't slow, didn't hesitate. Behind her the door clicked shut and she knew there would be no turning back. She felt the first curtain as she ran, a simple gauze veil designed to filter light. There were more curtains ahead, each layer heavier than the last, requiring her to push the fabric aside with exhausted muscles. She barreled through chiffon and linen. Fought through cheesecloth and velvet. She heard voices. Muffled at first but growing stronger. She pushed and shoved and muscled through. She heard cheering. The tunnel grew brighter and brighter.

She burst free of the passageway and stumbled into bedlam. A giant tent unfolded around her, the canvas sheltering row after row of packed bleachers. The big top crowd thundered. The air smelled like popcorn and cotton candy. One sawdust-covered ring dominated the floor, and a man stood in the center. Dominated it, despite his stature. He was small and tan, vaguely European, perhaps Spanish. He wore a purple tailcoat, dapper black vest, and orange pants. On his head a black flat cap, and on his feet pointed shoes. He seemed both exotically foreign and strangely familiar, the kindly uncle returning from far away with magnificent stories to enthrall nieces and nephews. There was no missing him, his face and name everywhere, on T-shirts, shopping bags. The banners hanging from above. SEBASTIAN LUNA'S CONTEST EXTRAORDINAIRE. He would crown her the winner.

But Tommy stood under Sebastian's arm, grinning from ear to ear.

The shock stopped Gillian cold. Even the water in the tank hadn't numbed her like this. Unreality enveloped her, as if she piloted her body from deep within her brain, a control center cut off from feeling. She pulled levers to stir her legs. She attempted to steer her head from side to side, to take in the cheers meant for someone else. She plodded toward Sebastian and Tommy and stood before them, waiting for Sebastian to notice her. He had eyes only for the victor.

"You did it, my boy!" The man lit up from within. When he looked at you, you believed he saw no one else in the world. "I knew you could do it."

A lavalier microphone cast his voice throughout the tent. Although the magic of Sebastian had you convinced his voice could carry unamplified for miles and miles.

Tommy was electric. He bounced in place. He could hardly

believe his luck – or, more appropriately, his skill. Gillian knew exactly what Tommy was feeling. She'd imagined and practiced her reaction to winning the Contest for months. She'd crafted the perfect version of what was to be and replayed the scenario in her mind every minute of every day until ten seconds ago.

Her lips parted but she didn't know what to say. She saw the jeans, the T-shirts, the Nikes – all Tommy's size. The giant million-dollar check. The lawyers holding photos and paperwork, talking new cars and residence in a five-bedroom house, today.

The other losers had disappeared, Sebastian's team artfully shuffling them offstage. Gillian was the only failure to stand front and center. Bathing in defeat.

At last Sebastian took notice. His eyes fell on her like she was a loose thread poking from one of his buttons. His mouth quirked. "And here's little Gillian."

Little Gillian. As if she was a bauble he'd all but forgotten.

"But," she said.

That was all she could say. *But.*

Sebastian's eyes twinkled. "But what?"

"I stopped to help Martin," her voice croaked. "He... He couldn't swim."

Sebastian squat on his heels. It was another of his trademarks. Bringing himself to eye level with children. Gillian had always appreciated the gesture.

"But that's not true," he said.

Deep in the recesses of her mind, deeper still than her imagined control center, something stirred. A dark suspicion. A truth she'd suspected but avoided because she hadn't wanted to face the ugliness. Gillian knew the words before Sebastian could say them.

"Martin can swim just fine."

The crowd had quieted. There were laughs. A few sympathetic groans. And then finally applause, rising from behind and growing in a wave until the stands were alive with sound.

Martin Ellsberg shuffled past Gillian and went to stand with Sebastian and Tommy.

Gillian's eyes burned. Anger and shame and disappointment coalesced and threatened to pour hot tears down her face. But she would not cry. She would not let them see.

Ellsberg wouldn't make eye contact. The little shit was too guilty.

"He was working for you," Gillian said.

Sebastian shook his head. "That's not the point, child. The point is you made two mistakes."

Two wrongs.

"The first was stopping. Never stop. Never stop chasing the prize when you know you are right. If you hesitate, if you second-guess, that's when you will lose."

He said it with such conviction. This man who had built himself and his empire from nothing. He knew what he was talking about. She wished she couldn't believe him.

"And your second mistake," he said, "was helping Martin."

"So I was supposed to let him drown?"

She hated the reckless anger in her voice. But the words washed over Sebastian and left him untouched. He set his hand on her shoulder in a tender expression that still managed to feel dismissive.

"You were supposed to chase your dream," he said. "And trust I would never let a child come to harm in my Contest."

Sebastian stood tall. "Conviction," he said, more to the

crowd than her. "Strength of purpose." He released Gillian and again brought Tommy close, the boy lost in his realized dreams of wealth and privilege and access until the end of his days. "I saw these things in Tomas Kundojjala. And I knew he would win."

The crowd stormed to their feet, their cheers deafening. Pandemonium swelled the tent, the confines increasingly hot and close and threatening. Gillian didn't know what to do. This wasn't how it was supposed to be. Fury lit inside her chest. Passion fired her throat and a blast of words erupted.

"I could have won!" she said. "I could have won the whole thing."

But no one heard her, or if they did, they no longer cared. Subtly, Sebastian summoned his handlers: pleasant-looking people with strong hands who guided Gillian from the center ring, which was now meant only for Tommy. His family dashed in as the handlers escorted her out. They ran so very fast from their old life, confident they'd never have to return.

You did the right thing, Gillian told herself, the words firm, even as she was led back to the life she'd failed to escape. *Saving Ellsberg was the right thing to do.*

But it was the words she'd said out loud that haunted her. *I could have won.*

Two
September 4, 2018

Gillian Charles, Age 30

"And those of you sitting in traffic will be pleased to note the LA area fell to sixth on the list of the country's most car-clogged cites."

Gillian tried to ignore the radio and drummed her fingers on the steering wheel. She blew a wisp of curled hair from her forehead. Cars inched along the 101 with the torpid advance of a snake. "Come on," she murmured, ignoring the voice in her head reminding her she had only herself to blame. She'd known Los Angeles traffic was waiting when she'd thrown herself in the car at 5 am. But she'd wanted to watch the Newton woman – an insurance scammer supposedly on long-term disability with a back injury. Catching her upright and frisky, on camera, would have meant a fat fee from the insurance company. That gig had been a bust, but there were other cash benefits to driving.

She let a hand drift out the open window, the Corolla's AC on the fritz. The yellow-tinged air made everything heavy and slow. There was another smoke advisory, but air quality warnings were as constant as the traffic. She crinkled the loose vinyl corner affixed to the door, one of three wraps covering the car. Her advertising gig required thirty miles a day to earn out the $300, every inch counted with a miserly exactitude by the company-installed GPS.

From the corner of her eye, she caught a man staring. White, swept-back hair, trimmed beard, flashy suit. He drove a BMW and looked like a Rolex advertisement. She weighed his appearance – attractive, or just gross? Then she realized he wasn't hitting on her. He was sneering at the ads slapped to the skin of her vehicle.

The nape of her neck burned. Her anger simmered between brain and spine, and she could feel the heat all the more since she'd chopped her hair. The undercut advertised her emotions, for those familiar with her. But BMW wouldn't know she'd lost her cool. Not that she cared if he knew.

"Hey," she shouted out the open window.

BMW's gaze came up, and Gillian gave him the finger. He made a face like he'd deepthroated a grapefruit. Directed his eyes forward and focused on the unmoving slog of cars.

Gillian laughed. Assholes were assholes, always. At least she could count on that.

When possible, Gillian preferred to run her hustles in twos. As she inspected the price tag hanging off a rose gold necklace, she also eyeballed the deadbeat dad shopping for engagement rings with his latest pretty young thing. The necklace was a lightweight bauble, 18 carats, and encrusted with thirty-some-odd diamonds.

"Charming," the clerk had suggested, his eyes lingering on Gillian long enough either to undress her or to wonder if she'd pocket the jewelry. And no way *she* was purchasing the necklace, not with her credit. If Gillian bought the jewelry, if it was sufficiently bougie, she'd acquire it on Chantal's credit. Her personal shopping client ran both a small cosmetics empire and a juicing company, raking in sufficient cash to *keep houses* in various destination cities. The necklace was very modern. Simple, in a one-percenter sort of way, and very much to Chantal's taste. Gillian had the clerk wrap the thing while she used her phone to snap pictures of Bria's lecherous ex.

Bria lived in Gillian's apartment building. She was loud and funny and competed in Ninja Warrior competitions when she wasn't managing the coffee house down the street. She had three kids with her ex, Clay, but all three lived with Bria full-time. Clay was a pilot, and his schedule and income didn't allow him to shelter the fruit of his loins. *Times are tough for the airlines,* was the story he'd fed Bria. *I can't afford it, babe.*

Clay paid cash for a gaudy diamond ring. Earlier Gillian had watched him enter a bank – one not on the list of accounts provided by his attorney – and emerge with a smile. Gillian assumed he kept a hidden safety deposit box. She'd get inside the bank and obtain proof if she had to, but she expected a judicious application of the jewelry store photos would be enough to make the jackass fold. Bria deserved better than this man she'd latched herself to for five years, but then everyone made mistakes.

The lech himself glanced Gillian's way, but she turned before he could make eye contact. Her gaze settled on a magazine the clerk kept behind the counter. The pages were folded back to expose a crossword, the puzzle maybe a quarter finished. Before she could stop herself, she'd solved three of the clues.

"Instinct," she muttered. "Arafat. Wham." A sour taste on

her tongue as the words escaped. She'd fallen off the puzzle wagon with so little temptation. And so loudly. The clerk shifted to block her view, upset that she'd nosed into his belongings. The twerp didn't know upset.

She returned to tracking the happy couple. Clay's new lady glowing, hanging on the arm of her man; he, smugly wrapped in his own charm. Gillian was struck with the sudden feeling that Clay would wiggle free from all of this. The photos would be dismissed and the bank account explained; Clay would jet off to a new city where he'd woo another lonely heart. He'd emerge clean and coiffed. Looking like a winner. Smiling like one.

Gillian put the necklace on Chantal's account and hustled from the store before she did something she might regret.

Back in traffic, Gillian squeezed opportunity from every precious second. Her phone was nestled face-up on the passenger seat between the small, crisp bags transporting luxury items for her personal shopping clients. The speakerphone blared tinny, Bria sounding more dejected than Gillian had anticipated.

"Are you sure?" Bria said. "I just... Even for him—"

"He's trash, sweetie." Traffic eked along, enough so Gillian had to pay attention. A box truck had crashed and cleared on the 71 hours ago, but the automotive snarl persisted. "He paid cash for the ring, at least ten thousand. I talked to the clerk – Clay has been in there before. He bought a watch. An anklet for her kid. I don't know what bull his attorney's been shoveling, but he's hiding assets."

"Maybe there's some explanation."

A hardness invaded Gillian's chest. She'd spent all day

tracking this asshole, and Bria was making excuses for him. "There's no explanation – he's out for himself. He was always out for himself. I'm sorry I can't make him be faithful or honest. People are true to their character. I wish the world was different, I truly do."

The silence crackled. Gillian rubbed her forehead. She'd hoped her efforts would have made Bria happier, that the woman would have felt more satisfaction at having cornered her slippery ex-husband. But Gillian should have known it wouldn't be easy for Bria to drop her emotional baggage. The revelation of her former lover as a snake was only painful, not satisfying.

Gillian used to think her strength was reading people. Some days she wasn't sure what her talents were at all.

They began to wrap the call as Gillian swung into her parking space. No ocean view. No porte cochère. A covered spot the only glamour she could afford.

"Look, I just pulled up," she said. "I've got some stuff to put away and I want to shower. I'll drop by after that. We can have a beer, wash this whole thing away."

"That sounds nice. Make sure to knock, though. The kids will be down and–"

"I'll be careful. You'll barely notice me."

"You're the best, Gil."

Gillian snagged her phone from amid the evidence of other people's wealth. *The best at what, exactly? Just getting by?*

"Thanks," she managed, and clicked off.

Defeated, Gillian stayed in the car. Out in the street a courier righted her toppled bicycle, surrounded by a sea of discarded cardboard signs. *Not Another Life. No Justice No Peace.* Earlier there'd been a protest – another Black kid shot dead by cops. Gillian had wanted to participate, felt maybe she should have participated, but the hustle wouldn't wait, or so she'd told herself. The reality was that she wasn't sure anything would change. Someone would co-opt the cause – someone charismatic and media-friendly – and the movement would become a vehicle for their success. She'd seen noble campaigns twisted before.

Eventually, her conscience won out. She exited and helped the courier align her twisted bike, brush dirt from the frame. There were some scratches, but the woman seemed unbothered. After thanking Gillian, she slung her backpack and pedaled away to deliver food or documents – whatever would get her paid.

Aware she'd left a small fortune in her crapheap, Gillian retrieved the litter of boutique bags and hung them across both arms. She used her narrow ass to bump the door closed, leaving the car unlocked – with other people's valuables draped across her body, what was there to protect?

As she squeezed through the front security gate, propped with an orange cone as always, she shook off her maudlin attitude. All in all, it hadn't been a bad day. Three gigs had paid out. Tomorrow promised opportunity – she'd earmarked the morning for grocery deliveries. LA's laziest were always game for someone to rescue them from the Trader Joe's carnival. And there was a product testing gig in Fullerton the landlord had told her about, promising an easy fifty. If nothing else, maybe she'd give ride-sharing another shot. Tonight even, if she could keep her eyes open.

One lonely tree greeted her in the courtyard. She went up the stairs and down the walkway before reaching her apartment. Her phone buzzed as she negotiated the dangling packages and tangled keys. She managed to wedge the cell between her shoulder and ear and regretted the decision to answer instantly. The dour voice of her sister stabbed into her ear.

"So you do answer."

With a key twist and a shove, Gillian's apartment door unlocked. She slipped into the cozy space, the interior lit by the warm glow of a single rice-paper lamp. "Hey, sis. You just caught me going out."

She swung her arms over the kitchen table and let the bags slough free. One clunked into last night's wine glass and only fast action saved it from toppling to the floor. She parked the glass at the sink next to a stack of dirty dishes and the crumpled wrapper to a breakfast bar she'd consumed before the sun came up.

Her sister was unperturbed by any pretense of Gillian having something better to do. "Have you talked to Mom today?"

Gillian dumped her keys on the counter. Momentarily lifted the bills stacked next to her potted barrel cactus, then lost her enthusiasm and dropped them. "I texted her last week."

"I mean called. On the phone, like a human being."

June talked like she was the only adult. She always had. Gillian escaping across the country hadn't changed anything. She was still the odd child. Still the disappointment.

Gillian navigated to the couch. She sidestepped the nightstand she'd drafted into service as a coffee table, to avoid dislodging the ancient laptop she'd covered in stickers. Caught a glimpse of the bedroom, where an unmade mattress and box spring lay on the floor with three days' dirty laundry piled on top. The place was hers and she was proud of it, but every time she returned home, she felt a pang. She lived like a college student, and she'd never even been to college.

"Is this what you wanted?" She collapsed on the faux leather cushions and tugged at the frayed edges of the giant armrest hole. "To hassle me?"

A dramatic sigh. "The clinic wouldn't fill her prescription."

Gillian sat up straight. "What do you mean? I sent the check."

"The problem is not the check. I told you last time. The steroids she's on – there's another pharmaceutical company making the drugs. At the last appointment–"

"Give them the check."

"It's not the *check*, Gil." Pots clattered in the background, and a young male voice asked about dinnertime. June was so domestic. "Mom is sick. She has a disease. I can't babysit her and keep tabs on Dad twenty-four-seven."

"He's supposed to be clean. You shouldn't have to *keep tabs*."

"Dad is clean, but that doesn't mean he's not fragile. He's working as a counselor. He talks to other alcoholics. He's helping them–"

"Is that a good idea? Seems like an easy way back to the bottle."

"Do not drag me into your petulant nonsense. If you have problems with Dad, talk to him yourself."

Gillian raised her eyebrows. "Petulant nonsense?"

"Give him a call – on the phone. Or better yet, come for a visit. Stay a while and carry your fair share of the family baggage."

"Dallas is fifteen hundred miles away."

"And who moved to California? Don't give me your excuses. You ran as soon as you could, all because of that stupid–" June bit off the angry accusation. Huffed into the phone. "You know you could just call him."

"Would you back off about Dad."

"I don't mean Dad."

A malignant silence invaded the conversation.

"Sebastian would help you," June said.

"Stop."

"He has money, more than enough to–"

"Stop it. He has strings and hooks and promises that go nowhere."

Gillian had fled the family drama at age eighteen, moving to LA. But family wasn't the only reason she'd left Dallas. "Just leave it, OK?" she said. "I can't do this now."

"You aren't ever going to do it. Lie to yourself, but don't lie to me."

Gillian tried to keep her voice calm. "It's a fantasy. It was always a fantasy. He's an adult playing kids' games." She squeezed the phone, as if she could wring opportunity from the cheap plastic. "There's got to be something else."

"Such as?"

"I don't know. Why is it on me? Why am I the only one sweating this?"

"The only one? I think you should check yourself. There's responsibilities here, and I'm managing all of them, despite never being asked."

Gillian toggled to speaker. Sometimes fifteen hundred miles wasn't far enough. She dropped the cell on the couch and listened to June's husband Todd shoo their oldest from the kitchen. Somewhere in the background there was the halting start-stop of their youngest practicing keyboard. "Für Elise." Gillian had played violin and piano when she was young, dual threat from age eight to twelve. She'd imagined touring the world and absorbing applause. Even when she'd switched to solving puzzles, she'd envisioned a future without boundaries, opening every oyster life had to offer.

If only she could get out from under. If only anyone would let her.

Outside, the orange sun dipped low. If Gillian wanted to profit from evening rideshare, she'd need to get moving.

"I'll call Mom," she said. "Maybe I can figure something out."

June's tone changed. Her vocal cords tight. "This isn't a puzzle, Gil."

"I'll figure something out." Gillian stood. "I gotta go."

A cluck in the back of her sister's throat. The lie catching there, June unable or unwilling to swallow it. "I'm sure you'll do what you have to do."

"Goodbye, June."

But her sister had already hung up.

Three

Burdened with the oversized and flimsy cardboard box, Gillian didn't see the man at first. She'd maybe have been better off missing him entirely.

Although her rideshare agreement prohibited individual commerce, Gillian hawked home-dyed viscose scarves to select passengers. She had a sense for those who'd see the sample deliberately yet casually draped at her neck and be drawn to the fabric and the colors, to the melange of something exotic and foreign, luxurious yet affordable.

In the moments where Gillian entertained fantasies, she imagined a celebrity plucking one from the box, snapping up five or six, wearing them to some premiere and addressing the paparazzi with irresistible nonchalance. *Who am I wearing? Oh, I'm so glad you asked. This is Gillian Charles. You simply must get one.*

Her neighbors spent their evening hours out of doors, sitting in plastic chairs planted in their front doorways and strolling the common walkway connecting units. Kendra, her neighbor across the courtyard, watched Gillian wrestle the box with amused pity. She was tall and gangly, ebony with dyed strawberry-blond hair and the demeanor of misplaced royalty. She ruled over the top floor in her purple silk robe from a throne of green plastic, nursing a dramatic cigarette.

"Not going to find a man that way, Gil." Kendra's voice boomed over the gap. "Not even if you wrap that scrawny little body of yours with a whole box of scarves."

Gillian carted her wares over the doorstep, carefully pulling the door closed behind her. "What do you know about men? Your last paramour was of the feminine persuasion."

"Paramour? I like that word. What does it mean?"

"For you? Let's say... special friend."

Kendra let loose with a cackle. "I do have a number of those." She got serious. "For real. Thank you for helping with the police. That last time, I didn't know what she brought into the house."

The gratitude made Gillian uncomfortable. She charged the wrought-iron fence, hoping to wedge the box between her hip and the balusters. Momentum nearly took her over the railing. "Don't you worry about it. That wasn't your fault. I just helped them do the right thing."

"Police don't do the right thing. You know that. We'd all be no place without you." She watched Gillian struggle. "You talk to Reuben?"

She managed to place the box atop the railing. Slid the beast toward the stairwell. At the corner she got too casual, nearly toppled her possessions into the courtyard. "I have."

"What'd he say about rent?"

The stairs presented a new challenge. Gillian wrapped both arms around the box. Shifted the load away from the railing. She couldn't see the steps.

"I don't know what Reuben told you, but we're not dating. We drink. That's it."

"But he talks to you."

"He wants in my pants." Warily, Gillian descended. "There's a difference."

"He talks to you." Kendra leaned over the railing now, casting her wisdom down upon Gillian, whether she wanted it or not. "If this place goes condo, we're all out on the street."

"Reuben doesn't even own the place. He's just the manager."

"His uncle owns it, that and those EZ Autos out in Long Beach. They're family. Family looks out for each other."

Gillian found enough oxygen to produce a cynical laugh.

"I'm serious, Gillian."

The last step beckoned. And then the car and a night of productive commerce, if she played her cards right. But the apartment complex was full of Kendras. Single parents and waitressing actresses and unprivilegeds who couldn't sign a new lease without the two months' rent they didn't have. "I hear you. I'll see what I can do."

At long last Gillian hit bottom. She found the perfect equilibrium and blitzed toward the gate and her car. Everything moved forward exactly as she wanted, for half a second. Money and opportunity shimmering on the horizon – hers for the taking, if she moved fast enough. Then she tripped, almost face-planted directly into the box of scarves; only the man's steadying hand prevented her from literally crushing her dreams. Somehow the box wound up in his arms. She righted herself, flustered, as he gently lowered her belongings to the ground.

He wasn't much taller than her. Aspirations of dashing, which he mostly achieved. Gray suit, three-piece. A shockingly white dress shirt open at the throat, no tie, with a white linen pocket square edged in crimson. A bit gaunt, but the suit's athletic cut streamlined his physique. His beard was carefully manicured and close-cut. His brown eyes were lively and his matching skin positively glowed. "Are you all right?"

"Fine," she managed. Her brain, frenetic at the best of times, manifested a kaleidoscope of history. The hot flush of success she'd felt having navigated the stairs went cold. "Tommy?"

He smiled. "Gillian Charles, our best and brightest. You look well."

Tommy looked great. Confident. Magnetic. An adult now, but something of the kid remaining.

"Do you have a minute?" Tommy lifted his chin toward the apartment Gillian had so recently vacated. "I've got something to ask you, and I'd rather not do it in public."

She hadn't seen him in almost twenty years. Left him half a country away, outside Dallas, along with everything he represented. She wanted to hug him. She wanted to shove him into the street. Regardless, all that confusion was meaningless. Advantage waited for Gillian out there. The big sale or the right contact. The words formed in her head like a slow rolling fog. *I really need to get going.*

"I need your help," Tommy said.

And there it was. *Help.* Gillian regarded the word with an ex-junky's fear of relapse. Maybe Tommy remembered that about her, all these years later.

She studied him. Noted the way his hand bounced off his thigh. How his right eye didn't track with his left, the orb no longer lazy, but a prosthetic. Life had happened to Tommy Kundojjala, only she still saw the boy she once knew. The Winner, sure, but more. Him laughing at her Schwarzenegger impression. Sharing his M&Ms, despite the competition. Staring at her in the Deduction Room, as they realized one of them was about to start the Contest in last place.

She wasn't her father; she had willpower. She could hear Tommy out and still say no.

She heaved her wares from the sidewalk and hiked the collapsing box up to her hip.

"Let's go upstairs."

Four

Set adrift in her confined apartment, Tommy prowled restlessly, his eyes scanning the bare walls and counters as if hunting for the bric-a-brac most would have spent years accreting. Gillian wasn't much for surrounding herself with the past, and rarely had visitors, at least with the lights on. Although Tommy wasn't any taller than Gillian, she felt suddenly cramped in her own space.

A pause as he took it all in. "It's nice."

He said *nice* like she'd gifted him a desk calendar. Only people with money complimented her apartment.

"Can I get you anything?" She dropped the box on the floor. "I have water. OJ. Beer."

"A beer would be fantastic."

Gillian pulled two Stellas from the fridge, remnants of beer night with Kendra – she enjoyed the hoppy bite and the fact they drank anything fancier than Coors. Gillian uncapped the cold bottles and delivered one to her guest before retreating to the dead space between kitchen and living room. Tommy took his bottle and sat on the couch, one leg crossed over the other, exposing purple socks. He took a long pull of the beer, closed his eyes, and let out a breath. Gillian watched him as if she'd just let a panther into her apartment.

"Long way from Dallas," she offered.

The remark drew a laugh. "You have not changed."

"OK, let me try again. You look well. Business must be treating you good. How's life? You married? Kids?" Gillian sipped at her beer. "Is that what you were looking for?"

"It's called Miscellany. Sebastian doesn't like to call it a business."

"What Sebastian likes or doesn't isn't something I worry about."

A tightness around Tommy's eyes, which he quickly smoothed. He took another long drink, draining the bottle over halfway.

"Do you ever regret entering the Contest?" he asked.

Gillian squeezed the neck of her beer. "I don't think about any of that."

"It's a shame. I always thought you should have won."

"I'm not going to do this. Reminisce."

He nodded. *Fair enough.* He did his best to swallow the remainder of his beer in one go, then set the bottle on the floor. "You're aware of our success? Since?"

"Tomas Kundojjala, resident of *Miscellany* since age eleven, employee since 2006? MBA with distinction from Stanford? Marketing Director, President of Consumer Products, now COO? Yes, I'm aware you've done well."

"I don't mean me, I mean Miscellany."

Tommy stared like Gillian's every emotion burned through the skin. She covered her bitterness with another sip of beer. "I'm aware the business is Fortune 500. Bazaars open around the country. Making some noise about expanding internationally. You did that thing with sanitation in Uganda."

"They have challenges with latrine coverage. Infection

and malaria and a dozen treatable, if not preventable, diseases. We helped them engineer proper hygienic practice and facilities."

"But you're looking to build there. And run games."

"Every Bazaar might offer a different localized experience, but there would still be puzzles, yes."

"Like a virus, with a payload." Gillian turned and set her beer on the kitchen counter. She didn't want a drink. Not even the appearance of distraction. "So noble."

"The humanitarian efforts are rewarding, but the puzzles are our bread and butter. We can't accomplish one mission without the other. Children who visit our Bazaars emerge with sharpened cognitive skills. Advanced emotional skills. Not to mention the access and opportunity only Miscellany can provide." After a brief hesitation, Tommy reclaimed his beer. "You know we never ran another Contest."

"Couldn't have been cheap to buy a house for you and… how many brothers and sisters? Six?"

He stared, daring her to squirm under his prosthetic's gaze. "My parents say hello. They always liked you."

She almost reached for her beer. She was showing her ass, no question.

"The public," he continued, "they wanted more. But Sebastian wouldn't cheapen the original. So ever since, we've only had the daily park games. Nothing as involved as what you and I went through. The events are shorter, the prize money less dramatic. You win knowledge, as Sebastian likes to say."

He was like one of those Jurassic Park scientists. Extolling the wonders of their creation while the raptors ate the guests. "Look, I hate to be rude, but what does this have to do with me?"

He smiled tightly. "Still so impatient." He wrung the sweating beer bottle. "Circumstances have changed. We're looking to hold another Contest. What they're calling Season Two."

Her DNA vibrated as she pictured word jumbles and ciphers and entanglements. The disappointment of water and two tunnels and standing in front of Sebastian as he judged her.

"We've been qualifying children from Bazaars across the country," Tommy said. "Quietly. Eight – twice as many as before. Sebastian wants everything bigger. Twenty million in prize money, a six-bedroom house on the grounds. Internships with NASA. Berkshire Hathaway. Pfizer."

"Tommy–"

But he wasn't listening. "They're taking advantage."

"The entire operation takes advantage. Jesus, it took you two decades to figure that out?"

"I mean it's a setup."

Tommy had come off the couch. No longer fixated on her, he paced in the small space, picking up steam.

"We're so big," he said. "I can't control every little detail. Three hundred people on Season Two alone. I used to interview everyone we hired. We had a circle of trust, and we knew Miscellany. But now we're a monster, and we're only growing. I've tried to warn people. I explained the risks to Sebastian. Diocletian – do you remember him? The emperor who divided Rome? The empire was too big to govern, so he split their conquests into east and west. I tried to warn Sebastian, but of course, he knows his history. *All Diocletian did was make Rome weak,* he told me. *The Visigoths sacked Rome within the next hundred years.*" A weak laugh dribbled out. "That's what he's worried about. A hundred years from now." His left eye was red.

"You're not making any sense," Gillian said.

"The kids. The qualifying kids." Exasperated, like she should have grasped his point. "Not all of them – the first two were maybe legit, but the rest performed well outside their historical averages. Someone is giving them answers. They want these specific kids in Season Two."

Giving them answers. The beer bottle in his hand like a dagger.

"I've tried to tell the others on the Executive Team, but no one will listen. Everyone is too enamored with being a global entertainment conglomerate to remember why we're all sitting at the table in the first place. They don't understand what we're doing. Our puzzles were a challenge – solving them meant something." Tommy noticed Gillian's stare. He relaxed his grip on the bottle. "Sebastian always told us there were rules."

"Sebastian liked to *talk* about the rules, if that's what you mean."

Tommy seemed to grow thinner as she stared. "I never asked Ellsberg," he said. "That day, at the lake. I never asked him to distract you."

At the mention of her betrayer's name, a yawning chasm opened inside Gillian, tilting her carefully constructed world. She almost fled back to the kitchen. "I told you. We're not talking about it."

He fell silent. She was tempted to let him suffer, but she took pity, if only because he seemed hurt and broken in a way she recognized. Of someone let down by the people they believed in.

"Look, you're upset," she said. "Maybe it's stress, the damage of working for Sebastian. You'd be forgiven for being a little wounded. But again, I don't understand what any of this has to do with me."

He seemed – this man with a billion-dollar entertainment and philanthropic powerhouse at his fingertips – at a loss. Wincing, he said, "There's a reunion."

Again the vertigo feeling struck her. "What the fuck? No. No."

"That's not exactly why I came."

"What did I say? What did I *just* say?"

Tommy approached, his face pleading. "The Reunion is simply a reason to get you there. To get a look at Season Two."

"Clearly." Gillian retreated toward the door. "Look, it's been great seeing you. Really. I always liked you, and you played fair. But I have a life here, and all this talk about what happened before isn't going to pay my rent, so–"

"I want to hire you."

The words stopped her short. She spun around so quickly Tommy raised his empty beer bottle in self-defense. "For real," he said. "Off the books, but it's a job."

She squinted at him. With enough effort, she could almost spot the fishhook. "I'm not working for Sebastian."

"This isn't for Sebastian. Well, not exactly. You'd be working directly for me." He snuck a little closer, arms spread as if he was harmless. "Something's not right here, Gil."

"Why do you think I left?" Under investigation, and after guzzling a beer, Tommy wasn't nearly as put together as she thought. His clothes slept in, a sheen of sweat on his skin. The temptation to assuage whatever ailed him surged, not unlike her instinct with Bria or Kendra. But Tommy wasn't a lost puppy. Taking an eye off the prize with people like him frequently led to disaster. And disheveled or not, the look on his face was still crafty. He'd seen the cardboard box. He'd been inside her threadbare apartment and her working-class Pomona address. Puzzle kids since birth, neither of them had lost their muscle-memory observational skills. He would have already drawn conclusions.

No, this conversation wasn't about favors. This was about matching wits with a skilled opponent.

"What's it pay?" she asked.

"Fifty thousand."

Gillian rocked on her heels. "Why so much?"

"I meant what I said. You were always the smartest one."

"Quit kissing my ass. Why so much?"

He tongued his cheek. "Fifty is how much it costs for one year of your mother's treatment."

Gillian clenched her jaw and nuclear anger fused her flesh and bone into a single immutable wall. In the Contest days, the kids had shared dorms through the qualifiers and up to the main event. They'd slept in bunk beds and whispered secrets at night. Alliances and friendships and feuds formed and fractured over the days and weeks. Her mom hadn't been as sick back then, but Gillian's love for her had burned no less hot. Tommy had listened, and remembered enough to use that fact against her. "That was cold."

"This isn't charity," he insisted.

"You came here." Her voice hard. "To use me."

"I wouldn't–" He assessed her demeanor. The hot glare and the rigid posture, the anger radiating from her in waves. He set the empty beer bottle on the kitchen table among the clustered shopping bags. From his front pocket he produced a black-and-silver card case, his name engraved on the lid. He extracted a sharp-looking business card from inside, one of many, and slid the card next to the bottle. "Think about it. The offer is real. The money is real. I'm not here to trick you into working for Miscellany or helping Sebastian. I'm here because there are kids, Gillian, thousands of kids who trust what Miscellany is supposed to be. And I don't know what we are anymore."

She stepped aside, so Tommy had a clear path to the door. No fool, he took the hint and opened the door, stepping out into the warm early evening. He turned to face her.

"Thanks for the beer," he said.

She closed the door in his face.

Five

After chucking Tommy out, Gillian lacked the will to ferry the inebriated and the soon-to-be. Although her taste for booze had fled, she needed something to help her unwind. Since she'd quit the dispensary and lost her discount, she rarely allowed herself edibles. Instead, she peeled off her shoes and socks and grabbed a bag of peanut M&Ms from a drawer. She appraised the candy, not immune to the irony, then popped a few in her mouth and chewed as she dribbled water over her cactus. The barrel cactus was small and spiky, graced with occasional blooms of color – an apt metaphor, and a comparison she steered into. She loved plants, the hard-to-love ones especially so.

Fuck Tommy for trying to use her. Showing up here, song and dance about the kids, about the Miscellany mission, pretending as if they'd only stopped puzzle clowning last week instead of two decades prior. And trotting out the money, the *exact* amount she'd need for Mom's treatments. Jesus. Pissed her off something fierce.

She went barefoot into the bedroom. Opened a window to let out the damp, the LA air hazy but breathable, the temps cooling. The city's angry car-horn-air-brake symphony matched her mood, but she didn't like her mood. She battled the noise with her phone's tinny music, a smooth cut of

The Temptations' "My Girl". She chewed on her M&Ms and breathed through her nose.

She thought about Tommy's story. She thought about the money. It sparkled in her mind – a lure, no question. But any such enticement had a man tugging on the other end of the line. Sebastian would be behind this, despite Tommy's objections, and being Sebastian, he'd have more than one lure. More than one hook. Fifty thousand dollars bobbing right there, and if that didn't satisfy, the temptation of a contest in trouble, an appeal to Gillian's sense of fair play. She wanted to say she didn't care, but she'd poured her heart and soul into that damn Contest. She and her fellow Contestants had disassembled, cracked, or otherwise annihilated every puzzle set in their path. None of them started with the answers; they'd earned them. And none of their families had the means to buy victory – a couple of sock drawer twenties amounted to a laughable bribe. Gillian could believe there were moneyed assholes unconcerned with smarts, chasing only Sebastian's blessing. His name and recommendation carried college admissions, Wall Street hires, elections. To think there were rich pricks out there, slimy flyboys like Clay, who'd bought their kids a spot on something they considered a Contest? Leaving some new Gillian frozen out, some girl who needed to qualify to change her life, to change her family's life?

Gillian realized she'd been standing in front of her closet for untold minutes. Grinding M&Ms to dust between her teeth.

Yeah. She cared.

Despite her limited means, Gillian was a clothes horse – thrift shop vests and Oxford shirts and gabardine pants. While admittedly fairly bare, the closet still held the expression of who she was today, but it also obscured her past. Behind the clothes lay a box she'd kept from the before times. A tumor she couldn't quite bring herself to excise.

She finished her candy and wiped her hands on her jeans. She hauled out the box, placed it on the bed, and gently removed the top. It wasn't especially full – imprisoned memories rising only to the halfway point. Dusty papers and clippings and photos from her puzzling days, from the era of Gillian on her way to the top.

Even in her lowest moments she'd avoided this dark heart of the apartment. She'd moved the box with her from Dallas to Los Angeles, from lease to lease, untouched. Over the years she'd had stretches where she'd managed to forget, weeks or even months where the adventure-seeker inside was a stranger. Ultimately weakness seized the controls, a craving she could defer but never expunge, and everything came flooding back. With the internet at her fingertips, sometimes drunk but distressingly often sober, Gillian would stalk those she used to pit herself against, and the man for whom they used to perform. The box, though, was harder to reach. Deliberately.

The topmost sheet rose with her fingertips. Foil certificate paper. Heavyweight stock. Elaborate script blazing across the surface:

*Thanks to your tremendous display of skill and
intelligence you,*

GILLIAN CHARLES

have won entry into
SEBASTIAN LUNA'S CONTEST EXTRAORDINAIRE
*Please call the number below to arrange transport to Dallas,
Texas, before September 1ˢᵗ, 2000, where you, and only you,
will be admitted entry to The Bazaar, for a chance to win the
ultimate prize.*

Congratulations, Gillian Charles.

You deserve this.

Gillian set the award aside. She fished through the snarl of
objects inside, once as essential as black coffee and scrambled
eggs. She found her trusty compact binoculars. A pocket
calculator, the number 7 worn away. A nearly stripped roll
of duct tape stuck to a walkie-talkie with a snapped antenna.
A flattened matchbox. Her Victorinox Swiss army knife, the
blade sharp enough to split skin. Weathered papers tattooed
with ASCII and Morse and Braille translation. Additional
trophies and awards, proof of contests she'd won on her
bullheaded path to the Bazaar. And underneath the hardware
of her success, photographs. A snapshot of her with her
parents, she just a baby, Mom hovering, Dad heroin-riddled
and strung out. A later 4×6 of the house on Lemon Ave, a
cozy brick-and-wood affair secured during one of Dad's
infrequent employed periods; June out front dribbling a blue
Champion basketball, the kind of carefree play Gillian could
no longer associate with her sister.

And, at last, *the* photo.

Their handlers had insisted on a picture, eager to capture the over-achievers before the Contest ate them whole. The original Bazaar just a building in the background, blurry, a four-story Victorian nightmare. In front, four kids between the ages of ten and fifteen. All heights and weights, different genders and census checkboxes, the faces excited or pensive. And, off to the side, with that squirrely look halfway between amusement and disdain, Sebastian. His buttoned orange vest and voluminous purple pants and the newsboy cap he'd doff as if fresh from the 1930s.

She looked at herself. Braids pulled back from her doorknob forehead. The smile she kept on a short leash. Big eyebrows and elephant ears, at least she'd always thought. Young Gillian looked straight at the camera as if she knew she would win. Because she had known she would win. Right up until the moment she'd lost.

Tommy stood behind her to the left. His chin raised high, as if to exaggerate his height. A hard part carved in his gelled hair. Big ears and thick eyebrows, same as Gillian, but otherwise in a league entirely his own. His grin all mouth and mismatched teeth and a joy that leapt into three dimensions. He seemed ready to take on the world. He had taken on the world.

She thought of the man who'd visited her apartment. The beer he'd chugged and the way his fingers danced against the neck of the bottle. The sweat and the nerves and how he'd paced. He hadn't done anything wrong, except win the Contest. Climbed the ladder to the very top rung and now, he was falling. Easy to see from the outside, which made Gillian uniquely suited to help.

Staring at the photograph only made her regret sending Tommy away. She set it aside.

Under the group snapshot was another artifact. Her old Discman, a CD still inside. She knew what the disc held. Other than the paper invitation, it was only thing she'd taken from the Contest.

She plugged in the Discman, and the CD spun. She dropped the ragged foam earpieces in place and heard Sebastian, the man interviewing each of them, asking what they hoped to be. Sitting on the floor, she listened as he asked, and the kids answered. Leah: "None of your business," a response that even now made Gillian smile. Tommy, the kiss-ass, told Sebastian he wanted to be him. Then came Ellsberg.

"I don't know," said Ellsberg. And Gillian could see him, back then. So goddamn young. Confident but fragile all at the same time.

"You don't know?" Sebastian said, slightly annoyed. "How can you not know?"

"Well," the hesitant response. "I thought I might like to be in plays."

Ellsberg had written a play, a fact he'd revealed to Gillian just before the interview. The production was about a boy – a boy with a German accent – who'd constructed a playmate from scavenged twigs. The twig-boy came to life. Resembled its maker. This caused all kinds of trouble: mistaken identities, otherwise avoidable confrontations. Gillian remembered finding the idea weird, but even as a kid she was struck by the immensity of the thing. Ellsberg writing a whole play, crafting an entire life from his imagination – that had blown her mind.

Sebastian laughed. His laugh that sounded entertained, from a distance. "An actor? I see. And what play would you be in? How many years will you toil away in this regard?"

Ellsberg knew he'd stepped afoul. "Well. Or a spy."

"Oh?" Genuine interest. Sebastian had gone from cold to hot. "And how would that work?"

"I could break codes." Gaining confidence. "Or make them."

"You could, at that," Sebastian said, in his corner. "I imagine you could be quite useful to government efforts. You'd be responsible for national security."

"Like a superhero," young Ellsberg agreed.

"Don't be ridiculous." Sebastian steering now. "You would be practically valuable. In reality." A shuffle as he leaned in. "You'd be responsible for thousands, perhaps millions of lives."

A silent pause in which you, the listener, imagined those words sinking in. Young Ellsberg absorbing the heavy reality of lives in his hands.

"I think you know, Martin," Sebastian went on. "Who are you going to be?"

"I want to be a spy," the boy said, as if this was the only answer. "And I'll be the best there ever was."

The audience of the day entertained. This clever boy who knew his destiny all along, only toying with Sebastian. And Gillian could believe Ellsberg had wanted it, how he took to the idea. Only days later playing with her life as if he owned it. You could draw a long nasty line from there to here.

She rewound and listened to the question and the loud silence again. The audio was poor quality, but maybe under the hiss, a sigh. With years of perspective, after hours listening to hustlers and scam-artists obfuscate unpleasant truths, the line didn't seem so straight. Ellsberg's pause was perhaps not an epiphany, but the moment when the boy abandoned his dreams. Ellsberg the actor, stowed away in a dusty box, never again to see the light of day.

Who are you going to be?

Sebastian hadn't only stolen the Contest from Gillian. He'd stolen Ellsberg, and replaced the boy with a creature who looked just like him.

She shook her head. Once before, she'd stopped to help a Contest kid, and look what happened. Charlie Brown with the football. She'd be an idiot to set herself up again. Besides, she had rideshare. Hustles. Bria and Chantal and all the others. The life she'd committed to, here.

Gillian jammed the Discman back in the box, along with the famed photo. She reached for the lid and paused. There was another picture in the box. Gillian, after she won the final qualifying event. Behind her, Mom, standing free and clear of walkers and wheelchairs, her daughter proudly positioned in front and facing the camera. The love so clear, Gillian's knees buckled.

All Mom ever did was support Gillian's dreams. It wasn't her fault those dreams had turned to ash. Gillian owed her mother, and $50,000 went a long way.

The kids in the picture stared. They were younger, so much younger. Gillian saw the bike messenger and imagined a version of herself at forty, pedaling through the cold streets, delivering crap destined for shredding or deletion. Her back sore, her knees shot. Her hopes and dreams ground to dust.

A hollow laugh. Going back just for Mom? June knew. June had pegged her one hundred percent. *Lie to yourself, but don't lie to me.*

Gillian sealed the box, then ventured into the kitchen where she retrieved Tommy's business card. She dialed the number and waited. When he answered she spoke before he could say *hello*.

"When do we leave?"

Six

Between the navy-blue herringbone tweed, the leather attaché, and the casual way he boarded his jet, Tommy looked every bit the success America taught its children they could be. The pilot greeted Tommy at the door, but he was on the phone, and only nodded politely. Despite her inclinations, Gillian suppressed the urge to gawk, instead manufacturing her own air of jaded nonchalance. *Here I am on my private jet, again.* She hadn't flown in years. Not since she'd spurned Dallas for LA, and that had been a long miserable trip wedged in coach.

The jet's interior was all leather and metal and wood. Gillian felt like she was flying in a European sports car. A crew of three staffed the plane and there were sufficient oversized seats for sixteen passengers. She and Tommy were the only people on the plane.

Dallas was expected to be unseasonably cool, a September day typically as warm as ninety, today only fifty-nine. Gillian wore her oxblood boots, white skinny jeans, red wide-lapeled blazer, and a pink tie over a starched white shirt. The outfit was intended to provide a certain confidence. Headed into the lion's den, she'd need it.

The jet taxied, then lifted into a gray Los Angeles sky. Tommy opened a laptop, but never broke from his call.

Gillian caught snippets of conversation. He danced around inquiries from someone Gillian guessed to be his wife, the questions he fielded apparently quite pointed. Where was he? Who was he bringing back, and why? Tommy responded with the callous honesty of the long married. Evelina should have known this trip couldn't be avoided – what did she think would happen? No raised voices, but instead the clipped tones and barbed questions a marriage under stress produced. He wrapped the conversation with a perfunctory *I love you, too*. Afterwards he looked to Gillian, as if he had to explain.

"Evelina, my wife." He tried to smile. "She works for Miscellany. Director of Park Communications. That's how we met."

"Sounds tricky. How do you keep work and home separate?"

Tommy's laptop chimed – another call. He wiggled an earbud into place, the laptop incessant. "It's the opposite. No separation. That's supposed to mean no secrets."

"Supposed to?"

But he was lost to the call, the first of several over the next hour. Financials to review. Puzzles to approve. Fielding requests from politicians and celebrities and journalists.

"They always want to do a jigsaw puzzle," he told some functionary. "The problems are the same as they've always been." Pause. "I don't care how many sides it has. We can't manage the pieces, and a puzzle with missing pieces is just a waste of time." Pause. "You don't have to tell them you said no. Tell them I said no."

Another call, voice only. Tommy on his feet, leaning into the back of his chair like he needed the support.

"Of course. No, of course your son is special. And I'm

sure we can get him into a local Bazaar, or really any Bazaar you'd like." Pause. "Well, as I said, the Bazaar at Miscellany is no longer open." Another pause. "For you, certainly, let me check with Sebastian." Tommy dropped his head and rolled his neck for a solid ten-count. "As I suspected, Sebastian said there's just no way it can be managed. I apologize."

Another audio call. Tommy sat again, hunched over the laptop. The lack of video allowing him to multitask without the other side being aware.

"This is in Changzhou?" Pause. "Chongqing, OK. And they need the qualification letter?" Pause. "They already have that?" He quietly typed out an email response while fielding the call. "No, you have my complete attention."

Gillian watched him. She imagined this jet was hers – she was fielding the calls, solving problems and creating puzzles. Being Sebastian's best and brightest.

She picked her cuticles, savagely. This was about the money, not Sebastian's approval.

When Tommy finished, he looked tired. He rubbed his eyes and worked his jaw. His movements sluggish, like he'd been dipped in cement. He caught her watching. "Jet lag. I've been working more than sleeping."

"This is the thing you want me to save?"

He smiled. "It's worth it. Trust me."

Tommy she might trust. But Sebastian was another animal entirely. "Why me?" she asked.

"What's that?"

"If you think these kids are cheating – an insider giving them information – you have, like you said – a couple hundred ass-kissers ready to lift rocks and twist arms. Why do you need me?"

"Because I know you."

"To hell with that. Nobody knows me."

The fogged smile faded. "You left Dallas after the Contest. And since then, you've done, what? Personal shopper, suicide hotline counselor, rideshare. Whatever it took to make the rent, I imagine. Eighteen years, and not one contest, capital C or otherwise. No chess, no Bazaars, no puzzles. Not so much as a crossword. You went from twenty-under-twenty to a gofer." He noticed her stone face. "No offense intended."

"Kiss my ass."

"What I'm saying – you aren't losing. You're not even playing."

The spot on Gillian's neck burned Chernobyl-hot. She'd forgotten what it was like to be under the microscope.

Tommy went on, in a kinder voice. "You're not connected to the puzzle world, or Miscellany. You made a clean break, which the rest of us haven't."

A flight attendant came down the aisle with a tray of food and drinks. Gillian snatched a croissant. Tommy took two diet sodas. He drank one while Gillian chewed.

"You see the others?" she asked.

"Occasionally. They're both involved with Miscellany. Leah's flying in today."

Gillian rubbed her throat. *This deal is getting worse all the time*. "All the people involved – you're making it sound like too many to count. Do you have suspects?"

"Access to the Season Two puzzles is limited." Tommy guzzled soda. "We're talking select members of the Executive Team. The Puzzlemasters. Sebastian, of course, along with myself. And the Head of Security."

"What about your security person? My experience, the person controlling the cameras is the first one dipping into the till." She aimed her chewed croissant. "Who watches the watchmen, know what I mean?"

Tommy took a long drink. "Ells is Head of Security."

A cold slug of emotion crawled into Gillian's throat and died.

"He's like me, Gil." Tommy leaned across the aisle, selling her. "He loves the place. I understand the history, and I'm not defending him, but I can't imagine him giving answers to kids."

Ellsberg had backstabbed Gillian without his accent so much as slipping, and he'd only been thirteen. Who knew how adult Ellsberg might ethically contort himself? But she could tell Tommy wouldn't believe anything different without proof. "And Sebastian?"

"What do you mean?"

"He's not above a little theater. It's all well and good to push the kids, but if you're not minting a new Banksy or Buffett, if you're not churning out child geniuses and they're, say, failing to solve the puzzles – that looks bad."

Tommy crushed the first can. Opened the second. Gillian wondered how many he drank in a day.

"Sebastian would never hurt the kids," he said. "If he learns the game has been tampered with, if he's given proof, he'll end it. Immediately."

Sebastian would never hurt the kids. Gillian squashed a cavalcade of acidic replies.

"Does he know I'm coming?"

"I haven't told him."

They both knew that answer meant nothing.

Gillian considered what she was up against. A frazzled COO. Her betrayer in charge of security. The kingpin, a man who derived joy from manipulating people.

Tommy put his hands together as if to pray away the doubts she entertained. "You can make Sebastian listen," he said. "He's not like you think. It's hard for him, at our scale. He's insulated and, I think, lonely. It's a delicate time. We're expanding. There's money on the table, and he doesn't know who to trust. If you make the situation clear – Sebastian will have to investigate. We can fix this. Go back to putting the kids first. All I need from you is enough to start the process. Do what you do. Ask questions, get people talking. Your relationships will open doors, and your mouth can do the rest." She dead-eyed him, and he put his hand over his wool-vest-covered heart. "You were always easy to talk to."

Gillian could all but hear her sister's cackle.

Having said his piece, Tommy escaped his seat and headed for the rear. She heard the bathroom door lock.

Trust him? She knew almost nothing about Tommy the man, and, if she was being honest, maybe nothing of Tommy the boy. They'd spent a few weeks together. A few hard, intense weeks that made them friends, if not quite family. She'd always liked Tommy, and back at the apartment she'd looked into his eyes and wanted to believe him. But in those eyes – the organic one – she'd also seen craving. Tommy wanted things. Wealth. Success. Control he clearly didn't have. She'd had that kind of person in her life before. The type who'd tell her anything, then promptly turn around and do the exact opposite. Justifying it to themselves throughout.

A glance at Tommy's laptop. *Trust him?* No.

Trust… but verify?

She moved into Tommy's seat. He'd left his laptop unlocked, because of course he did. She scanned email subject lines. Whenever she saw the words *Season Two* or *contest* she kept reading. She found a number of logistical items. Budgetary emails. The subject line *Re: Shares* caught her eye.

Back in the bathroom, the toilet flushed. She heard tap water run.

Gillian skimmed the content. *Ongoing talks. Shale and Kone. Headman Ventures. Path to IPO. Sensitive.* She saw a strike price and expected public valuation that raised her eyebrows. Investment banks. Initial public offerings. Tommy wasn't kidding when he said money was on the table. Big money.

The bathroom door opened. Gillian hopped across the aisle and nestled back into her seat as Tommy approached. His pants rattled with a pill-bottle shake she hadn't noticed before. He stopped and stood next to her chair.

"Did you get what you wanted?"

She looked up at him. "I don't know what you're talking about."

"Your questions? Did I answer them all?"

He'd been gone for more than a quick shake. His left pupil was wide, like he was breathing through his eyeball. Gillian's gut said *I told you so* and plummeted all the way back to LA. Tommy's behavior suddenly made sense. Frazzled fell way short. The man had a drug habit, it was only a question of which one.

"How many bathrooms this place have?" she asked.

Tommy frowned. "Excuse me?"

"You were gone forever. Thought I might have to find another sky toilet."

His bonhomie faded. "Did you want to ask me something else, Gil?"

When her dad was on the verge of a relapse, he'd get this

haunted look in his eye. A terrible self-awareness possessing him in his last few clean days, like he could see the drunk coming, like he was tied to train tracks and could feel the locomotive bearing down. Those moments of lucidity had often reached Gillian's soft heart and convinced her to forgive. Forgive, before he slipped. He'd drink and throw furniture and rant about success denied, then disappear. The family would pray for his safe return. Visit the local hospitals, searching for him. At least once Gillian had believed him to be dead. And gradually, after he reappeared, unemployed and ashamed, promising to dry out and never do it again, Gillian began to feel something different. Disappointment. Disappointment he'd come back. Disappointment they'd have to endure his spineless bullshit all over again.

Tommy stared at her expectantly. She supplied her best smile.

"I'm sure I've learned all I need," she said.

Seven

The black Mercedes SUV waited on the runway like a trained Doberman. The driver was Latina and wore a black suit, white blouse, and comfortable shoes. A scar creased her right cheek. She looked a smidge older than Gillian and wore her hair close-cropped. When she opened the door for her boss, there was an athleticism to her movements and, as the product of several ersatz judo schools, Gillian recognized a fighter when she saw one. Tommy's chauffeur following a proud comic book tradition of being more than a simple driver.

Her eyes flicked to Gillian, long enough to catch her checking out that scar. "Mr Kundojjala," she said, switching her attention. "I hope the trip went well."

"Smashing success, Jackie," Tommy answered with a smile. "Smashing success."

Jackie matched Gillian's stare with eyes like black tacks. The driver projected a particular kind of Texas hospitality, one of *sweeties* and *thank-yous* that masked an *eat shit* attitude. But bobcat friendliness aside, Jackie stowed Gillian's cheapass roll-around – decked in blue-and-pink pastel ferns – in the trunk. Gillian wasn't used to letting her scant belongings out of her sight, and kept close. She wasn't entirely sure what she saw. Only the empty sandwich baggie traveling from Tommy's luggage into Jackie's pocket. The driver threw a look over her shoulder. Gillian turned away before their eyes met.

They drove north. In the years since Gillian's departure, the terrain had changed. She stared at a paved horizon and marveled at the volume of concrete. Tons of willpower and money and ambition to carve something from nothing. The dream fueled by vast tracts of land and a low cost of living, a playground for entrepreneurs. She thought back to her first trip to the outskirts in 2000. There had been less development; anything north of Plano a desolate wasteland. The trek from northwest Dallas had seemed to take hours, she and June mashed shoulder to shoulder in their Integra hatchback, weaving through patchwork side streets to avoid the tolls. Mom could still drive back then, the lupus which would eventually confine her to a wheelchair manifesting as occasional lightning flashes in her toes. Gillian remembered only one stop, a detour to Dairy Queen. June insisted the Oreo Blizzard was best – *literally the best* – when everyone knew Peanut Butter Cup kicked a thousand percent more ass. The argument continued until they noticed the quiet. Mom a looker then, to be sure. Fewer wrinkles, a bright smile, loud – her beauty and sheer personality could stop a room, although given the vanilla sea of faces, the patrons gawked for other reasons. June and Gillian with their beige coloring. Mom with her darker skin. The DQ customers had an MO – ogle, then look away. Not staring the new staring. They got their Blizzards, but Gillian left the place angry. Angry those people made her self-conscious and doubt who she was. Although truth be told, home wasn't much better. Neighbors squinted at their coloring when they claimed to be Black, which they did. *Half-breed* one of the more polite slurs. As a kid, dwelling on race hadn't been especially satisfying. It was easier to focus on puzzles. In a puzzle, erasure and resentment weren't the only outcomes.

Looking at the political lawn signs stuck in grassy medians, Gillian reconsidered her first thought. She wasn't sure much had changed in the last twenty years.

Tommy also gazed out the window, fingers drumming against his leg, his eyes on the road signs. He downed an energy drink Jackie had passed him from a cooler nestled up front. "Take the next exit. I need to show Gillian something."

His remark drew Jackie's attention to the rearview. "There's an event–"

"I'm aware of the calendar. Take the exit, please."

Jackie stared into the rearview, but nodded.

They left the highway and weaved through side streets into a small neighborhood. Single-family starter homes and postage-stamp lawns, the dwellings an arm's length apart, but still houses free of graffiti and barred windows. They pulled into a cul-de-sac and parked. The house had a one-car garage. A ragged but readable welcome mat. Tommy insisted she follow him inside.

"I want you to see what I'm talking about," he said. "I want you to meet the Navarros."

The Navarros were husband and wife. He slightly overweight with a patchy beard and glasses. She taller, weightlifter solid, with a sad face and twin sparrow tattoos poking out the neck of her T-shirt. Mrs Navarro spoke while Tommy was still coming up the walk. "Please." Her voice tired. "What now?"

"This is Gillian," Tommy said, as if it explained everything. "She can help."

The woman looked to her husband, but he'd already retreated inside.

The house was quiet. No TV prattle, only a radio tuned to WRR, playing classical music. Tommy introduced the couple, Eddie and Katie. They stood awkwardly in the kitchen, and Gillian saw half-eaten PB&Js. A bag of white bread and a silo of peanut butter out on the counter, like they could make PB&Js for the rest of their life. A fidget spinner on the table. Crucifix on the wall. A refrigerator magnet showing mom, dad, and a ten year-old girl.

"Sorry to spring this on you." Tommy didn't sit, so Gillian didn't either. She felt like the 125th wheel. "But we were in the area."

Eddie returned to the table. He held a sandwich between his hands but didn't eat. Katie stood between the visitors and the heart of their home. Her eyes said she'd been through this before.

"I wondered if we could talk to Vanesa?" Tommy asked.

Katie again looked to Eddie. He didn't respond, only kneaded the bread between his fingers.

"My friend Gillian was in the Contest," Tommy said. "The original. I'm hoping she'll help us. Talking to Vanesa–"

"Is she a cop?" Eddie asked.

Gillian laughed, her voice loud in the house. "Jesus, no."

The response made Eddie uncomfortable. Gillian's eyes flicked to the crucifix.

"If you talk to her…" Katie spoke like she was suffocating. "This is the last time. After this, you don't come back."

Gillian's mother hadn't really fought with her, a more permissive parent who'd let fate play a big part in her daughter's upbringing, for better or for worse. But Gillian had witnessed the behavior of other parents in her apartment complex. Bria, for example, had a headstrong daughter who'd dyed her hair and somehow pierced her ears, all without parental approval. The screaming matches could be heard through the thin walls. *I hate you.* The hollows in Bria's cheeks clear for anyone who cared to look.

Tommy was oblivious to the family's trauma. "Of course," he said. "We don't mean to be a bother."

Eddie stopped massaging his sandwich. "What happened with my daughter – it wasn't right. You said you could make it right."

Tommy nodded, intent and sincere. "We will. We're going to fix everything."

"When? The lawyers cost money. You're suing us."

"I'm…" The accusation put Tommy at a loss. "We're going to make it right."

Gillian quietly seethed. She'd figured she'd fly to Dallas, ask some questions, maybe review video of the qualifiers. Emotional investment wasn't on the table. But Tommy had brought her here, and now they were inside the house and everyone was staring.

"Go on," Tommy said to her. "You'll see."

Katie led Gillian down the hall. Vanesa's bedroom said a lot. A bookcase jammed with reference books and dictionaries, a trophy – 2017 Dallas Regional Spelling Bee champ, a framed *Morning News* article on the wall reporting Vanesa's fourth place finish, under fifteen, World Puzzle Championship. Just walking into the room gave Gillian chills. And over in the corner, under a poster of Sebastian and his flat cap, was Vanesa. Sitting in a bean bag, her head buried in a fat book on the Moon landing. She wore a gray-and-purple MISCELLANY T-shirt and her black hair hung in her face. One eye was pinkeye red. Her knuckles were chewed raw. Staring at the girl was worse than a mirror – it was a time machine, sending Gillian all the way back to that house on Lemon Ave.

"This is Gillian, Vanesa." Katie spoke gingerly. "She knows Mister Tommy."

Vanesa looked up. Eyes full of hope. "Mister Tommy is here?"

"Yes. But he wants you to talk to this woman."

Vanesa's jaw clenched in a way not unlike Eddie's. She returned to her book.

Fuck Tommy for bringing her here. Even as a child, Gillian could have intuited the manipulation. She remembered the time in fifth grade when Mom – worried she'd puzzled through lunch – asked a counselor to check on her. The minute the woman circled the lunch table with her busybody air, Gillian knew.

Still, looking at this girl, winnowed down to nothing, Gillian had to admit she felt a kinship. A pang in her chest that hollowed her out. She squatted on her heels where Vanesa could be eye to eye, if only she looked up; a trick Gillian learned long ago.

"You like space?" she asked.

Vanesa shrugged. *Stupid fucking question.*

"I see you like games, too. I'm guessing you're pretty good?" No response. "Have you played the games at Miscellany?"

A deliberate sigh. "Yes."

"I played those games. When I was your age."

"Great."

Katie watched closely, probably ten seconds from throwing Gillian out. Maybe that pressure its own motivation. Could Gillian reach this kid in the time it took to pick a lock?

Vanesa's eyes flicked up. The color a shifting gray-green. "I've seen you before. Mister Tommy gave me a picture. You and some other kids. You had braids. You looked funny."

"I did look funny. My mom did that."

"Mom says I have to comb my hair every day. It's so annoying."

"Moms are like that."

Gillian tried to recall what it was like dealing with adults who simply didn't understand. "I hated losing," she said.

The jaw tightened.

"My mom always told me the fun was in solving the puzzles," Gillian continued. "She didn't get it at all. I wanted to be first. I still do."

Behind them, Katie sighed. Gillian remembered her mother doing the same thing. Her *can't we all just get along* worldview incompatible with her daughter's white-hot desire to win.

"I got second place." Vanesa's words burst loose. "I should have won. They cheated."

The words were a scary echo of Tommy. Of young, naive Gillian. "Why do you think that?"

"Because I was the best." Her chin out. Her nostrils flared. "I was first in Tetris and first at soccer spelling. That other kid couldn't get the balls in the right net, but I did, first try. And then in the escape room he just, like, knew all the answers and I didn't even get a chance. He got to go to Season Two. He's basically going to win everything." She broke then. Mashing her face into her hands. "Mister Tommy said I should have won. And some of the other kids said I should have won and even my friend Zane says I should have won." She got louder. "I told Mom and Dad but they don't listen. They don't understand because they're stupid. They're stupid and they never listen to me."

Gillian felt cold. She shouldn't be in this house with this kid. She wasn't the right person to make this OK. "I'm sorry you lost."

Fury nearly drove Vanesa to her feet. "I didn't lose!" she shouted. "He. Cheated."

Katie's hand was on Gillian's shoulder, the pressure something less than friendly. "You should go."

Vanesa dropped her head, staring hard into her book, the tears barely held back.

Gillian couldn't escape the room fast enough. She mumbled a goodbye to Vanesa, then hurried back to the kitchen, where Tommy had fixed himself a peanut butter sandwich and ate it with gusto. Crumbs littered his suit. When he saw Gillian he smiled, excessively cheerful. "How did things go?"

"We should get to the park, Tommy." Her voice sandpaper. "Now."

Tommy knew enough to stop smiling. He wiped the crumbs from his suit and stood, thanking Eddie for his time. Said he'd be in contact soon. Katie never returned from Vanesa's room and Eddie only chewed his sandwich. He didn't walk them to the door.

Once they returned to the car, Jackie started the engine and returned to the highway. Gillian fumed. Tommy rubbed one arm then the other, like an old man.

"Why did you take me there?" she asked.

"I told you." He didn't look at her. "Someone's cheating. Vanesa, the family – they got an offer. An insider promising to sell them answers. And they turned it down." He shook his head. "Can you believe that?"

"This was all just a performance, wasn't it? Bring me

back, show me the girl who finished second. If that was the best trick you had, you've lost your touch."

"Gillian, it's not always about you."

"Fuck you. You don't think you're part of the problem? That girl *worships* you. What are you feeding her?"

"I care about Vanesa. She wanted to play in the World Cup. She wanted to go to the Moon. These are dreams Miscellany is supposed to promote. We're not supposed to take her dreams away."

Gillian pictured the girl with her space book. The look on Vanesa's face as she replayed the games in her head. *Because I was the best.* "And yet you're suing the family?"

"Miscellany – the business – is suing them. Legal, the lawyers – it's always lawyers – got all in a twist. I could have made this go away."

"But the Navarros have evidence? An email? A name, a face?"

"They know, Gillian. They don't need evidence." Again, he sounded annoyed she wasn't keeping up. "You talked to Vanesa. You understand. Between what you discover and that little girl, Sebastian will have to see. Everything will change."

As a kid, Tommy could convince Gillian to do anything. He cajoled, dared, and bribed – M&Ms and a smile went a long way. She'd skateboarded downhill – blindfolded – because Tommy said it would be fun. Jumped out the first-floor window of the Bazaar, because Tommy said it would be faster than the stairs. He was a force of nature, and he might even have been right. But as Gillian considered the Navarros, as she recognized the smoking crater of Miscellany's impact on a family, she realized something else. Tommy never considered the cost.

Eight

Miscellany existed in the sprawling suburbs between downtown Dallas and Oklahoma, enclave after enclave of five-bedroom homes, strip malls, and twenty-four-hour pharmacies. Rabbits danced between car wheels and mad grackles dove for splattered roadkill. Eventually the signs appeared:

EXIT NORMAL LIFE. 10 MILES TO MISCELLANY AND WONDER.
NO LIMITS OTHER THAN YOUR IMAGINATION. EXIT 70.
MISCELLANY AND THE BAZAAR. NEXT EXIT.

There were other parks, of course. Six Flags wasn't far; the wood-and-steel Texas Giant dominated the skyline. Hurricane Harbor alongside that, promising wave pools and water slides. And for those who couldn't afford the big parks, like Gillian, there was even Sandy Lake, with its tame putt-putt and busted arcade games. But cost aside, the other parks had a different problem: there was no challenge. You strapped into a chair. You lay on a mat. Mechanics and gravity did all the work. Gillian wanted a challenge where she could think. Where she could win. As a child, only

Sebastian's Bazaars – only Miscellany – had provided what she wanted.

Why Miscellany? *Sounds small,* the criticism of an unimpressed Bill Gates. Say what you would about Sebastian, but the shade of global titans left him unfazed. *Miscellany suggests the possibility of various things,* he liked to counter. Miscellany did not dictate the normal or the boring, but instead the unusual, strange, eccentric. Bizarre. *Bazaars* themselves being a place where one might find the unusual, the strange, and the eccentric. The circle of references with no beginning and no end perfect for Sebastian.

The funk Gillian had been in since the Navarros faded. A cocktail of excitement and dread flooded her veins. Her body so high-strung, if Tommy flicked her in the arm, she'd likely fly apart.

A deliberately aged granite wall ribboned around the grounds and offered only tidbits and temptations at first. Sebastian was a showman who liked to reveal his cards one at a time. All they could see from the street was acres of parking. The road signs promised the public entrance was next, but there was no indication they were turning.

"Can we go in the front?" Gillian asked.

Tommy raised his eyes from his laptop. Calmer now, his nervous energy pumped into work. Jackie cocked her head, waiting to hear instructions from someone who mattered.

"It's a hike," Tommy said. "And I figured you'd hate the display."

"I need to see what everyone sees. Give me the show."

He shrugged. "Take us in the front, Jackie."

From the back seat Gillian could see the driver tongue her scarred cheek. But Jackie flicked her turn signal and steered them toward the main entrance. They drove through the lot, around eager beavers spilling from sport utility vehicles and honor student vans, license plates from Michigan, New York, and Florida.

They parked and Gillian exited, doing her best to appear unruffled. Across from her, Tommy did the same. He'd left his laptop in the car and had phone in hand, texting. He departed without a word, leaving Gillian to follow. Jackie remained behind, leaning against the car as if it were her personal property.

"You're not coming?" Gillian asked.

"Not my job."

"What *is* your job, exactly?"

A tight smile. "I keep him away from trouble."

Goddamn, the woman was pleased with herself.

"Be seeing you," Gillian said.

Jackie set forefinger along eyebrow in mock salute.

A long red-brick walk snaked toward Miscellany's filigreed gates, the trek designed to give guests maximum time with Sebastian's curated wonders: the boxwoods shaped into ponderous elephants and enormous blue whales; the faux-gas streetlamps, meant to evoke feelings of a Dickensian London, absent the disease and chronic poverty.

On the horizon, eleven flèches bristled, the structure too ambitious for walls to hide – the spires of the original Bazaar. The heart of the park and the location of the one and only Contest. The scene of Gillian's humiliation. When she thought of the place, when she tried to picture the inside, she saw only darkness.

Tiny voices nibbled at the edge of her consciousness. She was doing exactly as Sebastian wanted. Once inside the park, she wouldn't know up from down, right from wrong.

But she squashed those doubts. She'd left this place on her own terms and returned the same way. She'd earn her pay and leave with her psyche intact. She wasn't a kid. Sebastian was just a man.

The entrance plaza grew closer. Where the walls ended, the gates began, the opening flanked by towering menhirs engraved with seemingly innocuous objects like umbrellas and apples and milk bottles. Gillian could finally see the people of Miscellany. The brightly outfitted ticket takers dressed like Victorian-era carnival barkers. The buskers with bagpipes and barrel organs. Only the security guards were attired in modern-era slacks and button-downs, and even they gave a nod to theater with their short canvas half-cloaks.

Adventure and wonder and mystery hung in the air, the atmosphere meant to entice children and remind adults of the awe they'd once cherished. And although Gillian couldn't see the park's interior, she could almost smell the cotton candy and the sunscreen and sweat of her fellow tourists.

The park was a riot of people, packed to the gills; lines queued before lines. She could feel the heat and the rat-in-a-maze pressure; the park's layout designed to draw innocents past every attraction and hoover every dime from their pocket. But underneath the cynicism, Gillian remembered the view from waist-high. The opportunity. The way everything shined. The cracks between the people and the one glimmering half-second where space opened and a child could push forward and see what others couldn't. She remembered the thrill when she first laid eyes on a new puzzle. The way her pulse quickened. Challenge calling, and her desire to be first. The smartest. Like Vanesa said, it was about being the best.

Tommy marched on autopilot, buried in his phone, clearly dulled to the experience. He skipped the lines and bag check and cruised through the turnstiles, drawing no more than a cursory glance from Security. They didn't stop, or even slow down.

On the other side, Miscellany sprawled. Multicolored swirls of lawn and garden twisted around the winding cherry-brick path. Music piped through hidden speakers, the brass-heavy march peppy and inspirational. Banner poles soared overhead, snapping flags featuring images of Sebastian. Gillian stopped and stared. The serious young face standing in the parking lot of his first Bazaar. The goateed version ringing the opening bell at the New York Stock Exchange. Shaking hands with Will Shortz. And, of course, a picture of Sebastian with his kids. The Contest. The same damn photo Gillian had buried in her box back in LA.

Tommy pocketed his phone and came to stand at her shoulder. Always with the sweet tooth, he offered her a stick of gum. They chewed like children under Sebastian's watchful eye, staring at their younger selves.

"I had a lot of teeth back then," Tommy said.

"You got better looking."

"I had them capped."

"Very white of you."

Tommy watched her stare at the image. "There's a photo op later," he said. "For the Contestants."

"Hard pass." The media, with their relentless barrage of questions about her past, her love life, where she'd been these last eighteen years. She'd rather endure a root canal. And there were other concerns. "I haven't told my family I'm here."

"Lying to family – that I can understand."

Overhead, a rippling flag-bound Sebastian looked down on them, unblinking.

"He's speaking," Tommy said. "In about ten minutes."

Irrational suspicion. He knew. He knew she was here. "Is that unusual?"

"Very. He rarely speaks in the park. This is a last-minute event. Something to do with the Reunion. I only just got word."

The Sebastian in the flag looked older. Wrinkles creasing his forehead and mouth, signs of age they hadn't bothered to photoshop smooth. The telltale signs of wisdom. Or weakness.

He was just a man.

Gillian side-eyed Tommy. "Where is he?"

Nine

They approached the first Miscellany landmark. An enormous geodesic sphere hovered like a small moon above a proscenium stage. Creatures of history and myth played hide-and-seek in the arch. Feral goblins peeked through stone ivy. A burning cyclopean eye glared from the keystone. Symbology of Sumer, Greece, and Imperial China, to name a few. Back in the day, entertainers would prowl the stage and challenge audience members to solve riddles for trinkets. Gillian would track their movements, steely-eyed, always watching for clues and tells. The stage had been a portal to a magical place. An enticing escape.

The gloomy weather had done little to keep away visitors, the crowd a dozen rows deep. Food carts worked the edges, selling flavored popcorn, hot dogs, and even the cheesy cornbread sopa paraguaya. Guests filed in like lemmings, packed in tight. Gillian wondered how many might have bought one of her scarves.

Tommy caught the eye of a security guard, who muscled them a path to downstage. Once they reached a spot near the apron, he squeezed her arm.

"I need to be up there."

"Need to be?"

"I told you." The way he talked, he sounded almost like

ten year-old Tommy. Confident. Bordering on arrogant. "I believe in what we do."

He may have sounded like that kid with the elastic smile. But up close, she saw the bags under his eyes.

She shrugged. *Do your thing.*

"Don't forget the party tonight," he said. "7:30 at the Ballroom. Everyone will be there. It's the perfect time to ask questions."

"What do I do meanwhile?"

He withdrew a blue bracelet from his pocket and tossed it at her. She barely caught it. "You're staying at the Leonardo," he said. "It's the best hotel in the park. The wristband gets you into your room, among other things. Try to be responsible with it."

"Like a reverend with your Sunday donation."

Tommy flashed her a haunted smile. He paused, like he wanted to tell her more. And a memory flashbulbed the back of Gillian's eyes –Tommy's concerned look eighteen years ago in the Deduction Room. His lips moving. She didn't know what he was trying to say then, either.

He turned and disappeared into the crowd.

She felt momentarily adrift. How quickly she'd grown reaccustomed to Tommy's company. It unnerved her. She told herself it was better that he'd left. He and his troubles were a distraction. She'd think clearer with him gone.

She stood quietly and observed her surroundings. If something was wrong with the park maybe it began here, with the guests. They were certainly excited. Drunk with drama and anticipation. Gillian saw nearly universal adoration and was surprised Sebastian didn't lap this up more often. Did he suspect even a taste of hero worship could change him, or did he simply want everyone to think he didn't care?

And then, a cheer. Sebastian himself appeared.

He bounced out onto the stage, smiling big, his arms spread wide. He wore a green checked three-piece, spectator shoes in brown and white, and a russet-colored tie. Calfskin gloves concealed the shortened nub of his right thumb. His face the one from the flag, but younger than Gillian had expected. When he smiled, he seemed amused by a private joke. He looked healthy. On top of his game.

Around Gillian, people went batshit. They applauded like Sebastian had cured cancer instead of scaling three whole steps. People hollered his name and pumped their fists in the air. The atmosphere was surreal.

Other characters trickled onstage. Half a dozen Patrick Bateman types in Sebastian-derivative suits. A small, sophisticated woman with strawberry-blond hair and dark eyebrows, dressed in purple with a matching blazer hanging off her shoulders. And last but not least, Tommy, looking smooth and confident, waving to the crowd, the Winner nearly as well recognized as Sebastian himself.

Gillian watched Tommy and the redhead. Tension pulsed between the two, the redhead ignoring Tommy, his thousand-watt smile faltering. Gillian figured her for Evelina, Director of Park Communications, and the other half of the Kundojjala power couple. They and the other lieutenants filed to chairs arranged upstage and remained standing, waiting for their general to make his rounds. Gillian couldn't help but note the other executives eyed Tommy with a certain wariness. Tommy reattached his smile, but it seemed less full.

Downstage, Sebastian did a sweep. He dropped to one

knee, shaking hands with the front row, the Paraguayan Elvis. Parents lifted children so he could touch them. Pressed unauthorized biographies and pens into his hands. Obligingly, he placed his hand on downy heads. He signed the books with a smile. Gillian tried to remember what it was like to bathe in Sebastian's goodwill. But she felt only the crowd's sharp elbows.

He didn't seem to see her. But Sebastian saw everything.

Eventually he turned away from the adoring throngs. He ventured upstage and greeted his people, his gestures suggesting compliments and inside jokes. He spared extra time for Evelina, more than pleasantries exchanged. A squeeze on the arm for Tommy, along with a penetrating stare and a question. Tommy responded with a distant expression, as if he wasn't hearing the words. Nonetheless, Sebastian gave his arm an extra squeeze and moved on, having shored up the troops.

He strode to the podium. The pulpit constructed for his height.

"Welcome, my friends." Sebastian's smile was warm. "I'm glad you all could come. Today is a special day. A very special day. Everything we do at Miscellany is possible only because of the children. *Your* children. Every child who walks through the gates, to explore our park, is special. We have a legacy of over thirty years. Thirty years of children pushing themselves and finding out who they can be. And once, longer ago than I care to admit, we created a very particular opportunity for a group of talented children to make this discovery. The Contest Extraordinaire."

The crowd roared. Gillian remained silent. She watched the people lined behind Sebastian clap and smile. Tommy found her in the crowd, his smile fractured. Gillian couldn't be sure, but she thought Evelina had been watching her, too.

Sebastian waited for the crowd to quiet.

"Here at Miscellany," he said, "we don't like to live in the past."

Gillian eyed the flapping banners.

"But we would be foolish to ignore the success of what came before. Irresponsible if we failed to appreciate how our past success builds hope for the future." He paused and grinned mischievously. "Perhaps we can entertain both past and present simultaneously."

An excited murmur shot through the crowd. Even Gillian caught herself smiling. The old bastard.

Sebastian reached into his jacket pocket and withdrew a folded slip of cream-colored paper. He made a big show of opening it. "Many of you belong to Sebastian's Circle, our very popular children's club. Membership provides exclusive puzzle access and insider Miscellany information. But today, three of you, those between the ages of ten and fifteen, will be invited to take part in a little game. And why engage in any game if there isn't something to win? We have entertainments throughout Miscellany, each with their own rewards. Sometimes our prizes are monetary, sometimes they bestow recognition, and sometimes – *sometimes* – they offer merely the satisfaction of a job well done. But, in this case, I think we can do better. We can build your future with a little help from the past. Those of you keeping up with the news might be aware of the Reunion."

Gillian tightened like a bowstring. The crowd around her, oblivious, cheered.

"We have all our former Contestants in town to celebrate what was and what will be. All of them are on the Miscellany grounds. One or two are even here with us today."

Tommy wouldn't look at her. The cheers rolled on.

"The winner of today's entertainment – along with the parent or guardian of their choosing – will enjoy a private tour of Miscellany conducted under the personal guidance of a former Contestant. You will have lunch. You will ride the rides. You will solve puzzles together. And at the conclusion of your day, you will assist the Contestant in the creation of a new puzzle – one we intend to use in Bazaars around the country."

More applause. Sebastian smiled slowly, as if caught off guard by unexpected enthusiasm. But he never allowed the unexpected.

He called out three names. Those selected screamed and battered their way to the stage, followed by their guardians. A dark-skinned little boy with a broken tooth and an attitude; a freckle-faced blond girl with picked scabs on her arms and legs; and a little Black girl in braids.

A cold knife of déjà vu slid into Gillian's gut.

Assistants rushed onstage, bearing plush child-sized seats. Another approached Sebastian with three velvet bags, the openings knotted closed with gold cord. The bags were lumpy and roughly the size of a grapefruit. Sebastian picked fuzz from each bag and frowned when he found a loose thread. No less fussy now than he'd ever been.

The three children sat in their respective thrones. Cameras zoomed in, projecting their faces onto large monitors hanging from the arch overhead. The guardians hovered nearby, tablets with digital releases pressed into their all-too-willing hands.

Sebastian detached the mic from the podium. Backtracked to the overstuffed chairs.

"Here at Miscellany," he began, "we offer any number of

ways to stretch the human mind. Children are brilliant, simply put, and they are often not challenged to their full degree. Our puzzles, our games, push them intellectually. Intelligence is a key, unlocking the doors to success. Children – those of every color and creed – who have grown up with Miscellany are now captains of industry. They run governments. NBA teams. Puzzles, in fact, saved *me* from a life of poverty and allowed me to develop and demonstrate my intelligence. I was challenged, as well as entertained. And as such, I have made it my life's work to provide today's young people with the same tools, to advance their intellect through puzzles. There are any number of ways to puzzle – pattern matching, riddles..." The kid-in-a-candy-store grin. "Mechanical."

The chill spread up Gillian's spine.

The assistant unstrung one of the bags and dumped an object into Sebastian's outstretched hand. It was a reflective geometric puzzle composed of many small, irregular-sized blocks. In its current arrangement, the mechanism resembled a Frank Gehry building, not a cube but a hodgepodge of rectangular shapes. Sebastian held the object in front of Chipped Tooth. "This is a 3×3. Do you know what that is?"

The children had been mic'd. Chipped Tooth sounded insulted. "A Rubik's Cube."

"A name, to be sure," Sebastian responded. "Perhaps the most important speed cube. But this is of a particular variety. You'll notice the pieces are all one color." He spun the device in his hand. "This is a mirror cube. Mechanically similar to the Rubik's, but the monochromatic nature renders color irrelevant. The puzzle is solved only when returned to a cube state."

The kid's chewed fingers reached for the object, but Sebastian held it back.

"There is a solution, of course. If you're patient enough to see it."

Gillian clamped down the muscles in her face. She wanted to crawl on stage and knock the children aside. She could solve this puzzle. Sebastian knew she could. Her fingers might be older than the grubby digits currently twitching onstage, but her brain held more solution algorithms and pattern recognition skill than these kids could ever imagine. The quickness with which the competitive hunger surged scared her.

On stage, the other contestants received their mirror cubes. Each 3×3 was arranged in the same seemingly haphazard manner. Each child would start from the same scrambled position.

"When the horn sounds," Sebastian announced, "you may begin."

He let the microphone fall to his side. His eyes roamed the crowd. Grizzly bear eyes that moved so fast Gillian couldn't say he saw her – not with certainty. But he knew she was there. He had to know.

Smiling, Sebastian brought the microphone back to his lips. "Are we ready?"

A rousing cheer greeted his question. He raised his arm in the air, paused, then brought it down again swiftly, like an executioner. A loud horn blared, and the contest began.

The cube mechanisms rattled as the children twisted the sections. The crowd fell silent, the better to hear the relentless slushy hiss as the pieces spun. While these 3×3s were monochromatic, the strategies remained the same, substituting shape for color. Roux. Petrus. Fridrich. The methods well understood. This puzzle would be nothing for any of the former Contestants. If Sebastian were really pushing these kids, he'd opt for bigger cubes, or blindfolds, or solving only via feet. But these children were amateurs, as evidenced by their approaches. Had the children been experts, the cubes would have been slammed to the ground, solved, in ten seconds or less.

Gillian imagined herself in their place. Staring into the stubborn arrangement of blocks, the fractured mirrors emphasizing the blue in her eyes, the look others described as intense but she saw only as deer in the headlights. She saw herself cranking through the 3×3, rotating the blocks but also the mechanism itself, never slowing, never stopping. Ellsberg had always favored speed cubes. He'd loved breaking apart the known solutions and chaining the components together in new and interesting ways. The little snake had appreciated the structure.

She forced herself to breathe. These children weren't her or Ells. They came to impress, to quiet a compulsion, to sate some internal hunger for success. Their reasons and methods their own.

Chipped Tooth attacked his cube with LBL, or Layer-By-Layer. He'd likely solved cubes before – absorbed videos online or acquired tips from friends. He had one layer solved, all the pieces of the same shape and height, but the first layer was easy. He was already slowing down and had yet to advance to F2L – solving the first two layers. He'd need to bring an algorithm into play, construct a series of turns designed to keep the solved side intact. With his current approach he'd solve the cube, but might be the last to do so.

In a move that warmed Gillian's heart, Braids went Fridrich – her personal favorite. Fridrich was relatively easy to learn but more importantly faster than basic LBL, and the girl moved quickly toward solving the first two layers.

Gillian felt herself smiling, and stopped. The girl had the right look and the right traits. She could be a shill in some long Sebastian con.

The last contestant, Scabs, was using a method Gillian didn't recognize. Her hands moved quicker than the other two contestants. Right. Left. Up. Oddly, never down. Unlike her competitors, her edges were already oriented. She was engrossed. Between her teeth, the tip of her tongue was gnawed bloody. Her hands never left the cube.

This was what Sebastian looked for. Intensity. Drive. Focus that blocked all else. He stood off to one side, his hands behind his back, a kindly smile on his face. His eyes danced from child to child, but Gillian saw his gaze linger on Scabs.

The game continued. Chipped Tooth was clearly out of it. He'd already disrupted the solved face and was actually retreating from a solution. As for Braids, she had also slowed. She was still on the Fridrich path but had broken the last layer into stages, working the edges before tackling the corners. It was a completely legitimate approach, but not the fastest.

On the right, Scabs had her first two layers solved. Chipped Tooth cursed, and Sebastian frowned.

Braids' eyes lit up as she saw the last few moves.

You can do it, Gillian thought.

"Done!"

And it was over. Scabs held the solved cube aloft, the beating heart ripped from a slayed beast. The girl's mother stood behind her, clapping, the worry having fallen away like scales. Scabs was electric happy, a wild look in her face as she took in the crowd and all the people clapping only for her. Scabs liked the attention. Gillian remembered liking the attention, too.

Defeat exiled her competitors to different territory. Chipped Tooth winged his unsolved arrangement into the crowd, as Gillian tried not to stare at Braids. The girl held herself together well – perhaps too well. She spent another ten seconds solving her puzzle, not stopping until she had a cube as perfect as Scabs'. Her mother approached cautiously, one hand hovering over her daughter's shoulder but not touching. Gillian sensed a history there, a legacy of a kid so focused even a mother's love was a distraction. Or maybe Gillian threaded her own tangled past into their relationship. But that's what Miscellany did. Turned you around and upside down and emptied your pockets. You barely left the place with any idea of *you*.

Sebastian bounded down from upstage. The dry clap of his gloved hands methodical. He made straight for Scabs, as if afraid a similar crowd of entrepreneur moguls might chopper in to snatch her away. Pride lit up his face. He'd found this diamond in the rough – no one else. He paid no mind to Chipped Tooth and his dad as they stormed from the stage. He spared only a brief look for Braids, a slip of the eyes Gillian suspected few would catch but her. The girl stood and placed her completed cube on the chair and slipped her hand into her mother's before stepping quietly from the stage. The look was hard to read. Sympathy, perhaps. Respect. Disappointment, that this girl who clearly possessed the skills couldn't apply them fast enough. Or, most likely in Gillian's mind, satisfaction. Sebastian had known Braids would fail. Reality had only proven him correct.

Gillian turned to leave. She couldn't stomach watching another fete, especially one that felt arranged for her benefit. The crowd surged, eager to draw closer to the sun. Gillian couldn't wriggle free before Sebastian began to speak.

"A round of applause for our clever little girl," Sebastian said.

There were shouts and cheers. Gillian struggled against a crush of rabid fans.

"That was a very advanced solve." Sebastian's tone conspiratorial. He and Scabs just two puzzlers sharing secrets. "Remind me to show you a solution with two fewer moves."

Gillian frowned and elbowed harder. Behind her, Sebastian's voice rose.

"But on to the prize," he shouted. "I promised you all a glimpse of the future, and you saw exactly that. But I also promised you a visit from the past. And she's here, among us today!"

Gillian's stomach dropped.

"I'm sure you all remember her. She was fast. Clever. Above average with a word puzzle. Strikingly competent, one might say." A smarmy chuckle. "This one never held back. She wasn't afraid to take what she wanted."

The crowd pressed tight. Gillian's face grew hot. She couldn't push free. She wasn't sure what she'd do when Sebastian called her name.

"Ladies and gentlemen welcome to the stage… Leah Nev!"

The heat in Gillian's face flushed cold. The struggle drained out of her. She felt sick. On top of everything else, she'd fallen for another of Sebastian's tricks. She'd believed this was all about her.

Gillian found the edge of the crowd and broke free. She never turned around. She shut her ears to the crowd's adoring cheers, to Sebastian's cloying appreciation. She marched away from the stage and Sebastian and the taunting specters of her past.

Years spent crafting defenses. Building walls of distance and time that had crumbled within minutes. All the years and the lies she'd told herself. She was still the silly little kid in braids.

Ten

Gillian sat at the bar and ate mint chocolate chip ice cream. Dreary as the day was, she had the Formica counter to herself, the parlor an outdoor affair surrounded by a half-circle of stools. The ice cream was good. Nuclear green. The chips a buckshot of bittersweet chocolate. She licked an escaping sticky trail from her knuckles, kicked her heels, and felt, for a moment, like a kid again.

She was an idiot. The trip wasn't therapy or another opportunity to compete. She'd let the spectacle get under her skin, allowed Sebastian to manipulate her. He was still so sly. Confident. Able to work adults and children with ease. The years had treated him well. The touch of gray and the smile-line wrinkles lending him a certain savoir faire. He was a goddamn barrel-aged rye, stronger now than in the Contest days.

Funny, her thinking for even a moment she could help Vanesa. Gillian was no more clear of Sebastian's orbit than Vanesa was of Tommy's. It pissed her off that Tommy couldn't see the similarities.

Tonight was the party. Fine. She'd show Sebastian. She'd interview those intimate with Season Two: the Executive Team, the former *capital C* Contestants, and Evelina, maybe. Coax and cajole the players into revealing their secrets.

Uncover something concrete and turn puzzle promise into real-life reward – one Sebastian couldn't take.

Would Tommy make good on his promise? His behavior nagged her. He was off – the drugs, sure, but maybe something more. Was it possible he was playing her? Did he need more help than he'd let on? For a moment, she wished they'd truly recreated the Contest. Packed her and Tommy into a room for three weeks so they once again knew the other's every twitch, every glance. She wasn't sure if Tommy was on her side or using her to win some game she couldn't see.

Her mother always saw the best in people. Gillian could do worse than using charity as a guidepost. With generosity in mind, she withdrew her phone and texted Tommy. She waited for three dots that never came. A normal person would find distraction: play some cell phone game, chat with friends, or explore daydream getaways to beaches or mountains. Gillian eyed the crowd and wondered how they wrangled their brains. Why weren't they more stressed? How did they stroll through life and just relax?

The tall man derailed her thoughts entirely. He was visible even in the crowd. Beluga forehead, thinning blond hair, a continent in purple blooming on the side of his skull. He seemed older than thirty, his dress dull. Navy blazer, pleated tan slacks, mangy deck shoes. He walked with shoulders bent and neck thrust forward, a turkey protecting a papier-mâché heart. Martin Fucking Ellsberg.

She was off her stool without a second thought; never any question she'd confront him. Slithering through the park, daring her to appear, hoping to sidewind turn and strike? Like she wasn't familiar with his tricks? She thumbed chocolate from the corner of her mouth and approached from behind, giving her greeting some consideration. *Long time, no see?* Maybe something more direct, like a knee to the testicles? Ellsberg saved her the trouble. He stopped mid-crowd and put his hands in his blousy pockets. Let a grim little smile tug at his face. He waited as she approached.

"There's a shop in the northeast corner where they steep the mint leaves in cream," he said, when she was close enough. "This location uses mint extract." All these years and he continued to farm the German accent.

"You always did talk bougie." She circled him warily. "Although this look seems more JCPenney than Brooks Brothers."

"I enjoy the comfortable." He tracked her as she moved. "Why are you here, Gillian?"

"That's not much of a welcome. From an old friend."

He gave his smirk free rein. "Still nursing a grudge, I see. After all this time?"

"You cut me loose. Like I was a fucking boat anchor."

"Richard Nixon recovered from slights faster. Move on, I promise you'll be happier." He kept her at an angle, as if afraid to face her head-on. "Again, why are you here? You weren't invited."

"Maybe you don't possess all the facts. I was asked to be here."

"*I* didn't ask you."

"My dear sweet little Ellsberg, why should I give a good goddamn what you think? Tommy invited me."

Ellsberg considered his reply. When he spoke, his accent was a little less Teutonic. "Be that as it may. You're taking advantage."

"I'm taking advantage? Of what exactly? The multi-million-dollar theme park? The billionaire who runs it?

Tommy is a grown-ass man. You got a problem with his decision, discuss it with him."

"Every woman for herself, is that it? Just like before."

This arrogant motherfucker. She wanted to bring him down about eighteen pegs. "You know I'm doing you a favor, right? Your new contest is fucked up."

Ellsberg remained cool. Head up, composure in place. "Seeing as Tommy has been loose with the facts, I'll say this. There's no evidence of wrongdoing in this event, should there be one, but there is every bit of evidence that Tommy is overtired. This is not the 1980s. Excess doesn't have the same cachet. He works too hard and involves himself in too many details. Take this Reunion. I advised him not to take the Gulfstream to Los Angeles. And I certainly advised him against interacting with you."

She watched Ellsberg standing there, the world's biggest stick up his ass. Her presence upset him, unduly so. He was protecting something – Tommy's drug habit? Or maybe some impropriety in Season Two. Regardless, he didn't want her here, which was all the more reason to stay.

"Why are you so worried about me, Ells?" She got in his face. "Are you following me? That your job as Chief Head Mall Cop? To babysit all Sebastian's former kiddos?"

He didn't like her so close. He stepped back. "Sebastian doesn't have to babysit the rest of us, Gillian. We didn't run away."

The words stung.

"You haven't the faintest idea what this place is," he went on. "You haven't set foot here in eighteen years. You're out of your depth." He lifted his chin over the crowd. "The nearest exit is that way. Return to LA, flee to Paris or Rome, or the Yukon, for all I care. The jet will take you anywhere but here."

As a kid, she'd shared Jack London fantasies of running away to Alaska. Ellsberg seemed happy to throw that thwarted future in her face.

"Tommy is paying me to investigate Season Two," she said.

Ellsberg closed his eyes, as if his stomach disagreed with him. For a moment, she thought she'd sucker-punched him. "Tommy's broke."

If they'd been in Los Angeles, she'd have sworn the earth shifted. "What?"

"He's been placed on administrative leave. His spending, his personal investments – suffice it to say he has no access to funds. That definitely means company payroll, corporate Amex. He has no ability to hire you, or more specifically, to pay you."

She stood there, Ellsberg across from her, letting the news take her under, just like he had all those years ago. Now it was his turn to step close.

"I understand Tommy's stowed you at the Leonardo. It's a pretty penny. So what I've done is, I've allowed you to stay." He touched the band around her wrist. Waited a beat. "Take your taste of Miscellany life, at least for an evening. Enjoy what the park has to offer. And in the morning... well. The jet will be ready."

She'd flown all the way here, chasing a phantom. Another Miscellany promise as ethereal as cotton candy.

Ellsberg backed away, having turned the tables once again.

"I enjoyed catching up," he said. "And you look good. Very Los Angeles thrift."

He walked away.

Years spent imagining the taunts and barbs she'd rain

down on Ellsberg's pointed head. The accusations she'd bury him with. His artifice revealed, and the elation she'd feel at having finally confronted him with his betrayal. But in the end, she was left outmaneuvered and bitter. Tommy and Ellsberg working her all over again. This time Tommy the lure and Ellsberg there to push her head under the water.

She looked at herself. The blazer, the pants. Dressed like she was going to some West Hollywood club, meanwhile surrounded by guests in hoodies and tracksuits. She was playing the wrong game. Hopping on a plane with a fancy outfit as if she could razzle-dazzle the Miscellany crowd. Sell them a few scarves. This wasn't the Highland Park rich kids she used to outmaneuver on her way to the Contest. This group would never fall for flash and artifice, at least not in the form of trendy clothes and a few *you go girl* comebacks. And she knew better, had known better. A rage built inside, bigger and more powerful than all 5'6' of her stature.

Fuck Ellsberg and Tommy.

Fuck Sebastian.

She'd hustled and side-jobbed since she was eighteen. Scrapped for the clothes on her back. She'd come this far, and she *would* find some way to get paid for it. She wasn't finished. She wasn't beaten.

She went searching for the hotel. No longer wondering how the people around her relaxed. Relaxation was idle weakness. A luxury for losers.

Gillian was here to win.

Eleven

The sun broke through the clouds as Gillian wound toward the hotel, a stunning building that looked not unlike Leonardo da Vinci's helical air screw. Inside, the lobby was grand, the floor polished tile and the staff headshot attractive. The gloss reminded Gillian of the time she'd tried travel writing and took a flier out to Vegas. She'd spent the day walking the Strip's fancy places. The Wynn. The Bellagio. Lots of nice hotels – none as nice as this – with flowers and piped-in jasmine casino smell. She'd surfed the craps tables but couldn't stomach the twenty-five-dollar minimums. The free shows required an expensive room reservation. And ultimately, the games of chance reminded her too much of games of skill. Gillian found she had nothing to say about Vegas and returned to Los Angeles out the hundred for gas.

This place was just as predatory. Every pretty face smiling on behalf of the house.

At the front desk Gillian waved her bracelet near the contactless reader and within moments the staff conjured her particulars. They placed her in a room along the top blade of the screw, "just short of the penthouse." The elevator shot quickly past the lower floors, but Gillian felt almost no acceleration. She stared into the brushed brass, her reflection an insubstantial shadow.

Inside her room was white and modern. The mirrors full-length and the TV cleaver-thin. A bucket of iced beers sat in the sink, all LA locals she preferred. She stared at the beer, then at the band shackled around her wrist. What did it know about her, and who was it telling?

Ellsberg in her head. *I've allowed you to stay.*

Grabbing a beer and a bottle opener, she went to the desk. She set aside the bottle and eyed the laptop, a chic model infinitely lighter and more powerful than her aging beast. A sticky note clung to the screen. *For you.* She junked the note and went to the window to inspect the view. She noted this section of rooms hung out over hundreds of feet of open air. Apt. Very apt.

Tommy didn't answer his phone. Gillian left a message, asking him to call her back. Afterwards she stared hard at the phone. Started typing to Mom.

Hey, I know you're always wanting me to visit, so–

No. Delete.

Hey, how was your day? So, surprise, I'm in town. Work is keeping me pretty busy, though, so–

She should visit the care facility. Let Mom hug her and let herself be hugged. But then she'd have to explain why she was here. Endure the questions. *They aren't paying you?* The flood of failure drowning her all over again. And then how easy to crumble, to backslide. Stay a while, a while turning into months. Sleeping on June's couch, driving June's kids to piano practice. Telling any man she wanted to fuck *your place or your place?* And then to re-establish her hustle here… or worse. No way *He* would leave her alone if she lived in Dallas. It was hard enough to avoid his name in LA – in Texas she'd feel the heat of his presence twenty-four-seven. She couldn't orbit this close to the sun. Visiting was hard enough.

For a moment Gillian almost teared up. She could hear Mom's glorious cackle. See her toothy smile. The woman deeply loved Gillian, and all she got in return was disappointment.

Gillian deleted the message.

Pulling her shit together, she unpacked her old laptop, spurning Miscellany's too-slick gift. Work would steady her. She might have stayed away from games, but she'd dug up her fair share of dirt in the last few years. Chasing insurance scammers and deadbeat dads cultivated a certain set of skills. She'd apply those skills to Miscellany. Dig until she knew what was important to these people – how they moved, what they protected. And once she knew and understood the patterns, she could find weaknesses. Leverage.

Did leverage mean blackmail? She wasn't quite sure.

She connected to the Wi-Fi and ran searches. Nothing on Season Two, but a bevy of articles on Sebastian and his empire. State officials across the country drumming up tax exceptions, promoting guaranteed jobs and millions in tourist dollars. A big splashy photo of Tommy cutting the ribbon at a new Bazaar in Henderson, Nevada. The coverage by and large generous, save one article. A few weeks back a family filed suit against Miscellany, alleging negligence, fraud, and false advertising. The story wasn't in the mainstream media, instead covered in something unfortunately titled *Daily Miscellany*. The website quoted the family, the Navarros and their daughter Vanesa: *Miscellany and Sebastian have misled guests into believing they have a fair shot at a life-changing multi-million-dollar prize, so long as they try their best.* The Navarros insisted the park games were rigged. The victors only won because they had insider information.

The Navarro suit wasn't a class action. There were no

corroborating witnesses. Miscellany PR had, as of yet, no response. No scandal, merely the cost of doing business.

Gillian googled her one-time competitors.

Leah Nev. An entertainment lawyer by trade, she promoted herself as much as her clients. Navajo. Long hair that seemed to straighten or curl as necessary, she alternated between California approachable and East Coast *fuck you*. Bicoastal, she kept her fingers in a number of pies. She'd launched a YouTube show. Did a half-hour thing in NYC, *What's Hot* on Z100. Fame and fortune were close friends. Photos of her cozying up alongside Meryl Streep and Kerry Washington. Only one blip two years back, a quick spell in some Orange County treatment center for exhaustion. *Former Puzzle Wunderkind Can't Solve Addiction Nightmare.* For Dad, similar problems had limited him to starter jobs, competing for minimum-wage spots with high school kids. But such rehabilitations were de rigueur in entertainment.

Martin Ellsberg. Almost nothing of him online. He'd submitted biometrics questions in a security forum. Tried to sell an exercise bike. Information withheld, rather than simply absent. The fucker hiding, like always.

And then more Tommy. Smiling in a suit, both with tie and without. No indication the man lacked for anything, consuming every morsel of life, growing bigger with each story Gillian clicked. Reading only made her want to puke. The internet would teach her nothing of Tomas Kundojjala that Gillian hadn't already seen with her own two eyes. Miscellany-planted PR and a few handshakes didn't tell the whole story.

She chewed the taste from her gum. Was Tommy the problem? His presence on stage today had raised the hackles of his fellow executives, including his wife. His temperament ranging from desperate to euphoric, Gillian increasingly sure it was fueled by cocaine, at minimum. His behavior at the Navarros' was concerning – his near-mania, his failure to read the room, making a peanut butter sandwich while the family fell apart around him. And the capper – despite appearances, Ellsberg said he was broke. Tommy was clearly a train wreck.

But...

Tommy didn't live like a poor man. He flew on a private jet, cruised around in a high-end automobile with an honest-to-God chauffeur. And his behavior was maybe not that unusual. He did seem to genuinely care about Vanesa. His abrupt enthusiasm was perhaps the unavoidable intensity of a Type A, and the drugs just stripes on a tiger. The tension on stage could stem from simple jealousy, the result of his peers' thwarted ambition. Growing up with competition, Gillian remembered kids crying or throwing tantrums when they lost. Adults only pretended to handle defeat with more grace.

Gillian closed her laptop. It was tempting to chase this wounded animal. To figure him out, maybe fix him. But Mom needed money. Gillian couldn't make this about Tommy or the kids or Miscellany, or even her. If she couldn't shelve her emotions, she should fly home right now. Her suitcase sat on the folding rack next to the door. She hadn't even unpacked.

On her luggage, the neon-orange TSA lock. The combination one she'd used again and again. 2871. The Contest's first answer from the Deduction Room. The dice whose weight you multiplied to get the door lock code. The digits still fresh on her synapses.

Tommy had been last at that point. She'd beaten him out

of the room, fair and square. They'd traded a look, shared empathy, but the game was clean. No cheating.

She knew she shouldn't make this trip about Miscellany, or about herself, but she goddamn well was.

Lie to yourself, Gillian.

Over on the desk, the Miscellany laptop webcam stared, dead-eyed. What did they think, on the other side of the lens? Was this all according to plan? Did Miscellany think they had her right where they wanted her?

She took the gum from her mouth and thumbed the wad into the laptop's cold electronic eye with no small amount of pleasure.

Twelve

The Ballroom sat atop a grassy hill not far from the entrance. Music drifted on the air, the band playing champagne music as if Laurence Welk might appear and bubbles would fall from the sky. Black tie was the official dress, but Gillian saw all kinds of plumage. Contestants, VIPs, donors, industry insiders, Make-A-Wish kids, select members of the press, a Dallas Cowboy, two Dallas Mavericks, and a Nobel Prize winner. Clothed in everything from oversized jerseys to dresses by McQueen. Sebastian appreciated expression. If you could pull off biker chic, manage track pants and a barely-there blouse with blazer... more power to you.

Gillian had been tempted to push the boundaries herself – that kind of *give a fuck* outfit was within her means. Instead, she'd gone with her harem leg jumpsuit in a funky green and orange print, and plain brown sandals. She looked casually fancy, relaxed and loose. Inside, she felt like a coiled spring. All her worst fears gathered here. But she wouldn't run, not this time.

She went through security. Endured metal detectors and wands and some hard eye-fucking, although no one questioned her credentials. Once inside, the traditional setup. A big stage, a dance floor, bars positioned along the side. Less typical was the entertainment scattered around the perimeter. Table games like blackjack and poker, but also Skee-Ball and air hockey, Sebastian's mantra of continual play not forgotten.

The place was hopping, the Super Bowl in September, and the buzz made Gillian nervous. But she plunged into the crowd and allowed everyone a good look. Let them see their scrutiny didn't bother her, although she felt the eyes, imagined the whispers and judgments. Only after an unsettling sixty seconds did she drift from the center and retreat to the fringe. She stationed herself behind one of the appetizer tables, in the shadow of an ice sculpture crafted to resemble Theseus and the Minotaur. She nibbled on a crème fraiche tartlet and monitored the other alphas in the den.

She spotted Leah Nev in the confessional booth, breezy with her Panama hat and champagne – fashionable hobo, if Gillian had to describe the look. She found Ellsberg in a brown suit and red tie, radiating discomfort, like the world's most unsuccessful shoe salesman. But no Tommy and no Sebastian. Tommy's absence inexcusable, his pitch feeling more like a trap with every passing hour. As for Sebastian – the ringmaster would eventually show, no question. This was his circus.

There was no effusive reunion and group hug. The Contestants kept their distance, each similarly charged magnets, not unlike when they'd first met. A wariness had buffered them back then, the kids sizing up one another. Each assuming they'd win and assessing which rival was at best a threat for number two. Only after they'd found shared interests – languages, math, candy, board game throwbacks like Operation and Mouse Trap – had they let their guard down. Overcoming a similarity in background which drew them together, but also pushed them apart. *I may be like you, but I'm better than you. I'll rise above. I'll escape. And there will certainly be no hints, no mercy. If I know the Austrian national anthem is "Land der Berge, Land am Strome", I'm not humming a few bars before you whistle "Edelweiss"*. Those deviating from the me-first creed paid the price. Just look at Gillian. Had she not turned back for Ellsberg, she could have won the whole damn thing.

She watched the former Contestants stalk one another behind smiles and felt the Contest had never ended. They still competed for Sebastian's rewards – for his attention or his money, or both. They still played his game of winners and losers, where the roles could switch at any time.

Ellsberg found her, approaching slow, memories of their earlier conversation fresh. He inclined his head. "Glamorous as ever, I see."

He'd grown up in a literal trailer park in Alabama. He, of all people, should understand.

"Just because I don't own a Mercedes is no reason to dress like trash."

A small smile. "I am surprised they let you in. What if you steal the cutlery?"

"Nobody's watching, Ellsberg. You can say knives and forks."

"Someone is always watching." The smile disappeared. He scanned the guests, as if one might take a bite out of him. "Perhaps you'll benefit. The publicity from tonight is sure to raise your profile in LA."

"What do you mean?"

"I mean social media. Gillian Charles, the prodigal daughter returned. Your rediscovered fame is surely driving the livestream numbers." He gestured toward a raised platform, a pair of incredibly young women sitting with laptops and cameras, chattering away. Their cell phones swept the breadth of the party.

June was online. Always posting photos of family barbecues and band performances – two to three times a day, easy. Who knew how many times she scrolled through her feeds.

"You seem disappointed," Ellsberg said. "Did you promise someone an exclusive?"

"They didn't know," she muttered.

His smirk faded. "Your mother?"

"And June. I didn't tell them I was back. It seemed easier."

Ellsberg's silence felt accusatory. Surprisingly, he didn't offer any cutting remarks. "Jonas had a stroke."

He'd rarely mentioned his father. Gillian remembered stories of homegrown competitions for shoes and blankets, having to earn the right to sleep inside. He continued, lightly, as if discussing popular weedkillers.

"Twelve years ago now, if I recall," he said. "He was reaching for a bottle of tonic water. They found him on the floor, rocks glass clutched tightly. He died before the sun came up." Ellsberg shrugged. *C'est la vie.* "Mom still lives on that quarter acre. She has goats. I visit, from time to time, but she misses him, and I don't know what to say." He paused. "He took me to get my driver's license. Jefferson County, that governmental monstrosity. When I came out, temporary license in hand, he said, 'You did that, at least.' That's the last time we spoke."

She studied him. "Is this a teachable moment? Treasure the time I have with family?"

Ellsberg looked affronted. "Jonas could be standing across the room, choking on an olive, and I wouldn't take one step in his direction."

When Gillian put Miscellany in a box, she'd done the same with every memory of that time. She'd allowed herself to forget; all the Contestants carried baggage, long before Sebastian burdened them with more.

Gillian visited the bar, and to her surprise, Ellsberg remained close. To keep the stain off her teeth she chose white wine, a Chardonnay. Ellsberg ordered a lager and drank from the bottle. They walked, Gillian cradling her glass, scanning faces for Tommy but coming up empty, fruitlessly checking her phone. Ellsberg watched but refrained from comment.

She did spot Evelina through the crowd, dressed to the nines. The red dress fit the woman perfectly. She wore stilettos and her hair was up. Short in stature, but her personality took over the room. She chatted with some VIPs Gillian didn't recognize, mostly men who hung on her every word.

"She looks amazing," Gillian said.

Ellsberg smacked his lips as if waking from a millennia-long nap. "There is a species of mushroom, the destroying angels. Striking in their natural habitat, but trust me, they are toxic. After ingestion the consequences are severe. Vomiting. Diarrhea. Death."

"I know that mushroom. It's all white."

She batted her eyelashes at Ellsberg. He suffered the indignity in silence. Still, interesting he seemed wary of Evelina. All the more reason to secure a moment with the queen of PR, and anyone else connected to Season Two.

"Any of the new contestants here?" she asked.

Ellsberg looked askance at her. "No. As I said, it's unannounced."

"You've seen their qualifiers?" He didn't say anything. She persisted. "How do they compare?"

A grunt. "They certainly think they're smart."

Gillian laughed. "You don't like them."

"This batch has tutors. Miscellany Prep Courses. We didn't have those advantages."

"So they have money?"

He gave her a long look. "I'm not taking this Columbo journey with you."

She gave him a guileless smile. "Who's Columbo?"

The smile he returned was tight, and she worried for a moment. These exchanges with Ellsberg... After their opening salvos, she'd found herself enjoying his dry wit. That made her uncomfortable. The trip was becoming everything she feared, ghosts from the past.

On stage, the band wrapped their set and began packing their instruments. A Sebastian minion emerged from the wings and placed a single mic stand front and center. Gillian stared at the place where Sebastian would speak and felt like royalty before the guillotine.

Then it hit her – he'd want them all up there. The four prize ponies. His stable of cultured talent.

No, she thought sourly. *Two ponies. Two ponies, one rogue stallion, and one surly nag.*

An emcee took the stage. He banged a finger against the hot mic.

"Attention, everybody. Attention." The guy casual New Jersey. Such the opposite of Sebastian, obviously placed to disarm. "Going to need you to put down your glasses and bring the conversation to a dull roar and give the big man your attention."

Behind, other elves assembled the next entertainment.

Two tables. Four chairs. Gillian questioned Ellsberg, trying to keep her voice pleasant. "What does he think he's doing?"

Maybe a smile tugged at Ellsberg's mouth. "Seems we're expected on stage."

Gillian chided herself. Had she expected answers to be gift-wrapped, from this bunch especially? If they believed she was trapped, they'd relax. Walking into the cage – that was how she'd get her information, her leverage against Miscellany.

She tried to rekindle her childhood naiveté, the dead certainty of victory. Found mostly cold, jangly nerves.

Sebastian chose that moment to appear. Not so much appear as reveal his presence, as if he'd been at the party all along. He bounded forward from the wings. Today the three-piece was blue, with a blue-and-charcoal flat cap and vest. He waited impatiently as the emcee lowered the mic.

Gillian remembered when she first saw Sebastian. He'd spoken at the Majestic downtown, to a packed house. She'd won two tickets, and for perhaps the first and last time her dad was sober enough to attend as her guardian. They'd sat in the upper deck, the house lights down low, waiting. Sebastian had made them wait, letting ten minutes go by, then twenty. Then the lights came up and he was perched on the edge of the stage, kicking his heels as if he'd been there all along. Magic, in the flesh.

She'd wanted to be him so badly. Right from the drop, she knew he was different. For grown-ups, everything was about limits and fear. Don't go there. Don't touch that. But not Sebastian. He'd stared across the sea of faces and spotted Gillian in the back and twitched his lips, just for her. Like he knew everyone else was getting it wrong. Missing the point.

And if it was possible for Sebastian to resist the disease of fear, to maintain his real self and not get swallowed by talk of mortgages and taxes and the language of the dead used by every other grown-up, then it was possible for Gillian, too. She would fasten herself to him. Hold him close and do as he would do, and she could have everything he had and more. Sebastian would show her.

As she stared, she felt the longing again, like poison contaminating her bloodstream.

On stage, Sebastian put his hands together, one clasped in the other. "What a night," he said.

Applause. As if no one had hosted a party before.

"There's a mistake people make," he said. "They assume we hold these fetes in honor of Miscellany. Or worse, in honor of *me*. But nothing could be farther from the truth. We hold these events, we gather our friends and family, to celebrate the young people who take risks every day to make themselves better. To make the world better. It's not about me, it's about the children."

Gillian considered throwing up in her mouth.

"But of course, tonight is about no ordinary contest. It's about the Contest Extraordinaire. Do you all remember it?"

The crowd bit on the obvious and cheered. Sebastian smiled indulgently. "It has been a very long while since we've had these people in one room. The children who are no longer children, and yet are still my family. I've missed them, and I'm happy to have them back under our roof." He paused and took time to find each of them. Gillian dropped her eyes, yet still felt Sebastian's stare. "And while we would be remiss not to celebrate the Contestants' return, it would be an insult to their talent not to take advantage of this special opportunity. So…"

He paused, long enough that Gillian looked up. His eyes were electric.

"Let's play a little game."

He swept his arm to the side, toward the stairs leading up. Ellsberg turned to her, his expression a dare. *After you.* In his look, Gillian saw the boy pretending to drown, revealing enough with one hand to stab her in the back with the other.

If they thought she wasn't looking, they'd make their move.

Gillian went up the stairs.

Thirteen

A staffer guided Gillian to her table while the emcee entertained the crowd with patter. She sat across from Leah. Ellsberg sat across from – surprise – Evelina.

"Unfortunately, Tommy couldn't be with us tonight," the emcee explained. "But we're lucky enough to have his wife, the lovely Evelina Kundojjala, in his place. How about some applause, please?"

The guests complied. Evelina's answering smile gave no indication how she felt playing spouse, this woman who commanded a seat at a Fortune 500.

As for Leah, she remained fixated on the crowd. Didn't seem to notice her former opponent until Gillian said her name aloud. A blink and a slow turn; Leah stared blankly until recognition dawned. "Oh my God." Her face brightened. "Gilly. What are you doing here?"

People kept asking Gillian that question, as if she were trespassing.

"Tommy invited me."

Leah was a bowl of Sweethearts. "What a wonderful surprise."

The burgundy Courtnie dress with tiered skirt. The overly elaborate lariat necklace. This was quite a chameleon switch from Contest Leah. She'd been edgy and angry as a kid, and thus drew a lot of attention. The goth girl. The metal girl. Raised by her chill grandmother, who probably let her drink Cabernet at fourteen. Back then, Gillian had been too scared to approach Leah, intimidated by the older girl's smarts and cool. It was Leah who took Gillian under her wing. Makeup. Sharing crushes and silly pictures. They'd been close, until they weren't.

In the years since, Gillian had caught Leah in interviews. She talked in a raspy voice, like she'd stolen Joe Cocker's vocal cords then chewed through a pack of Newports for good measure.

A server brought them drinks, their orders predetermined. Champagne for Leah, Gillian more Chardonnay. She sipped at her beverage. Funny to be allowed anything, really. As children there had been no treats, the game too serious for soda and chips. Tommy's gift of candy all the more satisfying – not only were the M&Ms good, they also broke the rules.

In the lull, Gillian caught herself scanning the stage for Sebastian. Ever the entertainer, he'd slipped back into the wings after his tease. But he'd be close. He'd be watching.

The emcee once again begged for the crowd's attention. "The game," he said, "is draughts."

Gillian laughed out loud. The audience responded largely with blank looks.

The emcee leaned into his mic. "That's checkers, for you and me."

Checkers. Less sexy than chess. Essentially solved, computers having mapped the moves and pursued every outcome to a draw years ago. But disruptive variants existed, and none of the four likely played enough to think thirty moves ahead. This game would be decided by those who spotted their opponent's mistakes and capitalized on them. The goal not perfection, only to be more perfect than your opponent.

A vulture-necked staffer placed an empty board and digital timer between Leah and Gillian. The timer meant blitz – a maximum of three minutes per move. He then produced a flat cap fattened with playing pieces, letting Gillian blind draw. She came up with red, making Leah white. Lastly, he presented a stack of ballot cards, meaning move restriction, the card's face contents dictating the initial starting positions. Timers and move restriction were good news. Alterations forcing competitors into less cautious play and reducing the likelihood of draws. Gillian's brash, damn-the-torpedoes style lent itself to exactly this type of game.

She could win this thing.

Leah drew a card, a number on the other side. *Four.* Gillian drew a card, six opening moves listed on the other side. As dictated by Leah's card, they'd play the fourth set.

The moves: *11–15 (red), 23–19 (white), 8–11 (red).* The numbers indicated the dark squares on the board, 1 through 4 left to right, then 5 through 8, and so on. Per the ballot, Gillian's opening move diagonal from 11 to 15, a move the pros called Old Faithful. Taking the center in a show of strength. Gillian would have chosen the move regardless.

Across the table, Leah seemed unconcerned with the game's details, instead sipping champagne. Leah had always been cool, and maybe Gillian had worshipped her, a little. She remembered days the two had spent playing speed chess, slapping down the pieces, laughing. She'd lost more games than she won, but hadn't cared. It wasn't part of the Contest, just fun during downtime, Sebastian and his calculating smile nowhere to be seen. But over time Leah had treated that worship, that friendship, as some right to boss Gillian around. Leah the grown-up highlighting gaps in toddler Gillian's education, an expert criticizing her solves. *Should have studied your hieroglyphs, Gilly.* That had soured things.

Leah stared back at her. "Last time I saw you was the Tile Room," she said. "I stood on that pressure plate so you could escape."

"So I could pull the lever outside the door, and *you* could escape."

Leah shrugged. *Tomayto, tomahto.*

Gillian reminded herself she was thirty, not twelve. The point was to gain information, not win. "What happened to you?" Gillian asked. "After the Drink Me challenge?"

"I puked for a week, GI problems north and south. They were worried about my liver – Miscellany is lucky we didn't sue."

"And now you're a lawyer. Fighting gastrointestinal distress from the inside."

"Nothing so dramatic. OU on a softball scholarship." A bigger drink of champagne. "Law was just another thing they said I couldn't do."

One table over, Evelina laughed as Ellsberg made some joke. Despite his earlier comments, the two seemed chummy. Their banter took root in Gillian's chest, sent barbed thorns into her lungs. She could just as easily have been at that table, enjoying the friendly continuation of a decades-old competition. Ellsberg could have been making her laugh. She could be enjoying his company.

But no, that wasn't right. She should be playing him. *Beating* him.

"Here we go, folks," the emcee said.

Gillian yanked her attention back to the board.

"Yee-haw," said the emcee. "That means go."

Right off, Leah went 22–17. Combined with the ballot placement, a challenge for center control. The move made Gillian uneasy. It was the kind of aggression she preferred. If Leah seized Gillian's strategy, where did that leave her?

Outsiders probably fooled themselves with Leah. Saw a vapid socialite with diversity cred, someone more interested in selfies and parties than anything of substance. But Leah had been in the Contest. No one qualified for the Contest by solving the crossword in the back of the in-flight magazine. You qualified by being perceptive and smart, and often you concealed those traits. Leah seemed like popcorn. A few minutes of fluff and insubstantial fun. You wouldn't think she had grit until you looked up from some optical illusion puzzle, going cross-eyed hunting for the solution, only to realize she'd already crossed the finish line.

Case in point: Leah, smiling, asked, "How much is Tommy paying you?"

Gillian let her fingers hover over the board, like she didn't know her next move. "Who says he's paying me at all?"

"Backsolving. Know what you're looking for, before you look. Tommy – and I love him – is an idealist. Idealists talk too much. You're here to investigate the Navarro allegation."

Leah would be seeking to minimize Miscellany's risk. Sebastian's iron fist wrapped in sequins and lace.

Gillian went 11–16. Not giving up the center without a fight.

"Who would I investigate?" she asked. "You?"

The remark drew a laugh. "I wish. But no, I didn't give any of those kids answers. I don't think I could. Back then, I'd finish a puzzle and I felt smart. I liked feeling smart, didn't you?"

Gillian wanted to answer flippantly, but the wine was making her meditative. She missed competition. Proving herself. "It was a nice feeling."

Leah advanced, coming at Gillian on the left and leaving a piece exposed in the process. The rules required Gillian take the jump – she didn't like it. No way Leah accidentally abandoned a piece. But with no other choice, she took the jump. This dumped her right into Leah's retaliatory jump, and a subsequent exchange teed up Leah's double jump. In no time at all, Leah gathered a nice collection of red trophies at her elbow.

She'd bullied her way out, cleared space, and given herself freedom to move. Everything Gillian had wanted.

After, the game lagged. Gillian took more of her allotted time, and the party crowd drifted. Blitz or no, it was still checkers. A waiter appeared with snacks, and Gillian hid her frustration in food, snagging a bacon-wrapped hors d'oeuvre. One table over, Ellsberg also grabbed an appetizer, using the maneuver to study Gillian's game. She ignored him. Chewed aggressively and focused on her opponent.

"Imagine Season Two was rigged," Gillian said. "You'd know, right?"

A question too obvious to be a trick. Leah smiled, like she knew what Gillian was doing but wasn't threatened. "I'll tell you what I think." She swung her champagne glass freely. "If your scandal was real, there's one of three people, including me, who would be involved."

"Oh yeah?"

"The Puzzlemasters are out," Leah said. "They're all remote, everything is digital. One virtual office, everything controlled, nothing leaves. Anyone with puzzle access – we audit the home offices, their personal emails. They don't even get final approval."

"Who runs the qualifiers?"

"Operations. When they set up a game, they work in teams, so none of them has the complete puzzle or solution. They'd have to collude. And with eyes on them constantly, how would that work?"

At the other table, Evelina and Ellsberg had fallen silent. Lost in their own moves and countermoves.

"You said three suspects?"

"There's special tablets. Legal, Tommy, and Sebastian, we each get one. No way to hack them, supposedly. PR is dying for one, but at the moment, Evelina doesn't have access."

Leah enjoyed hearing herself talk. She barely looked at the board.

"Honestly, the only person we have trouble with is Sebastian," Leah said. "IT found him emailing parts of a puzzle to Tommy, in cleartext. Sebastian said it was easier. They begged him to stop, and I guess he did. But who can control the boss, you know?"

Gillian reluctantly moved a piece out from the back row. While seeming lost in the details of company culture, Leah responded quickly, attacking, more aware of the board than she let on. Her hand forced again, Gillian jumped an exposed white checker. And Leah smirked, moving almost before Gillian's fingers left her piece.

Control was the operative word, and Leah had it. Gillian was handcuffed. The game on rails. All this time, Gillian had believed she could beat any of these people, and right out of the gate she ran into a thresher. Sweat rose on her neck. Her face flushed. Everyone felt close, too close, especially Leah and Ellsberg, watching. Even Evelina, a stranger, knew how this game was going down. Goddamnit, what was Gillian thinking? Running up on stage, for a game of fucking checkers? Pretending she was still a Contest kid, only to wind up like Vanesa, like Gillian of eighteen years ago.

She glared at the checkerboard pattern, imagining flipping the board, the table. Storming off stage, giving them all a fuck you and then... what? Showing them she'd lost again? That she'd run away, again?

She closed her eyes. The board stayed, phosphenes branded into her retina. The game chasing her, no matter where she went.

It hit her then. Endorphins pumping, her skin pebbling. Position, not possession. Leah might have more red checkers in her collection, but the board told a different story. This early in the game, her pieces were very far forward. Which limited their moves.

The game within the game. Leah was working her, setting her up, on the board if not everywhere. Only, in her confidence, Leah had left herself committed and exposed.

"Gilly?"

Gillian opened her eyes. Across from her, the lawyer was impatient. Ready to get this over with.

Fine. *Let's get this over with.*

Pushing a piece forward, Gillian restarted the action. They traded moves and sacrifices, Leah continuing to advance aggressively. The subsequent exchanges were lightning flashes, ending in mutual jumps.

"This Season Two nonsense." Leah's hand hovered over a white checker. "I can't have you asking questions about an unannounced event. You understand the sensitivity?"

She moved another piece out from the back. One she shouldn't have moved.

Gillian could see the end of the game. It was all she could do not to lean back and cackle. Calmly, she responded down the right side. A seemingly functional move, not strategic.

"I just want to get paid, Leah. That's it."

Leah pivoted from prosecutor to long-lost friend with an ease that was terrifying. "I'm aware of Tommy's financial situation. And I'm sure we can reach an understanding. A few words with the Accounting department and they shake something loose from our consulting budget. Maybe pay you a stipend for services rendered, yada-yada."

A stipend didn't sound like enough money. "That might be interesting."

The lawyer smiled, thinking she had Gillian on the ropes. She returned her attention to the board and, for the first time, paused. She reached, hesitated, shifted and went for a protection move, covering a piece on Gillian's side of the table. Realizing she may have overplayed her hand, in any number of ways.

Applause from the crowd. One table over, Evelina had conceded. She was polite but exchanged only the slightest of handshakes with Ells. The man himself seemed pleased as punch. Gillian wished there was another round, that she'd get to challenge him directly.

As for her game, there was no more talking. Their moves became volleys, Gillian finally starting to push. The table continued to tell a story of a Leah landslide. Gillian advancing into a double jump, then another double four moves later and Leah acquiring the game's first king.

Maybe Gillian was wrong; maybe she wasn't good at games, hadn't ever been any good. This was why she lost, why she quit. She was fooling herself. She was a loser.

But Leah wasn't happy either. Now that she was paying attention, she knew the truth.

Confidence surging, Gillian moved. Under her hand, red hopped left and then right. Double jumping Leah.

The moment hung there. Leah staring at the checkers as Gillian removed them from the board.

"That was pretty clever," Leah said.

The move. The game. The conversation. Who knew?

Fatalistic, Leah jumped Gillian with her king, as the rules dictated. And Gillian took her king.

There was no point in continuing. Leah stopped the clock and raised her hand, summoning the staffer. Gillian and Leah stood, Leah all smiles and hugs in defeat. Up close, she murmured into Gillian's ear. "Word of advice?"

Gillian could afford to be magnanimous. She shrugged.

"Sit at the bar," Leah said. "Have a few drinks and enjoy tonight – you earned it. But tomorrow, go see him. Let him do his Sebastian thing. Smile, tell him what he wants to hear, play his game. Then take your money and go wherever you want. Otherwise, it's the same story, Gilly. He pushes, you have a meltdown and run away. And you're better than that."

Hardass or hipster, Leah still loved to lecture.

"I appreciate it."

Leah smiled. The best of friends. "You know, back then, I never doubted it. I knew you'd pull that lever."

Gillian smiled right back. "Roles reversed, I would never have trusted you."

More applause from the crowd, and the emcee summoned Evelina and Ells back to the stage. The four were guided up front, better to absorb the congratulations. Gillian told herself it was just a silly game. Checkers, a pastime for old men, not even chess. And yet her skin prickled. She felt ten feet tall, resurrected in marble and steel. She still had it. She could beat anybody. Granted, the Q&A with Leah had proved a mixed bag. Only three people with Season Two access, one of them the very man who dragged her out here. Sebastian's careless emailing perhaps an avenue, but that would mean talking to him, which she desperately hoped to avoid.

Once the four were arranged, they each received a sealed envelope. The emcee all but leering. "Go ahead and open them, folks!"

Gillian ripped open her envelope with a hooked finger. Caught Ellsberg unsealing his with the most incremental of finger moves, as if the envelope belonged in a museum. She imagined what might be inside. Miscellany stickers? Free passes to the park? She laughed as she tapped the contents into her palm. A single red card, with gold lettering.

TWO.

She looked to her left. Leah held a similar card with a different number: FOUR.

"Crap," Leah said, clearly understanding the implications.

Gillian's neck tingled.

The others freed their numbers. Ellsberg ONE, Evelina THREE.

"One, two, three, four," the emcee said, smug as hell. "Evelina's of course a proxy for the COO, yeah?"

He turned and looked to the wings. And sure enough, Sebastian materialized, annoyed, probably intending to appear in a puff of smoke. Instead, he strolled out like an ordinary CEO, his grin better than anything Satan could produce. He seized the mic and shooed away the emcee.

"How about that, folks? A nice little distraction, don't you think?"

Gillian could feel the gravity of having Sebastian so close after so long. But the big man paid her no particular attention. Seeming oblivious to the new satellites in his orbit.

"But did you feel it," he said. "The excitement? For a moment, a lightning strike. Intelligence. Inspiration. It's been too long, on that I think we can all agree."

Even the crowd lost him momentarily. Looks exchanged. A lull in their response. Gillian side-eyed the others and found no such confusion on their faces. They knew what was coming. Gillian stared at the number in her hands and wondered suddenly what she'd overlooked.

"I'm not supposed to do this," Sebastian said. "We were going to make the announcement tomorrow, but I think, tonight..." He looked down the line to Leah with an inquisitive face, like he was seeking permission. In response Leah shrugged, indulgent. *You've come this far.*

With a devilish gleam in his eye, Sebastian spread his arms wide. "In three days' time, here, on the grounds, we will reopen the original Bazaar!"

He let the announcement slither. Whispers ran through the crowd, question piled on question.

A chill raced up Gillian's spine.

"Why, you may ask?" Sebastian tamped down his smile. Serious now. Fireside chat mode. "I'd always fought the idea of another Contest. I couldn't disrespect the original Contestants – their commitment and execution. But I've come to believe the world needs another Contest. What we can offer a new generation is too great to be withheld."

He was about to announce Season Two. But panic

chewed at Gillian's nerves. She'd missed something.

"So we find ourselves with a quandary – how to reconcile these two incompatible ideas?" He paused, as if one of the attendees held the answer. "We allow the original Contestants to inspire us again."

Gillian felt the strong urge to run from the building.

"The numbers they hold are starting positions," he announced. "In three days' time, we celebrate the past. The Reunion, a reimagining of the first Contest Extraordinaire, with new challenges, and featuring each and every one of the original Contestants."

Mother. Fucker.

The crowd could no longer be restrained. A wave of excited chatter flooded the room, the dramatic reveal too much to bear. On her right, Ellsberg let loose with another of his sighs. "I was afraid he couldn't be talked out of this idea. It will be a stupendous distraction." He glanced at her. "It would seem you're staying."

From his place center stage, Sebastian watched. He dropped his head, his face with that look. The same look he'd worn eighteen years ago as Gillian struggled with the dawning understanding that she'd lost the Contest. His irritation with her emotions. His disappointment in her performance. The way she ran from Dallas and everything in her life since. It all came flooding back. He could still manipulate her, make her feel small and unimportant. This was the setup Gillian had feared. Lured back to Miscellany only to relive the past, to make another run at the brass ring. She reeled. From the booze, from the revelations.

And Jesus Christ, her first instinct.

Maybe she'd win.

Fourteen

Gillian slept in her clothes, over the covers. Hair wrapped in one of her scarves, otherwise no bedtime preparation. Only when the phone woke her did last night come flooding back. Disappointment, with a chaser of regret. No hangover, but she couldn't shake the sense she'd played too loose, somehow exposed her cards. If alcohol hadn't impaired her senses, the Contestants had. The Contestants and Sebastian.

Let the call be Tommy. She could leave before it was too late.

It wasn't Tommy.

"Hey there," Mitch said. "How are you?"

Mitch ran Mom's extended care facility. He was nervous, using his octave-higher voice, his talking-to-the-feminine-persuasion voice. Gillian rolled off the bed and went to open the curtains, hoping daylight would detoxify her. She stood at the glass, rubbing her eyes. Far below, the guests, their bodies reduced to reflections from sunglasses and cell phones. They sparkled – floated unfettered. She envied their freedom.

"I'm good. Out paying the bills." Letting Mitch know she was busy, in case he worried about her ability to pay, or desired an extended social call. "You need something?"

"I do. I wanted to tell you first." A noise like he was chewing his fingernails. "She's being discharged."

The glass seemed suddenly fragile. Gillian turned from the window. "That's not possible."

"I told you her Medicare is maxed. Didn't you get the letter?"

The mail would have gone to June. And, if Gillian was being honest, June probably told her. "What about the check?"

"Well, the check is short. That's what I'm saying. It's all in the letter."

"Look. I'm on a job right now. It's complicated, but it could mean money."

"How much money?"

On the plane, and even walking through the Miscellany gates, she'd told herself she could walk away at any time. "The whole ride. For a year."

"You have it now?"

"Soon. I just need a little time."

She was talking out her ass. But if she could convince Mitch to hit pause on pushing Mom out the door, she could get back to Los Angeles. She knew people there, people with money. Her personal shopper clients. Chantal.

"I already signed the papers." He sounded guilty. "She's got thirty days. I fought for more–"

"Thirty days? Mitch, where is she going to go? She needs specialized care."

"I wish I could help, I really do. The owners are looking at what they're making per bed. They don't know your mom, to them she's just dollars and cents."

"This is ridiculous. June told me last time she's there, Mom had bruises. She fell in the bathroom? You guys aren't even watching her, and instead of fixing the problem you're kicking her out?"

"It's not my call. What do you want?"

"I want you not to kick her out. There are options. We can get an extension."

"Gillian, I'm on thin ice already. I need this job. I got the condo payments. My car. I can't go back to my parents' place in Fayetteville. I mean, I like you, I really do. I wish—"

She was sick of Mitch and his games. Sick she was failing her mother, the woman who had given everything for her and been the light in a hellscape of dark. "No. No, I get it."

"I feel terrible."

"I understand." She kept her voice neutral. "Thirty days."

She could hear him breathing. He was always talking about getting into shape. "Look… if you can't make it… maybe I could make some phone calls. Reach out to other places?"

"Don't worry about it. You've done plenty." She swallowed. "This is my problem. I'll think of something."

"You're sure? You don't need—"

"Yeah. No, I got it."

He fumbled with the phone. "We'll talk? If you get the money, I can stop the paperwork."

"Sure. Yup. Thanks for calling."

She hung up. Listened for ticking clocks or chattering guests or any sign the world carried on, but she heard nothing. The room was acoustically baffled and dead quiet. Sebastian really did spare no expense on his hotels. Much like every other corner of his life.

The Devil whispered in her ear. *You know who has the money.*

She'd told herself she was never coming back. What

a joke. She'd always known she'd come back.

Her luggage still waited on the folding rack. Unpacking, she traded ballroom chic for theme park cool and casual. Out went the rumpled jumpsuit. In came her white-and-red Atari tee, jean shorts, a hoodie tied around her waist, and blue Chucks. She enjoyed being put together as much as anyone, maybe more than most, but at this moment she needed to feel free and unencumbered. Confronting Sebastian was a game, and like any game, she needed agility more than style.

She packed very little inventory. A string bag. Sunglasses. Pen and pad, because her brain worked better when she wrote things down. A paper book, in case she needed to sit and eavesdrop undisturbed. And her smart mouth.

She hooked the bag over her shoulders and went to find Sebastian.

Fifteen

Riding down the elevator, Gillian installed the Miscellany app on her phone, an emoji Sebastian smirking at her as the app loaded. She activated the logic puzzle account protection, the answer an additional access key. The problem was straightforward – a grid of pilots, parachutists, and jump times. *Buford jumped 1,000 feet higher than Margaritte. The parachutist who jumped from 15,000 was Paul.* The solution required matching the jumper to pilot and to height. A scenario steeped in the kind of relationships Gillian could chart in her sleep, although she did enjoy the process. She flew through the exercise and after finishing felt knife-blade sharp.

In. Out. Extract what she needed from Sebastian and avoid his temptations and detours. She worked marks all the time. She could do this.

Out on the grounds, the guests had slung jackets and affixed ballcaps, sunlight bleaching the landscape – typical Texas weather, turning on a dime. Gillian stepped into a river of humanity and found the experience less unpleasant than she expected. The sun warmed her skin. Chatter washed over her: normal talk about ballgames and movies. She could pretend the park was hers to discover. Go anywhere, do anything. She passed under raised train tracks, the arch overhead supporting an anthropomorphized locomotive laden with screaming children. She threaded the kids' zone with its rebuses and palindromes, noted the brightly colored signs for the Young Persons' Detective Agency – an interactive Miscellany caper. The place was both more and less than Gillian remembered. Eccentric touches commodified.

The forbidding turrets of a Victorian-style house appeared. Gillian remembered this building, a turquoise nightmare of styles and structures. Ornately trimmed fascia and exposed eaves. Crooked chimneys and narrow dormers and long fenced porches. A tall wrought-iron barrier separating the property from the rest of the park – the original Bazaar, the location of the Contest. Despite the heat, Gillian's skin pebbled. The beast stretched four stories above ground and burrowed a few thousand feet below. It had been closed shortly after the Contest, never to reopen. Until now.

She stared at the building. Sebastian was bone and gristle she could wrestle. The Bazaar and what it held – that was a ghost.

As she turned, she thought she saw her. For one second, Jackie's slash of hair and ballpeen eyes. Then a blink and nothing but people texting, glazed anonymous faces carting Miscellany-branded swag. Gillian didn't budge despite the annoyed glances, keeping her eye trained on that one spot. She stood watching for a solid sixty seconds and earned nothing for her trouble except crushed toes. She didn't feel any less disturbed, but she moved on.

The attractions thinned as she approached the edge of the park. A barbershop promised "Sebastian-style" haircuts. Bathrooms offered relief for victims of the hundred-ounce soda. Every five yards another mega-park staple leered. Sebastian always said he'd wanted to be big, but unlike previous moguls, he'd do things differently. Bigger, but better. As Gillian scanned the park she saw celebrity chef restaurants, saw merch, saw entertainments not covered by the initial ticket price. And always within eyesight, something branded with Sebastian's face. All the usual trappings of a top-tier theme park.

On the horizon, one structure rose above the scenery – Miscellany HQ. Gigantic steel girders and reclaimed oak posts framed an enormous glass curtain wall. Vast doorways disgorged cast and crew and employees. There was constant conversation, not so much a beehive hum as the excited chatter of Santa's workshop, a diligent group of enthused workers – *family*, in Miscellany parlance.

Gillian drifted inside, the interior bigger than an airplane hangar. A polished concrete floor stretched over a football field in length, dully reflecting the millions of shoeprint scuffs produced by Sebastian's army. Absent the security barriers and armed guards, it was a Restoration Hardware wet dream.

Had Gillian won the Contest, would she work here? Could she have kept her tongue in her mouth, or at least her comments on-script enough so that she'd navigate the transition from awed kid to inspired worker? Would Mom and June live on the grounds and shop in Miscellany-branded stores? Would Gillian have been on stage with Sebastian, warmly shaking his hand?

To hell with that. Sebastian could shake *her* hand.

At the barricade a body scanner and the de rigueur contactless reader. Her bag was inspected, her body digitally undressed. She bristled, wondering if everyone received the same profiling. Regardless, the guard seemed to expect her, called her by name. Sebastian waited in his office, a retreat annoyingly known as The Aerie. *Third floor, green door at the end of the hall, then all the way up.*

Gillian found the elevator, ascended with a group of fresh faces talking about the new AR experience and the invite-only locked room whodunnit being staged at the park's newest restaurant. No one discussed rigged contests. Everything seemed the bee's knees.

On three, Gillian walked alone through a space that seemed more laboratory than office. Color swatches and pencil sketches. A Boggle game and a giant Jenga tower and a whiteboard scored with hieroglyphs. She observed a few people in suits but plenty in board shorts and flip-flops. The low-bar Miscellany dress code of *you must be dressed.* Everyone looked happy and relaxed, like they weren't working for money. They swarmed to Miscellany because they wanted to be here.

At the end of the floor a single weathered green panel door was set in the wall. The door looked out of place – it belonged in an old wooden house, not embedded in a flashy glass-and-steel office building. Nevertheless, there it was, flaking paint chips onto the floor, the black security rectangle alongside blinking its alligator eye. Another wristband press triggered a click and then Gillian was through and up a winding staircase, a creaky low-ceilinged affair that didn't let her see what was coming. A rainbow of short painted steps took her away from the offices, the sconces on the wall flickering low. She expected organ music. She felt like she was in church.

At last, she reached the top, the door cracked open. She pushed through into a cramped room full of wooden bookcases and handmade furniture. Natural shafts of light fell from clerestory windows and a cheval dressing mirror stood watch opposite. The room was devoid of photos, a monument to the man's professed credo of not looking back. Papers accumulated everywhere, but she also saw a giant computer monitor mounted on a swivel arm over a tiny rolltop desk. Sebastian sat at the desk, angled away, perched on a chair that seemed designed for a child. Today the three-piece was olive green. He'd removed his gloves and massaged the nub of his right thumb with his index finger, focused on a collection of documents.

Somewhere a clock ticked. Sebastian didn't turn. Didn't acknowledge her at all.

Gillian was sick of it. The long pilgrimage and the eccentric lair and the calculated indifference. The nearly two-decade weight sitting on her shoulders, a weight she'd allowed to roost undisturbed. The desire to tear into Sebastian for a lifetime of manipulation competed with an interest to appear unruffled, to beat him at his own game.

Sebastian lifted his head, almost certainly having spotted her in the reflection on his screen.

"Why?" she asked.

"Why what?" His manner was puckish. As if he was dealing with another wide-eyed innocent.

"Why do this? Bring me back. Hide Tommy."

"I'm not his keeper. That's not how things work." He spun around and threw his arm over the back of the chair. His eyes goddamn twinkled. "It's good to see you."

"Don't change the subject."

"You were always angry. I'd hoped you would have conquered that emotion since our time together."

"Fuck off."

"I understand why, of course. To come that close. It must be hard."

"I'm not angry." Her angry face watched her from the mirror. She moved away from her reflection. "You're playing games. To keep me here."

"I don't know where Tommy is. He's free to pursue his own interests, like any ordinary human."

"He won your Contest. He's more than ordinary." The head of steam that had propelled her here boiled away. She felt wildly unprepared. She wished she'd worn something more professional before barging into Sebastian's inner sanctum, then regretted the thought.

Sebastian lifted an enormous stone mug from the desk. Latin script scrawled along the outside.

> *Exiguum corpus, sed cor mihi corpore maius;*
> *Sum versuta dolis, arguto callida sensu;*
> *Et fera sum sapiens, sapiens fera si qua vocatur.*

Gillian knew the answer to the riddle, but kept her mouth shut. Over the rim of his drink, Sebastian studied her. He drank slowly and when he replaced the mug, he kept the script face out.

"What yarn did Tommy spin to get you here?" he asked.

"Excuse me?"

"You didn't come for the Reunion. We didn't invite you."

"I keep hearing that. It's very flattering."

"You wouldn't have accepted. I knew better. Tommy must have set the hook, appealed to your intellect. You weren't going to leave your scarf-and-shopping empire for anything less."

"Here we go."

"Don't be silly. I don't mean anything by it. And you can't say it's not true."

She caught herself picking her cuticles. Which he'd see as weakness. She pointed at the riddle mug. "Is that for me?"

The look on his face suggested he was seeing the mug for the first time. "You remember your Latin?"

"Do not bring me that weak-ass shit."

Cursing in front of the man elicited a weird thrill. She'd always been a child with him. Never a real conversation as adults. As peers. Sebastian adjusted the mug and folded his arms. "And?"

"*Small is my body, but greater is my wisdom. I am versed in trickery, cunning and keen-witted. And a wise beast am I, if any beast is termed wise.*"

He considered her response. "That's essentially the translation."

She crossed her arms. "*Vulpes.* The fox."

He clapped, a grin stealing over his face. "Yes."

"It still suits you."

A head nod, his version of a bow. Pleased with himself, and her. "So many today stop at the text," he said. "As if rote memorization was the goal."

"Do the kids even know who Symphosius is? Can't they just google the answer?"

"It is a problem. But we try to arrange the puzzles such that an over-reliance on the internet sends one down false paths. We want to teach the children to rely on themselves for critical thinking, not someone else."

She'd been listening to him. Taking instruction. "Unless that someone else is you."

He watched as she drifted, taking in the many obscure instruments – a theodolite, a brass plumb bob, a Baroque pendulum clock ticking away on the wall. She inhaled and got a lungful of dusty vellum. This room was a trap, and Gillian pressed her luck every moment she lingered. "Tommy said something about cheating."

Not a blink from Sebastian. "Season Two. There's a nuisance suit, the lawyers won't let me discuss details. But the case is baseless. Run-of-the-mill greed." He pulled his gloves close but didn't put them on. "Tommy didn't bring you all the way here for that, did he?"

"He was upset."

"He's in a vulnerable place. He's lost access. To decisions. To expense accounts. By rights, he shouldn't have been able to take the jet to LA."

Gillian had assumed Tommy's financial issues were of his own creation. But perhaps some measure of his struggle was the trials of Job. Sebastian playing both God and Lucifer.

"*Stretch out your hand and strike everything he has*?" Gillian said. "Seems a little Old Testament."

"Don't exaggerate. We're a family, and we will take care of Tommy. But he has to stop with these public accusations."

"You've cut him off. Left him alone."

"No child of Miscellany has ever been alone. Present or past." He straightened the mug and his keyboard. "How much was he paying you?"

The elephant in the room. Trumpeting for all to hear. "I was doing Tommy a favor."

"You can be rewarded for a favor." He tracked her from the corner of his eyes. "Gasoline is not free. Rent is not free."

Gillian faced the wall. She watched the clock's pendulum swing, back and forth, locked into the same path.

"Maybe we can help each other," Sebastian said.

Not too quick, or he'd set all the rules. "I don't think so."

"I'm concerned about Tommy. He's the future, I can't do everything anymore. But you're here. You're smart."

"You've just described your right-hand man."

"I need someone I can trust, Gillian."

"I thought you found that person eighteen years ago."

The clock ticked.

"The Reunion is in two days," he said. "I need the situation managed by then. Help me solve a problem. I'd be paying you to solve a problem."

He looked at her. Foxes were opportunistic hunters. They'd eat whatever was dumb enough to enter their territory. "I'm not cheap," she said.

"Bill Gates pays his people fifteen hundred a day. I'll give you three thousand. That's six thousand for two days' work, in case your mathematics are rusty."

A number so much less than what Tommy offered. The disappointment must have been written on her face.

"You tell me the number," Sebastian said. "I'm sure you'll be fair."

"Again. Fuck off."

"Gillian. Tell me the number."

She hesitated. Could she ask for all of it? At what price did she owe Sebastian, instead of the reverse? "Ten thousand."

"Done."

He could have been agreeing to new napkins. A lamp for the living room.

She should have asked for more.

"I need you both at the Bazaar on time," Sebastian said. "Presentable. There's a media event prior, and Tommy cannot appear hobo chic. I want three-piece. Gray, perhaps. If he must wear a pinstripe, it should be subtle. Your fashion sense I trust, of course."

Gillian reminded herself this was only temporary. Find Tommy. Get him to the Reunion. Take the ten thousand, settle Mom, and fly far away from here. "I'll get Tommy to your game."

"And you. You're both competing."

"Don't push me."

"I never stopped pushing you."

She felt unsteady. She moved toward the door.

Sebastian put his chin in his palm. "You'll keep me informed? Two days is a long time. I'd like updates."

She paused at the top of the stairs. "I'm not running up here every time you get bored."

"I wouldn't dream of it. This problem speaks to Security. You'll report to Martin."

Cold sludge in her throat. Like she was back under the lake, watching the bright surface pull away. "That's not necessary."

"If you want to get paid it is."

The thought of Ellsberg evaluating her every move. Waiting to pull the rug out from under her.

"Cool," she said. "Good luck with Tommy, then. I look forward to reading about the scandal."

She took a step down the stairs, and Sebastian chuckled. "Don't be so dramatic." He looked at his computer but didn't focus on the screen. The nub of his thumb tapped against his mug. "Keep Martin apprised, if nothing else."

"Isn't he capable of spying on his own?"

Sebastian swirled the contents of his mug. Didn't rise to the bait.

"I don't report to Ellsberg," she said.

He chewed on the words. Inclined his head.

"You'll tell him?" she asked.

"Don't concern yourself. Martin will cooperate. He always does." Sebastian extended his hand. "We're agreed?"

Gillian fed him a look like he'd offered her a severed limb. "We trust each other, right?"

He drew back his hand and laughed. "Gillian Charles. You have gotten better with age."

The comment made her flush with pride. Her blood pumping and her synapses firing. She enjoyed this. Enjoyed matching wits with Sebastian.

A warning, from way back in her skull. *This is what he wants.*

She turned and accelerated down the staircase.

Sixteen

Gillian held phone to ear and listened to the electronic ghost of Tommy's voicemail. Regret chased her through Miscellany's wishes-and-moonbeams hallways. Eighteen years since she'd seen Sebastian in the flesh. Nearly two decades in which she'd built Sebastian into some dapper bogeyman. He was witty, powerful, and smart, but he was just a man. And yet, it had taken one day. Less than twenty-four hours in the park and she was already working for him.

"Bohemian motherfucker," she muttered.

Nothing struck her dead. No lightning cast from Miscellany's most eccentric tower.

The Reunion. Sweet Jesus, another Contest. Exactly the kind of rigged game she'd sworn off. If the Proscenium event – if the checkers game – taught her anything, it was Sebastian's games were a mirage. They led to nothing but disappointment.

But what if? What if she competed in the Reunion, and won? Took their money, took their game, got everything she deserved?

Fuck. What was wrong with her?

Tommy's voicemail greeting played out.

"Tommy," she said. "You need to call me. I don't care if you're on a mini-vacation, took leave of this earth, whatever.

Sebastian's got me looking for you now, and you don't want that, let me tell you."

She stopped at an intersection. Her look scaring the interns. She held back.

"I think..." she told the voicemail. "I *think* you brought me here to help, one way or another. I can do that. The Navarros – that's not good, anyone can see it. Maybe Miscellany should do more. Can do more. But someone loses, that's how the game works. Of all people, I know. You, Leah, Ells – you all called it. I ran away, I quit. You think I'm proud of that? And now, what? You're into achievement trophies, everyone's a winner? Tommy, you better believe I got wise, and so should you, pretty damn quick, because there's a timetable. Sebastian won't wait, and neither will I."

Jesus Christ. She sounded like Sebastian's process server. She rubbed her neck.

"Don't turn this into a game. You don't want to call him, don't call him, that's fine. But call me. Let's figure this out."

She hung up.

He was ducking her, no doubt. Fine. She could track one guy. Tommy was eighteen years removed from life-or-death decisions, whereas Gillian's every day depended on doing the job fast, or her ass was on the street. Ten thousand for shepherding Tommy to the Reunion – easier than chasing Tommy's paranoid delusions. A life raft for Mom, enough to keep her afloat while Gillian searched for better answers.

Better in the end, she thought. Better with Tommy as the payday, rather than a friend in need.

She hunted for his office. Even in this egalitarian utopia, there were haves and have-nots. Cubes in the center, offices along the windows. Gillian hated signing autographs, but a

Jane Hancock later and a young thing with nose ring and multicolored hair pointed her at a nearby office. Tommy's executive assistant, Jessyca, hadn't seen the man all day. *That Tommy, never where you want him.* Jessyca seemed bored, and showed off her latest tattoo, something with seahorses and feathers, the artistry one might expect from a drunken bender. There were two heartbeats in which Gillian expected the girl to touch her hair, but she instead pointed a finger at Tommy's domain.

The office itself was, surprisingly, one of the smaller fiefdoms. The interior Scandinavian sparse, but still tech exec. A glass standing desk with widescreen monitor and loose connecting cables, no laptop. A Miscellany Lego set glued in its assembled state. Two guest chairs with no backs and a couch you could put to sea. Gillian positioned herself behind the desk, amid Funko Pop vinyls and a single unsolved 3×3. Holding one of the Funkos at eye level, she could see it was based on Tommy. Another under the monitor a giant-headed likeness of Sebastian.

No paper and no notes. Not even fingerprint messages on the glass. A look in the trash revealed only a drained paper coffee cup.

Gillian changed venues and ventured outside HQ. She questioned clerks, show performers, and the others who made Miscellany function. Most of them recognized Tommy; none of them had seen him recently. She had the most luck at the Transportation Hub, gray-green offices barnacled to the shared wall with the parking lot. An attempt to bum a cigarette from the off-duty crew failed – the drivers all vaped – but she chatted up a handful about their routine, how things worked on the inside. Her status as a fellow hack opening doors, the drivers sharing stories of drunk clients, clandestine pickups of "escorts", not to mention the hours spent hosing vomit and urine from back seats. Valuable details proved sparse. Gillian learned only Jackie drove Tommy, never any of the others. Occasionally he'd been spotted taking rideshare from the parking lot, thinking he was covert – when your face was on the park banners you were never incognito. As for Jackie, she wasn't around, and despite the proletarian bonding, no one volunteered information on her whereabouts.

Gillian's tolerance for shop talk and half-answers at an end, she moved on. She wondered – why sneak off in a Prius when you had access to your own private car? And a driver who seemed willing to conceal your drug habit?

Hungry, she stopped at Enigma's Sweet Treats, a shop stocked with traditional confectioneries, but also edible jigsaw puzzles and interlinked ring-shaped candies. She ignored all the fancy shit and went for her reliable peanut M&Ms. She queued up and pondered the heads in front of her. Wouldn't it be something to find Tommy right here, satisfying the same craving?

Back in the day, Tommy's habits had been more innocent. He'd poured that candy into Gillian's hand as they'd waited in the stuffy wood-paneled hallway outside the first Contest room and grinned like he was giving her answers. She'd grinned back, figuring she'd chomp them in his face after she won. Then the door had opened, and they'd flooded into the Deduction Room.

She and Tommy had escaped the room last. Gillian worked her puzzle calmly at first, but once Ellsberg left, and Leah followed, her insides had collapsed. She wasn't good enough. She was too young, too immature. She didn't know what she didn't know, and these smart kids – these *better* kids – were going to beat her. Sure, the Contestants had fun outside the games, but they weren't friends, not really. Who could be friends and still win the Contest?

In her memory, Tommy had played mint-ice-cream cool. Facing third place, at best, and he'd worked his puzzle like no big thing. Arranging the dice on the scale, counting the number of ticks down or up, although what that meant was uncertain. Checking on Gillian occasionally, like he was worried about her. The candy, the sympathy – what game was he playing?

The puzzle had swum before her eyes. Disjointed. The answers steel bars refusing to bend. Her breath coming faster and faster. Her face flushed, her neck burning.

Breathe, girl. Her mom in her head. *Breathe. You can do this.*

And she had breathed. Closed her eyes, accepted she might be last from the room. Before she could defeat the others, she had to defeat herself. Slay the monster of her own anxiety.

She'd opened her eyes, reread the clue, and the answer had Tetrised into place. Ticks down correct dice placement, ticks up wrong placement. The big X over top of the scale indicating multiplication, the lock code the product. Hell, yeah.

And funny, her first instinct was to share her excitement with Tommy. A stupid instinct. But Tommy had already been staring, his lips moving.

What did he say? Standing in this store holding peanut M&Ms, Gillian wasn't sure. She felt panic, then and now. Panic that, in her excitement, she'd given Tommy the answer.

"Miss?"

Back in the present, the register line had drained away.

The clerk giving Gillian that look. *Distracted, emotional, or batshit crazy?* Gillian fumbled through her string bag for her wallet, but the clerk waved her off, instead pointing at the bracelet around Gillian's wrist. Of course. She brushed the blue plastic over the register's contactless reader. The reader blipped and the clerk thanked her, wishing her a very Miscellany day.

Gillian paused in the shop doorway, studying the singular handcuff on her wrist. The bracelet was a key – it was access to funds. It was also a tracker. Miscellany scavenged data from every warm body, their pathway to more dollars. Even Tommy had worn one, the COO not immune to data collection. Nowadays every phone, watch, and eyeglass frame transmitted and received. Who knew what else the bracelet could do?

Gillian knew who.

Seventeen

Leaving the candy shop, Gillian sought an unmarked door flanking the park entrance. She knocked repeatedly until an irritated scarecrow in security brown appeared behind her. "Ma'am, that's a secure door."

"I know. That's why I'm knocking on it."

He adjusted his glasses. "If you need Customer Service–"

"Actually, I need Ellsberg."

The guy really wanted a hat and a tin star to adjust. "Ma'am–"

"Miss. I don't need the Texas treatment."

He didn't like that. Red-faced, one hand reaching toward his radio. She wasn't being subtle, or even polite, but she didn't need to be. Kick up a fuss, get him here faster – he wouldn't be far. And she was right. Behind the guard, his hair askew and his slacks rumpled, looking as if he'd been guzzling an increasingly ineffective cocktail of black coffee and energy drinks. The guard didn't spit ten words into his radio before Ellsberg walked up and called him off.

"I've got this, Connor. Thank you."

Connor glanced from Gillian to his boss. His face clearly saying *toss her out on her ass*. But he wasn't born yesterday. He abandoned the shit above his paygrade and resumed his patrol.

Ellsberg took a moment to smooth his hair. She tried to imagine bantering like last night. Could no more picture it than she could sitting at a desk, working a nine-to-five. But competing against him again? That was the kind of relationship she could imagine.

"I hear you were in The Aerie," he said.

Of course he already knew. Gillian munched her candy.

"You talked to Sebastian?" he asked.

"No, I dropped trow and told him to pucker up. Of course I talked to him."

"What did you discuss?"

She talked through a mouthful of chocolate and crushed peanut. "Stuff."

Ellsberg winced. "He made CNN meet with Tommy. *Teen Vogue* was a video call from a conference room. No one visits the inner sanctum."

She licked candy from her teeth.

"If Sebastian wants to employ you for some vanity project," he said, "you're not the first Contestant for which that's been true. If you're here in some misguided effort to make peace with your past, best of luck, may the journey heal whatever wounds you still carry. But do not interfere with my life, whatever *special assignment* he has you on."

"His assignment? He's hot to find Tommy, that's all. Do I tell him his Head of Security had no luck tracking the access band?" She watched Ellsberg's face tighten. "That's how you've been following me, right?"

"You are a pain in the ass."

"Am I right about the access band?"

"Pain. In the ass."

He glowered. She chewed. Eventually, he swallowed his irritation. "Get out of the way."

She moved aside, and Ellsberg used his band to unlock the security door. She wanted to laugh as he grumbled. There was no denying it felt good to get the better of him, on his own turf. An almost inebriated feeling – elation laced with nausea. She wanted this thrill. She needed it.

Ellsberg led Gillian through a low-ceilinged warren, the place decidedly un-fantastical. A couple of tired guards without their cloaks, the pair straightening as they barged in. Banks of monitors displaying activity throughout the park. Pens, sticky notes, a fancy coffee maker, soda machine, desk phones, radios, even paper. Ellsberg had carved out a small space in back, where he sat and unlocked his computer, only then letting Gillian come to his shoulder. Onscreen an overhead map of the park. Ellsberg entered Tommy's name and a time range – the last week. A fuzzy purple worm wound through the map.

"The bands are RFID," Ellsberg said. "We can track him within a few hundred feet of a reader, and we have readers everywhere."

He seemed proud, not ashamed. Gillian felt uneasy looking at the other monitors. Real-time stats on guest location. Ride wait times. Food court and bathroom occupancies. She twisted the band on her wrist. They knew everything in this room. A lot more than the guests realized. She told herself the knowledge would lead to Tommy.

She leaned in and touched the top edge, center screen. "He stops here."

Ellsberg removed her finger. "The Boardwalk, but the timestamp is a few hours old."

"The leash comes off?"

"He doesn't always wear his band, and he has anonymous duplicates, despite my best efforts."

"What about outside the park?"

"There's no GPS. Off the grounds, he's invisible. He could be playing hipster in Bishop Arts. Standing atop Reunion Tower. He could be on the Moon for all I know."

"We need to find him."

"Your observation is noted. I'll write it down, alongside *the Earth is round.*"

Ellsberg had grown more pompous in the intervening years. A giant balloon of ego. She wanted to stick him with a pin. "Did you know he takes rideshares from the parking lot?"

"Rideshare?" Ellsberg seemed surprised. "Why would he do that?"

"As Head of Security, I'd hope you'd know."

"He's an adult human being. I don't follow everyone around the park."

Gillian made sure he saw her scan the distance between them.

"You came to me," Ellsberg said.

Still, the look on his face. Irritated he hadn't known about the rideshare. Gillian couldn't keep the satisfaction off her face.

With Tommy's last known location in hand, they left the security room. Outside, Ellsberg moved briskly, seeming to grow taller as he walked, drawing power from the park.

He took a breath. "Given your assignment, perhaps the best strategy is to pool our resources. Share what we know."

Mom's health and living arrangements were tenuous – Gillian had no time to infiltrate over days and weeks. Ellsberg was a Contestant and a Miscellany executive. He had access.

"You have a theory?"

"He favors The Boardwalk. Even at his station, he still plays the games. It's quite possible we could find him there."

"Why do I need you?"

"I could detain him on park grounds, if it came to that."

She didn't ask why he needed her. No benefit to him doubting her usefulness. "I get my money, no matter who finds him."

Ellsberg flashed a smile. "The sooner you get paid, the sooner you're no longer my problem."

They cut toward the heart of the park. As they walked, Gillian scanned the crowd. The guests seemed more prosperous than in her day. Designer leisurewear. Ray-Bans. Expensive running shoes. Lots of money oiled the Miscellany machine.

"You mention Tommy engaging rideshare," Ellsberg asked. "How did you stumble upon this information?"

She recounted her time spent at the Transportation Hub. After a trip through Ellsberg's security domain – Big Brother stalking the guests from parking lot to puzzle room – she better understood why Tommy would spurn the Escalades at his beck and call. "You know why he's jumping through those hoops, right?"

A disapproving grumble preceded the words. "He's aware we LoJack company vehicles. He doesn't want his location tracked."

Gillian nodded. In classic puzzle kid fashion, Ellsberg was more upset Gillian uncovered the answer first than he was with Tommy outsmarting him. He all but kicked rocks in frustration.

"You've checked the house?" she asked. "Our boy's not parked on the couch, watching TV?"

"Evelina insists he's hasn't been home."

"She might be lying."

"Kuthodaw is a private neighborhood. The people there wouldn't appreciate disturbance."

As if Tommy and his wealth operated as a sovereign nation. *Supposed* wealth.

"We keep talking cars and houses. I thought you said Tommy was broke."

"Were you paying attention?" The frustration of a long-suffering teacher strained Ellsberg's voice. "Nothing is in Tommy's name. The winnings – they belong to Miscellany. We own the house, the jet, the cars. Tommy and his family won the right to use them."

Sebastian back in The Aerie. *He's lost access. To decisions. To expense accounts.* As an angry kid who'd just lost the Contest, Gillian had seen what she'd wanted to see: Tommy staking claim to a pirate's immeasurable bounty. But did he really? The oversized check, not cash in hand. The cars and house registered in whose name?

The spoils of the Contest prizes, but also shackles.

"So Miscellany pulls the strings. Use your authority, then. Search the place."

He arched one eyebrow, a theatrical arch he pulled off exceptionally well. "You know, it's the audacity I'd forgotten. The idea that nothing and no one were off limits, to you."

"You wanted help with Tommy – I'm helping. What are you so afraid of?"

"You have no idea how things work here." Ellsberg's birthmark flared red. "You have an axe to grind. You're dangerous." As he got angry his accent slipped, the Birmingham twang leaking through. "Miscellany does good in the world. Everything Sebastian did for us, we're doing for the globe. It's not simply puzzles and riddles. It's cognitive development. Hand–eye coordination. Increased confidence and self-esteem."

"I know. I read the website."

"You never believed in him, or the mission."

"I believed in me. My mission. You used to be the same way."

Ellsberg puckered his lips. She'd clearly agitated him. He rubbed his vast forehead as if she'd lasered a hole there.

The cacophony of The Boardwalk drew nearer. Gillian watched guests swarm the games. Ring toss. Balloon darts. Upright arcade cabinets like *NBA Jam* and *Gauntlet*. She remembered days spent at NickelRama, the old Garland arcade, thumb-feeding coins from her cup into every slot still lit, a tanker trunk of soda at her elbow. Those memories helped dampen her anger. Ellsberg relaxed also, at least no longer squirming like his underwear chafed.

"You used to be quite good at these games," he said. "If I recall."

"Let's keep watching. See if one of them sells out the others for a free T-shirt."

"If that remark is directed at me, the T-shirts were not free. They were $20 and I had to borrow against my allowance."

Gillian laughed despite herself. Ellsberg's dry wit had attracted her in the beginning, like she was discovering a secret person no one else knew. But then Sebastian and the Contest brought out a different side of him, and she'd walked away, wishing she'd never met any version.

Ellsberg pulled a pen from his pocket and clicked it distractedly. A childhood reflex that stirred kinder memories.

"Are you still failing at crosswords?" she asked.

"I do quite well, thank you."

"You never finish one." She beckoned with her open palm. "Come on. Give."

Making a big production, Ellsberg produced a crumpled brochure from his back pocket. It advertised Miscellany's daily activities and included a crossword on the back page, the kind with a riddle buried inside. Gillian inspected the layout, and Ellsberg's progress. "It's in Spanish."

"Sebastian is fluent. As were his most successful protégés."

"I didn't say I couldn't read it."

Ellsberg had done a decent enough job. The crucigrama was nearly complete, less a block in the corner.

"Inflatable raft is lancha." She jotted down the answer quickly, as if being timed. "Which means recipe direction is remover, not girar."

He leaned in. "Damn. I knew that."

"Perennial words of the second-place finisher."

Her eyes danced over the boxes. Again, she felt her heart rev, as if she'd been shocked awake. Ellsberg stretched his arm over her shoulder to stab at 5 down. "That's principio."

"I know," she snapped. "Didn't I just solve remover?"

Estibar. Libidinoso. Espada. Together they populated the block and revealed the riddle, circled letters composing both question and answer.

"Ríos pero no agua. Ciudades pero no edificios. Bosque pero no arboles." Ellsberg made a noise. "A map? Who writes this drivel?"

"Maybe you should request a transfer to the crossword department."

"I couldn't fuck it up any worse."

"Martin." Gillian's tone a dead ringer for Sebastian. "That language does not become you."

They both laughed, and Ellsberg lost years from his face.

For a moment, Gillian forgot everything but the shared joy of solving a puzzle.

The end of The Boardwalk arrived. Ellsberg stopped under a series of rope ladders, adjacent a trash can, the receptacle somehow gum- and graffiti-free. He scanned the surface contents, hands in pockets. Found nothing. He paused and, with a certain amount of dread, tilted his head back. An orange bracelet dangled from the nearest rope square.

Sighing, Ellsberg unhooked the tracker. Regarded the bracelet as if it had personally disappointed him.

Gillian wondered, was this real? Ellsberg appeared troubled enough. Like Tommy's absence meant more than a negative performance review. In the Contest days, Ellsberg was always weird around Tommy. Laughing too quick at his jokes, snapping too quick at his slights. A volatile love–hate relationship. Gillian had always wondered how Ellsberg felt inside, and which emotion prevailed.

Ellsberg struggled with what he wasn't saying, finally spitting it out. "Tommy has a drug problem," he said.

"Cocaine at a minimum. I'm aware."

A patented Ellsberg scowl. "I knew you knew."

"Sue me for not immediately playing besties." Children scampered across the ropes overhead. They seemed happy. "How long?"

"I can't be sure, but it's gotten worse over the last year." He hesitated, trying to figure out where the line on family was drawn. "I found bloody tissues. A logbook that suggested injection dosages."

"And you didn't say anything?"

"Of course I talked to him. But he had explanations. Stress. Fatigue." Ellsberg sighed. "We had the cast of *Stranger Things* here for a Halloween event – Tommy was not himself.

Irritable. He actually shoved the man who plays the sheriff. The big one."

Last October. Nearly a year of him dropping weight and shooting up, his body tattooed in bruising and pinpricks, and no one stopping him. Not his friends, not his wife. But then where was Gillian, the girl who saw everything?

"Who else knows?" she asked.

"I suspect Jackie Alvarez conceals his habit, at the very least."

"She pulled baggies from his luggage. She's involved."

Ellsberg didn't say anything.

"You've already questioned her?"

"For me to interrogate Jackie, and about Tommy's habit, would be politically indelicate."

"Why? She's his driver."

That put a twist in Ellsberg's shorts. "I'm not sure where you're getting your information, but per the usual, it's flawed. Jackie works Personal Protection, and reports directly to Sebastian."

"Protection for who? Tommy?"

"All the executives. And their families."

That explained Jackie's open hostility toward her.

"What about Evelina? What does she know?"

"About the drugs? I've never broached the subject with her. But she's a smart woman."

"Gasp. She might rise above her station."

"Don't get pissy. That's not what I meant. She's in public relations. It's very difficult to know the truth with that one."

Gillian remembered Tommy on the plane – the tension as he talked to his wife. Not only his wife, but another player in the corporate game. "Is she working Season Two?"

Ellsberg hesitated. "Yes, but that's not unusual. She's

involved in the launch of anything public-facing." He frowned. "You're not still on about this cheating nonsense, are you?"

The idea tempted her, investigating Miscellany with Ellsberg, the two pushing each other to solve a mystery, just like they had the crossword. But momentary détente aside, Gillian didn't trust Ells. His face raptor-sharp. His body leaning forward, hunting for answers. The concern stamped into his jaw seemed real, but even if he was sincere, that didn't mean his motives were pure.

Back in LA, Gillian had dealt with plenty of clients – friends – worried about a loved one's erratic behavior. Sometimes the client and the *loved one* were entangled in a contract, and the violation of a morals clause triggered a huge payday. For Ellsberg, friendship and loyalty were just tools. She'd need to remember that, now more than ever.

"I'm trying to solve a puzzle, Ellsberg. You remember puzzles?"

He straightened, as if she'd slapped him across the face. He stood there and considered with an almost Katherine Hepburn air before bringing himself around to an answer. "Evelina won't appreciate an intrusion," he said. "But I'll send a guard by the property. If he's home, I'll let you know."

"Sounds like you aren't going to do jack shit."

"I could always escort you from the park. Good luck getting paid, in that circumstance."

Gillian looked at the rope ladders overhead, trying to see the sky beyond. To chart a course through life's dark clouds. Irony was, the skies were blue and the clouds postcard white. The kids happy and carefree. One of the girls clambering overhead wore a NASA T-shirt. She was all elbows and knees and seemed to be having the time of her life.

"Fine," Gillian said. "I'll wait at the hotel."

He looked as if he didn't believe her. "Just like that?"

"You said it. It's not like I'm getting paid otherwise."

Ellsberg kept still, staring at her, like he could smell lies on the air. "Perfect. I'll be in touch."

He left then, meandering back to HQ and occasionally looking over his shoulder to see if Gillian was still there. As if she was a mountain lion that might attack if he didn't maintain eye contact. The bony-ass bastard was scared of her.

Gillian smiled.

Good.

Eighteen

Evelina and Tommy lived in Kuthodaw, the master-planned and Miscellany-owned community, occupied by park employees. The name was Burmese in origin, a collection of stone tablets inscribed with Buddhist text. The homes themselves were strictly vacation rental, open-plan villas with courtyards and fountains and circular driveways. Gated, protected by a rent-a-cop in a white button-down and iron-on badge. Fortunately, Gillian had bribed one of the Leonardo's valets. She knew someone at the Kessler, offered the guy tickets to the next Leon Bridges show. The valet drove her out, Gillian crouched low in the back. The guard let him through with a wave. Once out of sight, a fistbump and a drop-off, then the valet cruised away.

Gillian was never going to wait at the hotel.

There was no traffic, although there were plenty of cars parked in luxurious driveways. The neighborhood was something from another time. Grass so green as to look fake. The gentle *shush* of automatic sprinklers. Faint laughter carrying from carbon copy homes. So different from the neighborhood where Gillian had grown up – northwest Dallas, Love Field jets thundering overhead. Gangs and drugs prevalent, but the neighborhood vigilant. Largely Black, and willing to look out for their own. Dad a part of that community, Gillian thought, although if anyone had considered Mom a sellout for marrying a white boy, they never shared their toxicity within earshot. And once Dad got his drunk on and lost the El Fenix job, the family had to move. Gillian wondered if their house still stood.

The outside of the Kundojjala house was quiet. A sprawling Spanish colonial with ivory walls and blue flowerpots and a terracotta roof. A red Civic parked on the street, out of place among the BMWs and Teslas.

She wanted to hate this place. She imagined living here, everything in Kuthodaw the same and Gillian struggling to remain true to who she was. People might even tell themselves she was white, which in itself was reason enough to reject this Texas Malibu. But try as she might, she still wanted *this*, wanted this with an ache she couldn't deny. She wanted to drive the Lexus if the Jag wouldn't start. To let friends sleep over in the second guest room. Wealth afforded the opportunity to forget an unfair world. Money might not buy happiness, but it could rent amnesia.

As she stood there imagining different life choices, a tall blond man exited the house, texting and talking. His voice carried. *The dinner reservations are for eight, not seven. The car should be a black Escalade, don't screw me again with the white Expedition.* He had a shopping bag looped over his arm and a receipt clutched in one hand. Gillian took him for a personal assistant, the poor fucker. Every day spent orchestrating the minutiae of someone else's life, the toil unending and thankless. Gillian was reminded that Chantal and her list of wants and needs waited back in Los Angeles. She could sympathize with the blond guy, even like him. Especially since he left the front door unlocked.

Once he drove away, she went up the drive and stepped inside.

The interior of the Kundojjala house was very neat and very adult. An open tiled entry, an expansive sunken living room replete with white couches and sand-colored end tables. There were quartz counters and an oversized farmhouse sink. Lots of glass. She listened for other occupants but heard only her faint footsteps and nervous breathing. Being found here alone, old friend or no, would be bad business. If someone had seen her enter and called the cops, gunshots would come before questions. She moved quickly.

She found the home office on the far side of the immaculate living space. It was the only room the least bit disheveled. More cables scattered on another stark desk, but no laptop and no Tommy, only a long black slice of display. There were books shelved along the wall, tales of private eyes and humans gone off the rails. Dashiell Hammett. Elmore Leonard. Margaret Millar. Gillian fanned the books but incriminating evidence failed to drift out, only a photo of Tommy and Evelina in beachwear at some luau, smiling so hard their faces might break.

Gillian returned to the desk. She opened a polished brass box to find a pen cap, a nearly empty package of SweeTarts, and multicolored sticky notes. The top note covered in scrawl, a series of meaningless numbers. Flipping over the sticky revealed a list. *Photo book. Cards. Email perms – EK. Socks (2).* And crossed out, *Picture Frame* and *Team Gifts.* A man's idle to-do list, which he'd stuck in a box and promptly forgotten.

Email perms – EK. Evelina Kundojjala?

Gillian moved to the garage. It held three cars – a Tesla, a

BMW, and an Audi. Gillian opened glove boxes and popped trunks and found only ice scrapers and jumper cables. The odometers on each vehicle under ten thousand miles. The cars never went anywhere. They were expensive props.

She sat in the Audi, nestled behind a carbon-fiber steering wheel, and tried to put herself in Tommy's shoes. The man had everything he'd ever wanted. The trappings of wealth. Access to power. He designed puzzles and crafted entertainment for starry-eyed kids the world over. And he was miserable. Coked off his ass and convinced the system had turned against him.

When you were caught in a trap of your own design, where did you turn?

Back inside the house, Gillian went to stand at the windows to the backyard. She could see the golf course, just over the lip of the infinity pool. Music played from speakers she couldn't see. The scene felt staged. A house that existed for someone other than the occupants.

"I mean, can you believe the view?"

Gillian turned. The red-haired woman stood in the kitchen, smiling. Burgundy blouse. Black tie. Oversized sunglasses. Evelina Kundojjala came in for a handshake, not tall but her presence huge, the nearby oxygen molecules seeming to vibrate. When Evelina shook, her grip was strong.

"Gillian Charles. I've heard so much about you." Her nails were champagne pink and the cuticles unmangled. Her diction sharp and precise, almost as if English wasn't her first language, which maybe it wasn't. She removed her sunglasses and dropped them on the kitchen counter along with her handbag. "I'm making a doppio. Can I get you anything?"

The woman behaved as if Gillian was an expected guest. Gillian was content to play along. "Right as rain, thanks."

Evelina took her smile and aura to a massive espresso machine. She gathered coffee grounds and almond milk and a dainty mug. Delicate fingers danced over the machine's controls, causing the mechanism to rumble and spit steam. She kept an eye on her phone, her sharp eyes soaking up bits, in that way a lot like her husband.

"Tommy loves his coffee," she said, over the racket. "This is an automatic. Tommy got us a manual, from Budapest, but we never used it. It was too complicated."

Gillian noticed Latin script circling the outside of the espresso mug. She fought off a smirk as she imagined signs in giftshops all over the park. *Riddle mugs, only $30.*

Once the machine spat out her doppio, Evelina carried her cup and saucer and led them into the sunken living room across from the great windows. She eased her drink onto the massive coffee table and sat on the white couch all in one smooth motion. Gillian followed and sat in the leather chair closest to the door. Evelina smiled and looked at Gillian like she'd conjured her into existence. "Now, what about you?"

Calm and cool. As dangerous as any of the Contestants. "What about me?"

"I assume Stephen let you in. He's an excellent judge of character."

Evelina's eyes were sharp. Watching, maybe to see how she'd react.

"The door was unlocked, yes."

The smile stayed on. "I've wanted to meet you for a long time. Gameplayer. Chess – and checkers – champion. You even played the cello."

"Violin."

"Nevertheless. No other woman went as far in the Contest. That's amazing."

"First place would have been better."

"But then you ran into Tommy." Evelina lifted her cup, blew on it and took a sip. "You never blamed my husband?" She perched like a bird, her black porcelain eyes reflecting all Gillian's scrutiny. "Or aren't you here to talk about him?"

Which Tommy would Evelina love? The wunderkind, or the user, or Gillian's childhood friend? She shifted in her chair. "Your husband disappeared on me. We had business."

"If you're asking, he's not here. I haven't seen him since yesterday."

"How was he? He seems... stressed."

Evelina set down her drink and hooked a strand of red hair behind her ear. Her smile was a little less bright. "The job is very demanding. Tommy is under a lot of pressure."

"You mean Season Two?"

Her host paused. "I really shouldn't talk about it."

Evelina was playing coy. Either she needed a friend or something else was going on. Either way, the fencing was enjoyable. Matching wits with someone unburdened by Contest history.

"Tommy said something to me," Gillian offered. "About Season Two being rigged."

A pause. Evelina thinking. "There are hurt feelings," she said. "You were in the original Contest, you understand. These are competitions. There's one winner, no reward for participation. Color, creed, background – meaningless. But it takes smarts to qualify, this isn't charity. Sometimes the kids who fail take it hard. And the platform will be huge.

Huge. We're broadcasting the entire event. Twitch, YouTube, ESPN. There are millions at stake, for Miscellany and the families."

She talked like a commercial. Like Gillian didn't know how life worked. "You mean the IPO?"

Evelina froze. "What?"

"Running errands for the rich, you get to know the names. You're dealing with at least two different investment banks."

Evelina's smile resembled a grimace. "That's amazing. None of this is in the press."

"Puzzle kids. We work things out."

"I'll bet you do." Evelina used a long drink to collect herself. "We're fine. As you can see, we don't need money." She gestured, taking in the expansive estate. "I run the charity arm of Sebastian's Circle, I know true hardship when I see it. And without the investment, it's those people who will be hit the hardest. The ticket takers, the ride operators. The children."

Did Evelina know about the perilous state of their finances? Gillian could imagine the woman lying to avoid an uncomfortable truth. Convincing herself as much as anyone.

Evelina took another drink. "Season Two is a big part of making the dream work. And Tommy is the one who brought the revival concept to the Executive Team. It's his baby."

"*Tommy* sold Sebastian on Season Two?"

"Yes, of course. So when these parents complain, he takes the situation personally. He's a very emotional person. You know him. He's intense."

Strong-willed was the word Mom used to describe

her. Gillian ignoring homework in favor of studying flag semaphores and atomic weights. Earning detention arguing with teachers about who built the pyramids, who discovered America. She'd cost Mom hours in parent–teacher conferences. Being intimate with competitors – elite competitors – would be a nightmare. The highs and lows, the constant black whirlpool of self-doubt. Sometimes Gillian could hardly stand herself. Sparing Mom the emotional toll had justified moving half a country away.

Gillian changed the subject.

"I was going to call him charming."

"He is charming, isn't he?" Suddenly Evelina's mood deflated. Her eyes skittered around the room, looking everywhere but at her guest. "He disappears sometimes."

This was the family trauma Gillian remembered.

"Do you know where he goes?"

Evelina shook her head.

"Track his phone?" Gillian asked. "Rideshare? Credit cards?"

A helpless shrug. "We don't believe in all that. The tracking. Like we're property? It sounds naive now, I know."

The bracelet on Gillian's wrist felt a heavy counterpoint. But Evelina kept going.

"Here's the sad thing," she said. "Even when he's here, he's not here." She tapped a fingernail against her saucer and smiled a vulnerable smile. "He's in treatment. A program in Tucson, and it's not cheap. They have hiking. And yoga."

"He's in a program now?"

"He was. It was six weeks. A sabbatical. He came back and I thought he was better. I wanted him to be better."

Gillian had a flashback of Mom, swearing she wasn't going to put her life on hold for Dad but never leaving the cramped kitchen, tied to the phone, that damn landline nailed to the wall like a crucifix.

"Speaking from experience," Gillian said, "staying in the same place, with the same people – it's hard. Addicts, they get comfortable, they backslide. They don't see what they're doing to everyone else."

Across from her, Evelina nodded, her eyes misty. Being with someone who understood must have felt like such a relief. As a woman drowning, she'd reach for any extended hand.

Using empathy to exploit – Sebastian would be proud. The thought highly unsettling.

"I should go." Gillian stood, abruptly. "If you see Tommy, will you let me know?"

Evelina snuffled and nodded. Dabbed her eyes. "I don't recall seeing a car. How about I call our driver?"

All of Gillian's alarms triggered. "Jackie?"

"Oh, you've met."

By all appearances, Evelina was unconcerned she had a tiger as a pet.

"I'd be careful with her," Gillian said.

Evelina lifted her chin, exposing her pale neck. The tears and smudged eyeshadow gave her a look best described as glamorous raccoon. "She's been with Miscellany forever."

"I'm concerned she's enabling Tommy, maybe supplying him. She's helping him hide his habit."

"No, you've got it all backward. I asked Jackie to watch over Tommy. The drugs he's doing – the cocaine – there, I said it. The cocaine. If he's caught with that? You can't imagine. He keeps syringes in the house, too, Gillian. Syringes."

"You're sure?"

"As sure as night and day. Jackie is a rock. She's the gold

standard. She's the only reason we're pulling this off."

Gillian had believed Ellsberg a friend, right up to the moment he walked into that tent and stood at Sebastian's side. Smart people were the worst. They made snap decisions, then convinced themselves only facts drove their conclusions.

"I'll be fine walking," Gillian said.

The pair strolled to the front door. Evelina found her smile again.

"I hear you're competing in the Reunion. Back into the fire?"

"The jury is still out on that."

Evelina laughed. "You don't fool me. You're dying to compete."

Gillian couldn't object – the lie would be written all over her face, and Evelina was perceptive. With her arched back and sharp features, Gillian thought of nothing so much as a switchblade. Harmless one minute, deadly the next.

A number of emotions jumbled. Respect. Jealousy. This woman's life – this was what Gillian wanted. Not the looks or the impossible fairytale marriage. She wanted the influence. The ability to make a difference. But she was getting herself confused. Mixing professional and personal.

Evelina stopped her on the front steps. "You think you can find Tommy before the Reunion? Two days isn't long."

"Like I said, I'm a puzzle kid. We work things out. And I'm motivated."

That same look, the one Evelina wore when Gillian mentioned the IPO. But then she blinked and was all smiles. "Well, if you need my help navigating Miscellany politics, don't hesitate to ask. I have a way with the people here.

They act differently when they think they're among friends. Their masks slip."

The woman was indeed a switchblade. "You'd have done well in the Contest."

"Oh, sweetie," Evelina said, laying a hand on Gillian's arm. "I would have won."

Jackie Alvarez pulled up as Gillian approached the gate, driving the ubiquitous black Mercedes. The car barely stopped before she was out and arcing around the car like a missile. She wore her dark suit and white dress shirt, the top button secured firmly at her throat, no tie. All business.

"What are you doing here, cuttlefish?"

The name followed Gillian everywhere. "Where did you hear that?"

It happened fast. Jackie reached her in three steps, seized her by the wrist and brought her in close. Gillian was caught completely off guard. She'd taken judo as a kid, but her thirty year-old microwave-burrito body wasn't primed for combat.

"I said, what are you doing here?"

Jackie squeezed the bones in Gillian's wrist. The pain was exquisite. Lightning up her arm and, despite herself, tears springing loose.

"You're hurting me." Gillian's voice was wobbly. "Let go."

"I'll answer my own question." Jackie's grip was a vice. Locked in at just the right pressure to buckle Gillian's knees. "You're here to do whatever Miscellany wants."

Gillian didn't say anything. Her breath was ragged.

"The Kundojjalas are special," Jackie said. "But people try to take advantage. Evelina, in particular. She's a people person. She's trusting, and I don't like to see her trust abused. She's done a lot for me. You hearing me, cuttlefish? She's important."

Jackie squeezed tighter. Gillian made an involuntary noise. "I hear you."

"Next time you want to visit, you ask me first. You understand?"

The wind lifted Jackie's blazer. A gun holstered at her side. Gillian didn't wait for more pressure.

"I understand."

Jackie released her. Immediately Gillian stepped away, rubbing her wrist.

Growing up, Gillian had always imagined herself the sort of person who wouldn't submit to bullies. She'd puff out her chest. Use her mouth to good advantage. Even if the bad guys tried to beat her into paste, she'd never back down. She was steel and diamonds.

She walked away from Jackie, cradling her wrist to her chest, and tried her damnedest to stop the tears.

Nineteen

Gillian pressed the towel to her wrist, the ice inside crackling. After the encounter with Jackie, she'd retreated to her hotel room, examined herself in the bathroom mirror, holding up her arms like a post-scrub surgeon. The right side was a tree trunk, a fleshy stalk from forearm to palm, no wrist. Looking at it was disturbing, and touching the puffy inflammation nearly made her sick. So she stopped looking.

At the writing desk, Gillian contemplated the Miscellany laptop, the camera now pristine, gum scraped clean or the device replaced entirely. Gillian had no interest in Miscellany's Trojan horse. Instead, she grabbed pen and paper. The pen heavy. The paper Miscellany letterhead. She made a list, and crossed through it.

~~Call him (again)~~
~~Office~~
~~House~~
~~The park~~
~~Evelina~~
~~Wristband tracking~~
And last:
Fuck it, give up.

She'd thought herself in control. Strongest person in the park. Then Evelina with that face, the one June and Mom wore, emotions brittle from enduring one too many Gillian temperature swings. No wonder she wasn't ready for Jackie's ambush. Although if she was being honest, no amount of preparation would have prevented that ass-kicking.

Back in LA, Gillian wasn't in the people-finding business. The deadbeats she'd tracked were known quantities, marks who didn't know she was watching. Gillian wasn't a bounty hunter – she didn't do puzzles where the answers ran away. God's truth, she was out of her depth. Away from Dallas, she'd allowed herself to believe she was a shark. Turned out she'd been swimming in the little pool. Here lurked real predators – they moved quick, the stakes were cutthroat, and the violence was imminent. To think she'd been Nancy Drewing her way through the day. *The Case of the Coked-out COO*. What a fool.

She leaned back. Breathed in and out and let the panic riptide recede.

Sure, it would have been nice if she was the smartest and the strongest. But that had never been true. Back in the Contest days, she'd worked harder than anyone else. Threw herself at problems until they broke. In the years since, she'd gotten soft, replaced truth with myth, drank her own Kool-Aid. Gillian, the born prodigy. Gillian, the natural polymath. Then she threw a tantrum when Miscellany tore that myth to shreds? Cry me a river. The Gillian of LA was more persistent than this sniveling mess. Gutsier.

She removed the towel. Flexed the fingers of her right hand and winced. That bitch. Hand-to-hand, Jackie clearly knew her stuff. Repeat the encounter a dozen times and the outcome remained the same. Gillian wasn't that kind of badass, fine. If they ran into each other again, Gillian would strike first with her own weapons – persistence and her mouth.

She looked around the room. Her eyes fell on the hotel letter opener, sheathed in hand-stitched leather. Something sharp might also be nice.

Gillian withdrew the slim knife and gripped it in her fist, blade down. She made a double stabbing motion. She imagined herself back on the street with Jackie. *Now who's a fucking cuttlefish?* Gillian wouldn't count herself out. She'd never count herself out.

She set the blade next to her on the table. She looked again at the list.

She drew a firm line through *Fuck it, give up*.

Twenty

The desk phone ripped Gillian from sleep. A cool-voiced woman from Reception spoke. "Sorry to wake you, Ms Charles. You have a guest."

Blurry, Gillian rubbed her face. She immediately thought of Tommy, downstairs with hat in hand. She'd buy him a hat only so he could grip it contritely. "I do? Who?"

When they told her, Gillian was no longer sleepy.

"I need to clean up," she said. "Tell her I'll be down in half an hour."

The receptionist said something pleasant and hung up.

Gillian stared at the wall.

June seemed uncomfortable. She sat sideways in her chair and picked at her hotel breakfast buffet scrambled eggs with the tines of her fork. She wore something practical and looked askance at the tourists traipsing through the lobby in their swimsuits and tank tops. Gillian wore black pants and a white blouse and a pair of dangly earrings she didn't remember packing. She realized only now she'd dressed conservatively in anticipation of meeting with her sister. They hadn't met face to face since they were kids. Gillian's cuticles were picked raw.

"How's Todd?" She cut her sausage, wary of eating with her fingers. "He still running that taco place?"

"Pizza." June stirred ketchup in with her eggs. "Owned it five years."

"Oh."

Around them silverware clanked. Waitstaff hustled from end to end with water and coffee refills. By contrast, the sisters' table was church. June, undisturbed by the quiet, merely took the place in: the carpet patterned with maps from different ages and locales, the funhouse-mirrored ceiling. None of it seemed to meet with her approval.

"They're paying me," Gillian volunteered.

"Place like this?" More critical inspection. "Bet they can afford to."

The waiter asked if they wanted coffee refills. They both said no.

"I've been trying to call you." June's eyes found the battle-scarred phone on the table next to Gillian's plate. "I saw you online. Mom had to find out you were here from Channel 5."

Gillian had deleted June's messages, unheard. "I don't pay attention to the media. I've been working."

"You couldn't call?"

"We're going to do this? Now?"

June crossed her legs. The picture of discomfort. "They wouldn't give Mom her pills yesterday."

Gillian dropped her silverware. "Why in the hell not?"

"They said she was no longer eligible. Effective immediately."

That liar Mitch. "They can't do that."

"Then you need to talk to them. Get this fixed like before."

"That was a one-time thing. They did me a favor, and it was sketchy as it was. I can't ask them again."

"She didn't get her treatment, Gil."

"I know that. You don't have to keep telling me."

"Maybe I do." June lifted her coffee and smelled it. Wrinkled her nose but drank. "The people there know who you are. The woman on the phone said Mitch already talked to you."

Gillian sat back. Sometimes the trouble with June wasn't so much June herself. Her sister represented the disappointments of the entire family – the tip of the Charles disappointment iceberg. "They said thirty days. I was going to work it out."

June turned and stared. Waited.

"The insurance didn't cover room and board," Gillian said. "She's being discharged."

"This is you taking care of it?"

"What do you want from me?"

"Like I said, you know people. We turn on the TV and there you are together with that man from the Contest. The German."

"He's from Alabama, and we weren't together."

"There was a party. I saw you with the Puzzle Man, elbow to elbow with the governor, and then you're saying you can't afford some rat-trap clinic off I-30."

Every banished concern about Mom, and Gillian's inability to help, surged back to the fore. She was frustrated with herself, angry she hadn't solved this problem before June got involved.

"They've raised the prices twice," Gillian said. "They're grooming the property for sale – the city wants the land for the convention center. And I walked by the governor, it's not like he knows my name."

"Talk to your buddy, then. The Puzzle Man."

Gillian didn't answer right away. She stabbed a fragment of sausage but didn't eat. "I can't just ask him for a loan."

"You said they were paying you."

"Not until I'm finished. And maybe the money covers a few months at a new facility, but then what? This was the cheapest location we could find. Any new place is going to cost more. A few months and she'll be out on the street."

"Then stay here. Earn your keep. Work for Sebastian."

"You don't know how hard I fought to avoid that."

"You were nuts for his Contest. I thought that's exactly what you wanted."

"You don't understand."

"No, I don't understand. It looks like you don't give a shit. You come all this way and you don't see us. You don't call. And when I drive all across creation for help, you tell me *it's hard being smart*?" Her sister paused, then charged ahead when her words failed to deliver the expected coup de grâce. "How about the other stuff? The driving and the scarves and that shopping thing?"

Gillian had represented her hustles as a smashing success. Admitting otherwise about killed her. "Those jobs pay the bills," she said, her voice quiet. "Barely."

At first June didn't respond. She presented only her profile, her fingers tapping against her ceramic coffee cup. When she finally turned to face Gillian, she looked contrite. "I lied before. Todd doesn't own the pizza place, he's the night manager. He's got a line on a thing at Home Depot, it's his second interview – more advancement opportunities, but it doesn't pay as much. We can't make our bills either."

June had made herself vulnerable, a position no Charles but Mom ever put themselves in willingly. Her effort was the only thing making the next question tolerable. "What about Dad?"

"You want to put that on him? He's in recovery. He's got social security. What he makes as a greeter. He sleeps in the spare bedroom."

Gillian shook her head.

"You know people never gave Dad a chance," June insisted. "Unemployment down, but where's his paycheck? He tried to start his own electrical business. The permits, the inspections – all that money – and no bank would give him a loan. He was good enough to pull wires but not man the till."

"You sound like him. And his excuses. Dad had every chance – look at him. Instead, he leaves Mom and you and me and a pile of medical bills. Sure, he got a raw deal. Don't tell me about raw deals."

They stared at each other.

"She doesn't get that treatment, she's never going to walk," June said. "Worse, the disease could progress. Her kidneys could fail. She'd need dialysis."

"I know what happens, June."

"What is she going to do? You figure she'll live with me, share the room with Dad? No meds, she'll die there."

"I know, June."

Her sister finally swung herself around. "I get what you don't want to do. But we all make hard choices. I could have been a dancer. Maybe my dear husband is a college professor, in some other life. But instead, I spend my day doing charts, getting shit on by doctors. Todd slings pizza and comes home smelling of grease. And our mother is sick – deathly sick. You want to solve puzzles? Solve this one. The answer is staring you square in the face."

June dug into her eggs and didn't say another word.

She didn't have to.

Twenty-One

After breakfast, Gillian rode the elevator to her room alone. The journey silent. Punishing. She wished the car would stop and let someone – anyone – on.

June in the flesh was harder to contain than June online. In Gillian's face, driving her toward the hamster wheel she'd spent her life avoiding. Her sister never did puzzles as a kid. *Boring*, she'd said. June preferred activity, the girl a natural at basketball, dance, volleyball, anything achieved through muscle and sweat. The sisters alike in their stubbornness, if not wildly different in how they applied their skills. All the more frustrating given June had used her mind and mouth to whup Gillian's ass.

Mom needed her meds. Only days, maybe hours between her and the literal curb. This woman who used to drive Gillian across counties to contests, hunch in a cold car for hours, then maintain an even keel through an aftermath of euphoria or rage, depending. The time for hustling up a solution had expired long before Gillian set foot on Tommy's jet. She'd spent a lifetime chasing dreams, doing it her way. She'd walked away from Mom, from her family, like they held her back. Instead, she ran around pleasing every stranger in LA, those people who regarded her as more interesting than a failed actress, but not by much. And she couldn't afford to examine those choices; they were made and done. Now was her time. Finally, *finally*, she was in a position to help. Sebastian had money. Sebastian wanted her. She needed to take the money and be a goddamn grown-up.

In the Contest, hesitation killed. Above the lake, next to the boys, she'd been afraid; they'd all been afraid. And Gillian had jumped. Because that was how you won.

She stepped off the elevator, head up. Passed a housekeeper, a woman who greeted Gillian with a good morning and a smile. Someone who probably made tough decisions every day.

It's hard being smart.

Time to fucking jump.

Her phone vibrated. Tommy's name lit up the screen.

Gillian stared, doubting her own eyes. After an eternity, four rings, she answered. "Where are you?"

"The dinner party looked fancy." Tommy's voice sounded normal. "I see you're playing nice with Ellsberg."

Gillian turned around. No one there, not even the housekeeper. "Do you know how many people are looking for you?"

"I do. That's why I'll stay put, thank you."

She kept looking, as if she'd spy him behind a potted plant or in a ceiling duct with binoculars. "I can't help you if you don't let me."

"That's a very Sebastian line. I hear you visited him in The Aerie. Sounds cozy."

"Fuck you. You came to me, remember? *You* brought me here. *You* promised me things."

Tommy breathed heavy into the phone. There was noise in the background. Hubbub and clatter, like he was in a restaurant.

"Whose side are you on?" he asked.

"Whose *side* am I on? This must be the drugs talking. And yes, I know you're using. You're as subtle as a drag queen."

"Is that what they told you?"

"They who?"

"Evelina and the Executive Team. They know about Season Two. They know, they've always known. When I came to you, I thought the problem was the cheating, but the problem is the lies. They know how the Navarros live, they know the Navarros have a case, and they're going to squash it and the family. Ask them. Ask them about Target Practice. They've all seen it. Evelina has seen it. Right there, in my bed, my wife under the same covers. She lies. She knows about Target Practice." His voice was pressed against the phone. Manic and sweaty, like he wanted to crawl through the line.

Gillian thought about the kid who'd shared his M&Ms with a smile. "Look," she said, "you flew to Los Angeles to find me. You need me. Let me help."

"Help? No, no thank you, I don't need that kind of help. You investigate Season Two, like I said. You talk to the Navarros. They live in that house, it's a nice house, with a car and a job and a nice life, one they built from nothing but it's safe and full of love, and what did they ever need until we came along and told them their life wasn't enough? Wasn't enough, and they couldn't keep it? Can you imagine, Gillian, if someone came into your home, came into your mother's home, and said they were offering this once-in-a-lifetime opportunity for your family, to make everything better, to make your child exceptional, and this brass ring they were offering was the only way? That it was everything you ever wanted and your child would be important, and in the end, at the end of this yellow brick road, this pot of gold at the finite tip of this rainbow was a lie, a lie that poisoned everything. Vanesa, their daughter, she's nine and she's brilliant. She's reading books in French and Chinese and she calculates numbers in her head like she's a computer. She plays chess and she codes, or at least she used to, but since she lost the qualifier that's all vanished like magician's smoke. She's retreated, she sits in her room, she won't read. Do you understand, Gillian, what they did? They put something in her. They poisoned her with their lies and now they don't want to take responsibility. That family is fighting back, but good luck because there's Miscellany – there's Miscellany with investors and stock options and publicity to worry about, millionaires in the making. The Navarros have an army of lawyers threatening them, Leah and her henchmen suggesting not only – not only will the family not get the pot of gold, but they'll lose their stake, that the car and the job and the nice house that was full of love, are all the property of Miscellany. First place, second place, it doesn't matter. Play the game at all, Gillian, and you lose."

She listened to his forced breath. "You're scaring me."

"You're scared? I'm fucking terrified."

Tommy's fear was infectious. Wasn't the housekeeper standing in the hall a moment ago, lingering? Lingering why, exactly? One of Sebastian's eyes and ears? Ellsberg's? Jackie's? Hadn't Gillian been followed earlier – Jackie in the crowd, Jackie at the house. The road to Tommy's paranoia was easy to see, jumping at threats from all directions, with no idea if you were ten feet from safety or lost in the heart of the jungle.

Tommy's voice called Gillian's name and she brought the phone back to her ear.

"Tell me where you are," she said. "Let's get the hell out of fantasyland. We'll go to Grapevine. Euless. Somewhere no one is looking. We'll find a bar in a nowhere strip mall and you'll tell me whatever you want to tell me. Right now. What do you say?"

The noise in the background had changed. A high-pitched whistle. Underneath a more distinct voice emerging, someone talking directly to Tommy. A female voice. Someone who knew his name. *Tommy, you know you want to–*

"Who was that?" Gillian asked.

Tommy hung up.

Twenty-Two

Before braving the park Gillian changed, shucking the church-wear and reskinning in her Atari tee ensemble. She'd packed only so many clothes, and the pants–blouse combo made her itch, inside and out. She did throw a gray duster cardigan over top, bowing to practicalities. The weather was changing. A cold front blowing in.

On the way to Miscellany HQ, Gillian replayed the call in her head. *Target Practice*. What the hell was Target Practice? Another Tommy rainbow with bullshit waiting at the end, probably. He'd radiated crazy. Passionate, sure, but passion didn't equal truth. Gillian had wanted to press him for answers, but return calls went straight to voicemail.

Frustration dogged her. Tommy lurked. He'd monitored the Ballroom event, knew she'd seen Sebastian. He was watching, breathing the same goddamn air. With more time, Gillian knew she could find him. But she could still smell burnt coffee on her breath, taste the Leonardo cafeteria eggs on her back teeth. Mom used to make the three of them eat breakfast together every day, no matter what chaos ruled. Some mornings Mom was the only one to carry the conversation. The woman persevered, regardless how tough the road.

As June said, the answer was staring her square in the face.

Once at HQ, Gillian learned Sebastian was trimming hedges near the Bazaar, the news delivered like the CEO played gardener all the time. So, another journey to see the king, the Bazaar's spires disappearing then reappearing larger as she approached. When she finally reached the gates, she found a crowd pressed against the pickets, kids and adults alike. Their faces squished through the gaps, their phones held at the ready, hoping for a glimpse of the park's architect. Gillian threaded through the mob and approached the guarded entrance. She tentatively pressed her wrist against a pad and was allowed entry under watchful eyes. She dug her hands into her pockets as she hiked straight up, ignoring the switchbacked walk and the crowd's conspiratorial murmurs. The Bazaar loomed dramatically, as if Sebastian had built the thing exactly for this moment, for her.

A handful of groundskeepers worked the property. A few riding mowers but more exercising hand tools and finesse. The work quiet and the men sweating, despite the overcast sky. Gillian fetched water bottles from a nearby wheelbarrow and handed them out. One of the men was kind enough to direct her to Sebastian.

The Puzzle Man worked at the foot of the Bazaar, kneeling under a canted signpost. He was placing rocks the size of large potatoes into a hole at the sign's base. He wore a flannel shirt with the sleeves rolled and a gardening smock with various tools tucked in the pockets, as well as his flat cap and Joplin-style sunglasses. He faced away and didn't move as she drew near, although this time he really seemed ignorant of her presence.

"Sebastian?"

He turned and looked at her over his glasses. A hard

frown creased his face, one that didn't get any less severe for seeing her. Up close she noticed he was disheveled. Frayed, as if he hadn't been sleeping. His pits were sweat-stained and his hair damp beneath his hat. Gillian wasn't sure she'd ever seen him perspire.

"You didn't tell me you talked to him," Sebastian said.

Gillian left the path and crunched across patchy earth. "Who's that?"

"Tommy. I had to learn third-hand you've heard from him. He's talking to you, the Navarros. Everyone but us."

Gillian stopped in her tracks. "How do you know that?"

"By doing what you should have done. Focusing on the problem."

"How did you know I talked to Tommy?"

"Someone in Security must have told me. Don't get precious, I need you up to speed. We're in crisis. The position Tommy has put us in is a travesty I can't begin to fathom. Do you know he contacted his drug dealer from a company laptop? He's left explicit emails. The media will have a field day if they get a hold of the story."

Sebastian stopped to right the sign, but the post leaned over again.

"Security bugged his phone? And his laptop?"

"We didn't have to bug anything." The man took a deep breath. "You're aware of Tommy's behavior? With these families?"

"The Navarros?"

"The Navarros are nothing," he said. "Last month we ran a Sherlockian mystery – handwritten letters sent to a dozen children, ages ten to fifteen, who would be visiting the park. You know the type – all amateur Watsons. Children with different skills, each sent different challenges. One copy we sent in Braille. Tommy wrote the letters, every one of them. He said it was a welcome diversion. I thought – I'd hoped – running the mystery would help him."

He held up a hand, as if Gillian planned to object.

"He was euphoric. Manic. He ran around the park with the children, sweating, not making any sense. He actually removed his coat – the Brooks Brothers – his tie, and unbuttoned his dress shirt, then gallivanted around Miscellany as if he'd been tossed from some bar. The parents were there. Gillian, I swear to you, he revealed some of the answers."

Gillian could picture it. Cokehead Tommy with a hair up his ass and wild enough to lose his composure. But Sebastian was talking too fast. Steamrolling her concerns. "You know, Tommy mentioned something to me. The Target Practice puzzle. There was a contestant who gave a deleted answer. Like they knew an earlier version."

"That's Tommy's paranoia talking. That's a thing cocaine can do, correct? He's reading this vitriol, on Twitter or wherever he finds it, from the losing parents. And it is always the parents. Adults, the pride of the species. Is it any wonder our efforts encounter resistance? People who want to tear us down. They go on Fox with their red hats and froth about our liberal values. We can't vet the parents. Some of them vote red, white, blue, and apple pie, and they fear what they think we represent. We have to be careful with them, handle the PR very carefully, and then Tommy threatens to blow up the entire enterprise."

Sebastian continued to dump rocks in the hole. Gillian wanted to argue, to throw a little tar on this masterpiece he was painting. But she couldn't. She hadn't trekked out here to debate Target Practice, or Sebastian's dreams.

"My mother is sick," she said.

Sebastian stopped throwing rocks. He turned and put an elbow on his knee. "Stephanie's lupus?"

"It's worse now, than before. She's in a chair most of the time."

Off came the sunglasses. Sebastian tucked them into an apron pocket. "You're asking me for help?"

"I need to get her moved to a new place. Now. That takes connections. Money. It's something I would pay back."

Gillian felt like Sebastian had been winging the rocks at her chest. It was killing her to stand here and ask him this.

"You could have said something when she took ill," he said. "You could have asked me at any time."

"And come crawling back? I lost. I was second. You made it very clear I was a disappointment."

"You always took feedback too hard. You could have persevered. Ellsberg stayed. Tommy, for all his flaws, stayed."

"You wanted me as... what? Some prop, up there to spew lines?"

"Certainly not. You could have been designing puzzles. Entire parks."

He kept looking at her. Like this was the easiest riddle in the world to solve. "Maybe I didn't want that," she said.

"Bullshit. You're out there struggling, taking pictures of deadbeat fathers, doing anything a hundred kids with a phone could do, for what? Is that fighting the good fight? You could do good here. There's maybe one in a million with your mind. You're a unicorn. A Pegasus."

She wanted to be angrier when he took potshots at her life in LA. Only the thought of returning to the chase for the almighty dollar filled her with dread. The fact that she was thirty and barely making it filled her with dread. The knowledge that the woman who'd shown her more love than anyone was suffering, and only days from being thrown out in the street and Gillian couldn't stop it, filled her with dread.

"You want me to come back," Gillian said. "Is that it? Unless I come back you won't help?"

"That's not what I said."

"It's what you meant."

Sebastian dusted off his gloved hands and stood. He looked her in the face. Those eyes like mirrors of her own. Sebastian a version of what she could have been. What she could be.

"You know where Tommy is?"

"I'm trying to find him. A little more time and I–"

"A little more time?" He tugged off his gloves. Moved into her personal space. "You're competing tomorrow?"

Green Thumb Sebastian dropped away. Replaced with the man who could sell sand in the Sahara.

"I don't solve puzzles," she said. Her protest sounded weak, even to her. "Not anymore."

"You solve puzzles every day. Convincing people to do what you need them to do. *People* are the ultimate puzzle. And they can be solved." He tucked his gloves under his arm. "I need you. I need Tommy, too, but I need you more. You're stronger than he is. But you held back before and walked away. I cannot have that again. Tomorrow night is the great game. The Contest Extraordinaire – Redux. Any puzzle is the perfect arrangement of the unknown and the known. The known is family. *All* of the children. Ellsberg. Tommy. Leah. You."

Sebastian was in an ultimatum-giving mood. Much less subtle than he'd been in The Aerie. He watched her absorb the reality of his words. She'd hoped he'd require less of her than everything.

"I could hire you right now," he said. "Today. We're redoing the Bazaar in London. Paris is next year. We've got a shot at breaking ground in Brazil. You don't have to stay here, I know being here is hard for you. Take the mission, take Miscellany and go wherever you want. Tommy was great at talking but he'd get lost in the weeds. You cut weeds down. I've seen it. I remember."

This was more than competing at the Reunion. Much more. She glanced at the Bazaar; could almost feel the slimy water of the tank, her failure lurking somewhere below ground. Sebastian seemed content to let her stare, if only so she remembered a time when she had come to Miscellany willingly.

"If Tommy's behavior gets out," he said, "if he's caught breaking the law, it impugns our integrity and we take a hit. We're no longer on a mission to build the next generation – we instead bunker down and save ourselves. There will be no more expansion. No more hiring. I certainly can't entertain thirty year-old Uber drivers as if they're the next CEO. We've been searching for investment. That will all go down the drain. That won't impact me, of course – in the long run I'll be fine. It's the people of Miscellany. Thousands of people. We grow or we die. If we cannot succeed here, this could all go away."

Gillian side-eyed him. Her presence energized him, this lost soul he might save. He believed in his mission, believed he fought for the kids. And he could make all her problems go away.

His voice got softer. "With you and Tommy in the fold," he said, "there's a Miscellany that can help your mother."

Sweet Jesus. She was actually considering it.

Sebastian was done with gardening for the day. He stuffed his gloves in a pocket.

"We will do what we are meant to do," he said. "You will both compete. You will both do well. You are sharp, you are hungry, and you will remember what I have taught you. I expect a very close race. Although, if I'm being honest, I expect a different outcome this time."

He headed down the path, patting her on the shoulder as he passed. He could afford to be magnanimous. He'd gotten what he wanted. And she hadn't stopped him.

"This is what you're good at, Gillian," he said. "Never feel bad about that."

Twenty-Three

Gillian spent a few hours revisiting the same haunts. The Boardwalk, the Transportation Hub. She called Evelina, telling herself she didn't visit in person to avoid bothering the valets; certainly she wasn't afraid of Jackie. And although the chat with Evelina was pleasant – *Did you meet our cat? We call her chudo, chodovishche, the beast* – she still hadn't seen her husband.

Last but not least, Miscellany HQ. Late afternoon and the sun struggled to break free of the clouds. Gillian sat in Tommy's desk chair, for the moment queen of his austere palace, her posture such that nobody dared question her presence. She commanded the office that could have been hers. Maybe still could be.

Sebastian staring at her. *I need you.*

The idea mesmerizing and dangerous.

A year back, Gillian was deep into rideshare, driving at 4, 4:30 in the morning, early enough to encounter the really epic boozers from the night before. A car had clipped her going the wrong way near the Hollywood Freeway. Her Corolla lost a side mirror and a front quarter panel she'd replaced but never repainted. Afterward she'd felt exhilarated. The rush a close cousin to how she'd felt in her Contest days. Running on no sleep, taking chances, the kind of chances she hadn't taken in years. Stupid. A self-inflicted grind that had almost killed her. She'd quit rideshare for a while, swore it off, until the sad state of her finances drew her back. Another promise she'd gradually erased.

Did practicality drive her, or the search for thrills?

Returning to Miscellany offered potential. To step into a place of authority, to spotlight where they'd grown stagnant. To focus on new opportunities and new kinds of children – maybe children that looked more like Gillian. To challenge herself against Sebastian, to stand in his presence and not blink. Tommy played the game, or had tried to. Ellsberg, Leah. Why shouldn't she?

Shit, in the end it didn't matter. Mom needed Gillian to be strong. Not using her skills – that was an insult to everything her mother had sacrificed for her.

Gillian's gaze traversed the office. This space, spartan or not, said a lot about Tommy. He didn't like to be here. He didn't like HQ. Mr Best-and-Brightest had finished first in the Contest Extraordinaire. He'd leveraged that success into an officer position at a Fortune 500, partnered with an amazing woman, shaped hearts and minds with a coterie of like-minded individuals, and built the on-ramp to a new tomorrow. He'd earned the right to sit anywhere but The Aerie. Only, somewhere in the midst of his righteous mission, the Kool-Aid went sour. Tommy had turned to coke, appropriating the white male executive stereotype. He'd looked around and found not five or six fellow believers but a host of leeches and corporate yes-men. He'd lost his way, lost himself in a corporation grown too big, too strange, and too unfamiliar. Ultimately, he'd fled Miscellany and sought Gillian because he'd run out of people he could trust. He was disillusioned. He was unhappy.

Gillian replayed Tommy's call in her head. Sounds in the background. A crowd of people, the casual clatter of plates and cups. A restaurant, maybe, but the high-pitched whistle got her thinking of espresso, the machine Evelina had wrestled with in the Kundojjala home. The *empty* Kundojjala home.

On the call, there'd been a woman in the background. The voice intimate. Familiar.

Tommy had partnered with an amazing woman, to be sure. Gillian had met her. No doubt she was smart, funny, and beautiful. But men throughout history forged success with powerful women and then pissed it away for an entirely different stereotype.

Her friend always had his vices. First candy, later caffeine. And now? Tommy was a smart man, but he was still a man. And men were predictable when they were unhappy.

She leaned over and looked into the trash can. She fished out the paper cup.

Tommy loved his coffee, sure. But who did he drink it with?

The imprint on the cup two black-and-white photos of a coffee mug. *Turn to the front, turn to the side*. The placard the name of the place. *Mugshot*.

Gillian's phone told her there were only three locations.

Mugshot hid in the overpass shadow of the DNT and Sam Rayburn. The driver circled a few times before finding the place, even with GPS. One of the Transportation Hub guys took her – a favor, he said, although Gillian did offer to *put in a word* on his long-requested schedule change.

The coffee shop was hipster but cozy, and although the

cappuccino took forever to arrive, it tasted great. Gillian sat at the counter and waited until the barista seemed bored enough to talk. She had pink and orange hair, her forearms sleeved with spiderwebs and ravens. Gillian found her aesthetic kind of cool, and said so. The barista was willing – post compliments and once offered free Miscellany park tickets – to identify an online photo of Tommy and Evelina at some charity event, although Evelina wasn't the woman she recognized.

"Nah. Girl with him had tie-dye hair. Less perfect. Like, this one seems all hard edges – kind of badass. His girl had a nose ring and new ink – amateur work, seahorses and shit. She's in here all the time."

Seahorses and shit. The voice in the background. The voice Tommy heard every day, right outside his office, the two working closely together. Gillian should have seen it sooner.

A call to HQ and Gillian played Jessyca the Executive Assistant, asking IT about a laptop delivery on behalf of Mr Kundojjala. The laptop should have been shipped to her home – did they have the correct address? The overworked tech lacked record of a laptop, but when Gillian/Jessyca's questions came too fast he spit out the address anyway.

South she went, to Addison. Jessyca lived in a fancy brick townhouse within walking distance of the Belt Line strip. A Lexus nestled against the front curb. Gillian didn't want to judge, but having done secretarial work herself, she knew the job didn't pull down townhouse and Lexus money. The unit was ground floor, the shades pulled up. Gillian pressed her face against the glass windows, but no one moved inside and the lights were out.

After, she visited the sales office. She offered the twenty year-old "manager" Mavericks tickets she didn't have, but assumed she could secure through Sebastian. In her head a tiny cash register ringing, her debt increasing with every word over her lips. Manager boy promised to call if Jessyca or her male friend appeared.

Feeling more clear-headed since she'd left the park, Gillian decided to stay local. There was a pizza place right across the street, dead empty. They wouldn't sell her a beer without food, so she bought a slice and a lager and sat at the window. She played tiled word games on her phone between pulls from the bottle.

Her mom texted. She always sent out a text first. *You young people like texts.*

You young people.

Gillian called her.

"How are you feeling?" she asked, before her mother could work in so much as a hello.

"I can't complain." Her mother's typical opening salvo. "But how are you, dear? I heard you're in town. Otherwise I didn't get a lot of information from your sister."

"I am. I meant to call. Things have been busy." She drowned her guilt in a swallow of beer.

"You don't have to tell me. We saw you on the news. June told me you sat with the governor."

"I didn't sit–"

"She told me you're back working with Sebastian. I'm so glad to hear you've dealt with all that. I always wondered why you didn't make a career out of those puzzles and games. You're so good at them. You could be like one of those game show hosts. Like *Wheel of Fortune*. Or that *Carmen Sandiego* thing you were so into. You know some of those hosts get their own talk shows."

Her mother sounded croaky. There was a lot of noise in

the background. The clinic had always been crowded. The walls thin.

"I'm working on getting you out of there."

"Oh, don't worry about me. I can't complain. Grace – that's the woman in the room next to me – that woman can complain. Her daughter moved into their house, only she has a new baby. And the husband doesn't work."

Gillian had heard all about this woman last time. She knew more about the strangers around her mother than she knew about her own family.

"Mom, I talked to Mitch. I came back to Miscellany for a reason." She realized her voice had gotten louder. The two stoners behind the counter so bored they'd started to eavesdrop. "I don't know what June told you, but I'm going to work it out. We'll get you into a nice place."

"I'm fine here. They have those chicken sandwiches I like. They stock the machines with Diet Coke. I know I'm not supposed to drink Coke, but you have to have some vices."

Gillian bowed her head. Around her the sky was falling, and she couldn't keep the firmament up. "I'm going to come see you."

"You don't have to do that. You're way up north. The traffic will be terrible. You know those tractor trailers are always jackknifing. Why do they have so many of those darn things?"

She squeezed her eyes shut. "I don't know, Mom."

Her mother paused. "Are you sleeping?"

"I'm fine. I feel like a million bucks."

"That's what your father always says." The next question was inevitable. "Have you talked to him?"

Gillian retrieved her beer. "It's been a while."

"He misses you, Gil. You know he's sorry."

"Yeah." She imagined her mother searching the heavens for answers. Never a religious person, more the type for scrying and seeking comfort in crystals. Confident the energy of the universe would provide. Gillian was a part of that energy – a fractured crystal her mother never gave up on.

Across the street, a couple walked the sidewalk hand in hand. A smiling tattooed blue-pink-blond with a nose stud and a lovestruck grin. The man in a blazer with an untucked button-down, his hair disheveled but a looseness to his shoulders Gillian hadn't seen previously.

"I gotta go." She pushed aside her beer and pizza as she slid off the stool. "I'll call you later."

"Oh." Mom's faint note of disappointment was inescapable. "I know you're busy. I'll let you go. Call me later and tell me about one of those puzzles you're solving. I always loved hearing about those."

Gillian was already out the door. "I'm going to get you out of there."

"I love you, Gillian."

Her mom hung up. Gillian swallowed a bubble of beer vapors and heartbreak.

The lovely couple didn't immediately notice her charging across the street. Gillian approached from Tommy's blind side, although he was so engaged with Jessyca he wouldn't have noticed had she plowed into him with a Mack truck. She shouted his name twice before he turned. He murmured into Jessyca's ear. He stopped, but Jessyca kept walking, more briskly and with a concerned look on her face.

"That's your girlfriend?" Gillian pointed at Jessyca's retreating ass. "This is why you're not calling me back?"

"We were having dinner." Tommy stuck his hands in his pockets. Sheepish, because he'd been caught. "There's a fantastic poke place around the corner. The sushi is so fresh. I know the chef. I could introduce you."

Gillian stopped, close enough to knock him down. Tommy's eyes weren't particularly wild. He was calm. The peace of someone whose lies had been revealed. "What are you doing?" she asked.

"I told you, we were having dinner."

"Really? That sounds cozy – was Evelina invited?"

Tommy waved his hand, dismissive. "Evelina doesn't care."

"That's funny. She seemed very concerned with your behavior."

His chuckle was grim. "The PR business is tricky. You start repeating things long enough, and you believe them. I warned her how easy it was to get lost. I'd hoped she listened, but I don't know how to talk to her. She's gone. Just gone."

"So you found someone else?" Jessyca had already disappeared inside the townhouse. "Is this why you brought me here? To uncover your affair? Jesus, Tommy, you could have just hired a divorce lawyer. I guess I was cheaper?"

"That's not it." He shook his head vigorously. "I brought you here for a reason."

"I'm not sure I care anymore." The anger in her voice surprised her. "I'm back in the middle of all this, again. Playing second fiddle to you, *again*. You don't know what it's doing to me. I–" She caught herself. If she kept going, she might not be able to stop. "Everyone is looking for you. You want to divorce your wife – she's a kick-ass woman, she'll be fine. And Ellsberg is only doing what he's told. It's

Sebastian. You know him. He needs this done, and by his script. That means showing up for the Reunion. That's how you take your money and your girlfriend and stroll off into the sunset. You want new challenges – off you go. You want to spend more time with your family, or start a new one, Miscellany will write the press release. But you've got to do this thing, and then get help. Take the storybook ending, or close to it, because I'm here to tell you there's no narrative where Sebastian's golden child skips out on the Reunion and instead has a coke-fueled meltdown with his fucking mistress."

It was as if they'd changed places: Tommy a rock and Gillian flying off the handle. He shook his head throughout Gillian's speech.

"That's not what's happening?" she asked.

"It's not the drugs."

"Then you scared the shit out of a bunch of ten year-olds because it was fun?"

Tommy let out a long, shaky breath. "Sebastian told you about that?"

"To hell with Sebastian. I saw you at the Navarros'."

He chewed the inside of his lip. "Did he mention Target Practice?"

The lack of self-awareness was incredible. Chasing conspiracies while Gillian's mom ate plastic chicken in God's waiting room, a shithole they couldn't even afford. Mom crippled with an incurable disease and she saw a doctor – a physician's assistant – maybe an hour a week.

Without shame, Tommy carried on. "This is Evelina," he said. "Feeding you stories."

"Evelina can't be trusted now? That's an amazing reality distortion field. Sebastian-worthy."

"They're following me."

"Your wife is gorgeous. Trust me, you'd spot her from a mile away."

"I don't mean Evelina. I mean Jackie."

Gillian resisted the urge to look over her shoulder. It made her angry. Tommy's snake oil, selling Jackie the bogeyman. Like he knew she was afraid and hoped to exploit her weakness. "Nobody's following you."

But he ignored her. "Why are you here? Who sent you?"

"Nobody sent me."

"But somebody's paying you? Evelina? Leah? They promised you something."

A spike of guilt she quickly squashed. "You invited me here. *You* promised me something."

The accusation gave him pause. "I'm working on that. There's a liquidity problem right now. But I would never forget your mother. During the Contest she brought us homemade blueberry muffins. Because we were just kids, not because we won some Miscellany game. It's a shame you're using her as an excuse to do their dirty work."

He could have hit her with a car and hurt her less. "Don't you dare."

"The girl I knew would fight. She wouldn't take no for an answer."

"She died!" Gillian roared, the frustration boiling over. "She died that day. What did you expect? I couldn't be the second-place girl everywhere I went. The girl who lost. I had to find a way out, a strategy I recommend you start embracing pretty damn quick, unless you want to go crazy. Have you listened to yourself, Tommy? Your wife is out to get you? Your chauffeur? What you should be worried about is some fan with a camera-phone – the minute this shit pops on social media, you're screwed. Miscellany will nail you to the wall. You'll lose everything. Your house, the cars, Evelina, that girl who seems to really like you but who knows what she's going to think when you're plastered online, hands cuffed, clickbait. You abused Miscellany resources, injected enough cocaine to kill a horse, then chased a bunch of kids around your employer's showpiece theme park? You're not a rich white man, Tommy. After this, you'll never get a real job. You'll be driving cars and selling fucking ties for a living."

As agitated as Tommy had been, she was afraid he might take off running. But instead, he crossed his arms and frowned. "What do you mean *abused*?"

"Sebastian said you emailed your dealer. From a company laptop."

"I used my laptop. My personal property."

"It's the internet, Tommy. They're monitoring your accounts. It doesn't matter what computer you use."

"Sebastian is–" Tommy stopped. Swayed as he backtracked through the storm of his mind. "Then he knows everything." He looked up and down the street, quickly. "We can't stay here."

"What are you talking about?"

"He knows we're here."

"Jesus Christ, are you listening to yourself? He has no idea where you are. Trust me."

"He's doing this. He tricked you into coming here."

"*I'm* doing this!" she shouted. "It's brass tacks, bottom line. I'm here because Miscellany is paying me, pure and simple. You think you're out here, fighting the good fight, you'd better think again."

Tommy watched her, angry. She took a breath.

"Put it on pause," she said. "Go to the Reunion. There are options here. Graceful exits. I saw you on the jet, I saw you play the game. This is business."

He rubbed his face. Glanced over his shoulder, as if someone stood there with cue cards. The longer he waited, the more he settled. The anger drained. "I made a mistake, bringing you back."

"I just told you–"

"No, you're right." He was eerily calm. "I'll be there, at the Reunion. But I don't need you. I think I wanted you to tell me I was doing the right thing. I should have realized Sebastian would get to you. Again." He put his hands in his pockets, as if he'd decided something. "You should go home."

"What are you doing, Tommy?"

"Like you said. I'm Sebastian's golden boy. The number two man in the fourth largest entertainment conglomerate in the world. Imagine me walking into the Department of Justice. There's nothing they'd love more than a corporate whistleblower at my level. And whatever you think of my habit, I've concealed it for a long time. When the interview starts, I'll be wearing a nice suit, custom. I'll have shaved. I'm not blond-haired and blue-eyed, but I represent the second largest immigrant population after Mexico. I can impact not only corporations, but elections. Miscellany ignores me at their own risk."

He stared at her, unblinking. Gillian was breathing loud, almost sweating. She hadn't a moment's control since she'd stepped outside the pizza place, maybe longer. She was lost at sea, and she wasn't even sure how it had happened.

She looked at Tommy. "I thought you believed in Sebastian."

He stood there, the Tommy of old. Self-confident. Victorious. "I thought you didn't."

With that, he walked around her and disappeared into the townhouse.

Twenty-Four

A rabbit chewed the grass next to June's tumbledown front steps. Unafraid, it sat on its haunches, watching as they piled out of the car. June's husband Todd stomped at it, but the creature continued to eat, bland faced.

"Todd." Mom settled into the rickety wheelchair. "It doesn't mean you any harm."

Gillian kept herself apart. By rights, she should feel good. She had Tommy, he'd committed to the Reunion. Better still, Mom was free on a day trip. Bolstered with happiness, surrounded by family. The zest in her laugh, in her every movement, all the validation Gillian should need.

I thought you believed in Sebastian.

I thought you didn't.

Gillian stared at the rabbit's alien black eyes. Nothing she believed a week ago was true. She'd never return to Miscellany. She'd never compete again. She'd never work for Sebastian. Promises forged in bitterness, and best left behind. That's what she told herself.

Todd had to get within a foot before the rabbit shot off around the corner.

"Too damn many of them." He scratched his head, nearly dislodging his undersized porkpie hat. "They're pests."

"June." Mom waved an arm at Gillian's sister. "Can't you control him?"

"Don't look at me." June wrestled with a beach bag stuffed full of Mom's daily medications, her heating pad, and three one-liter bottles of Diet Coke. "Damn rabbits tore through my box garden. Cars can't flatten them fast enough."

June's house was out in Carrolton, a three-bedroom, one-bath rental in dire need of repairs. They situated Mom in Dad's buttworn recliner, then Gillian got the tour like the stranger she was. The inside nice but cozy, barely enough room for June's family, let alone guests. Transparent curtains. Water stains. Too many pictures. A look out the rear windows revealed a big old oak overlooking a one-car garage and a narrow lawn that stretched back fifteen yards or so. It was a place to call home, but Gillian could see where June's means ran out.

Mom nestled in with one of her Cokes. June's two boys mumbled shy hellos before retreating to their shared bedroom. Dad remained absent and unmentioned. The TV came on, broadcasting the typical anticlimactic end to the Rangers' season. Mom and Todd started up on what ailed the team – everything from the GM to bad pitching. Gillian was content to stand in the kitchen and watch how the family worked without her.

June hung her keys on a hook near the fridge. She scooted around Gillian to rustle up snacks. Chips and dip. Some leftover mac and cheese. A store-bought veggie plate, the contents untouched under plastic.

"They can't win on the road," Mom said, pointing at the TV as if the evidence was right there.

Todd waved her off. "They won last night, against the A's. Calhoun homered."

"What good is that going to do? Too little too late is what I say."

It was funny to hear Mom speak so mercilessly of the ballplayers, when she'd never been so cut and dried with her kids. She'd always been a softie.

June sidled up next to Gillian. Leaned against the wall with arms crossed and watched her husband and mother talk as if they were unemployed scouts. "I've got a casserole for dinner. We'll eat around 5:30."

"I can't stay that long. I've got to get back."

June eyed her. "I traded shifts to make this work."

"And I came all the way out here. They didn't fly me back for family time. I'm working. The Reunion is tonight."

"You leave before dinner, you tell her. I'm not making your excuses."

Gillian gritted her teeth. She'd made the pilgrimage because she owed her family. Sure, Gillian loved her mother, but her role was different. The one they could pin their hopes on. The problem-solver. Out here, where did she fit? The conflict on her face must have been easy to read. June adopted a conciliatory tone.

"We'll eat early," she said. "It's Saturday, there's no rush hour. Todd can drop her at the clinic, you'll be back in the 'burbs before seven."

Mom argued with Todd about designated hitters. Sounding more invigorated than she had in months.

Gillian made a face, like she was thinking about it. Then, while still frowning at her sister, lobbed a comment into the living room. "I say Andrus is done."

The remark hit Todd like a stick in the ear. "Done? At shortstop? What are you talking about?"

Mom looked disappointed. Shaking her head. "Oh, Gillian, don't say that."

Gillian let the frown slip into a smile, still looking at June as she waded into the conversation. She set a hand on Mom's shoulder, to let her know she was there.

June fussed like a mother. She gathered empty plates while simultaneously lecturing her boys, the two engaged in a rambunctious game of Uno with their grandmother, stacked Draw 2s generating some consternation. Gillian followed her into the kitchen, where June deposited plates in the sink, then retrieved two glasses of wine from the counter. She gave one to Gillian, who wrinkled her nose but kept the glass to seem accommodating. June then assumed a surveilling position outside her oven, squinting at her casserole through the tiny window as if it might disappear if she didn't keep a sharp eye. She'd hardly left the confines of the kitchen. Her favorite mug stowed behind the microwave. A pair of books stacked atop the refrigerator. Some knockoff tablet leaning behind the sink, playing Eighties rap. The kitchen was clearly June's space, and she was comfortable in her lair. She hummed a little and slurped at her wine. "Dad's coming."

Gillian looked at June, who focused on her oven and kept her face innocent. She didn't trust herself with words.

"He's better." June turned to face her, butt against the oven. "Would mean a lot to him if you acknowledged that."

"I don't owe him anything."

"Why is everything a transaction with you? I'm talking about a little human decency. If Mom forgave him, why can't you?"

"Don't put this on me. You want him in your house, fine. Mom takes him back, God bless. Respect my choices. You didn't need him like I did."

"Daddy's little girl got her heart broke? Come on. The rest of us moved on."

"He left me. More than once I had to take a bus. Remember the time he got drunk off his ass and I had to walk from the convention center? Fortunately one of the proctors saw me and gave me a ride home, although we won't talk about the risk I took getting into a stranger's car." She could tell June had forgotten. "You were older. More self-sufficient. I wasn't like that, not back then. So don't tell me how I'm supposed to feel."

June drank her wine aggressively. Found bottom and went to reload her glass. "If you came around more often, this would be easier. You'd see him more."

"Sure. We're a barbecue away from a happy family."

At the counter, June's shoulders hunched, instinctive. Gillian always the Molotov cocktail. Unstable and most likely to hurt the innocent.

Gillian swirled her wine. "There's a chance I'm staying."

A humorless laugh. "And St Nick is coming ass-first down the chimney."

"I'm serious."

Her sister half-turned, enough to catch Gillian from the corner of her eye. She sipped from her refilled glass, using the wine to collect her thoughts.

"We'll deal with whatever comes."

Not exactly what Gillian wanted to hear. But June came away from the counter and, with a tiny smile, clinked her glass against Gillian's. "Drink your wine. At least say hello to Dad before you leave."

June slipped from the room and went to watch the card game, leaving Gillian feeling as if she'd been somehow outmaneuvered.

Dirty dishes clattered as Gillian said her goodbyes. She gave Todd a wave as he sat in his chair, flipping channels. She bent down to hug Mom in her chair.

"You have to go already?" Her voice mournful in Gillian's ear.

"The life of a celebrity," June said from the kitchen. "Can't keep the cameras waiting."

Gillian squeezed Mom's hand. The bones dry leaves under gray skin. The hair more steel wool than black. Her cheeks puffy from the meds. And yet, Gillian saw Mom's smile, still vibrant after all these years. She wondered how the woman remained so positive. Mom from a different family, a different species. She believed in energy crystals and reincarnation, and although she voted Democrat, she wasn't sure a woman was ready to hold office. The woman impractical to the extreme, but she'd always believed in Gillian. A sincere belief that had shined through the cloud of crap surrounding Gillian's life. She'd never forget that.

"You want anything from Miscellany?"

"A jacket would be nice. It gets cold at the clinic – they turn the air down too far."

"A jacket I can do."

"Something sparkly. We play stud poker on Tuesdays. I want to make the old biddies jealous."

Gillian hugged her mother again. She'd have changed time and space to make things easier on this woman. "Clean them out, Mom."

She gave June a hug at the door. It was warmer than their embrace at the hotel. "Thanks for hosting."

"That's what I do." When they separated her sister looked worried, like she thought Gillian was headed for trouble. But all she said was, "Drive safe."

Outside the heat still shimmered off the cracked sidewalks. Gillian waited for her rideshare with arms crossed. As she stood curbside a dirty green Saturn pulled up, a black-and-gold dreamcatcher hanging from the rearview. Gillian's dad was behind the wheel.

She looked at her phone. The rideshare was two minutes away.

Dad levered himself free of the car. He was white – so damn white. His hair still long and brown, only lightly threaded with silver. Under his pronounced nose, the seventies-look mustache. The hangdog look of his youth only more pronounced with time and age, the wrinkles slicing under his eyes the most severe. The eyes themselves a dusty light brown, as if they'd burned too hot too long. He wore a loose blue dress shirt and linen pants. Gillian remembered her father as pasty and wet, but this man was withered like burnt corn stalk. He stood awkwardly next to his car, his hands hopping from his cuffs to his earlobes to his hair. Once alcohol drove the Wallace Charles train. Now, maybe just nerves. But then Dad had been on the wagon before, and always found a way to dive off head-first.

"I'm headed back," she said, her chin lifted.

He nodded. Looked down at the keys in his hands, the bundle knotted together with a twist-tie. "I've been clean two years. Five before that."

"Great. How long you planning to go this time?"

He raised his head. The patches under his eyes darker

than the surrounding skin, like bruises. They made him look old. A memory took hold, the smell of his cologne when he hugged her. Brut, in the green bottle. A guaranteed Father's Day gift every year.

"You wanted me to stay away so I stayed away," he said. "But I would apologize, if you let me."

"That's a lot of words, and none of them are *I'm sorry*."

"I am sorry."

"Terrific. It's too late."

A white Prius turned onto the street. The driver cruising slow, looking for the fare.

Dad drew closer. He could have reached out and touched her arm, if he wanted. "I'll do whatever you want, Gilly. Whatever you want."

She stepped off the curb and into the street. Raised her arm like she was hailing a cab. She was breathing heavy. Her jaw squeezed so tight her teeth creaked.

"You guys always do the same thing," she said. "You step all over people, do whatever you want, and after you've done exactly as you pleased, only then do you apologize."

The Prius found her. Accelerated and eased over to where she stood. She didn't wait for the car to stop before reaching for the passenger door.

"June made a casserole," she said, as she piled into the back. "You eat it, and you say thank you."

She slammed the door. The car pulled away, leaving Dad alone. She braced herself against the door and refused to turn around. Let him watch his children leave him and his mistakes behind.

Minutes later, her phone buzzed. It was June.

What did you say to him?

She considered. Typed out, *What needed to be said.* Her

thumb hovered over SEND but remained locked in place. She let her head fall back and she stared at the ceiling. She thought of her sister back in that little house, worrying about every little thing, including her flaky ass – the girl who'd never gotten her shit together, not since that day at the Bazaar. June was always the reliable one. The one in the family who did what had to be done.

I told him the casserole was delicious, she typed, erasing the original message. *And he should say thank you.*

She hit SEND and slipped the phone into her pocket.

Twenty-Five

The press junket was theater of the first order. Held in one of the older buildings adjacent to the Bazaar, the aesthetic Cold War bunker – low ceilings, yellow cinder block walls. Gillian fielded questions in her dressing room – the one Miscellany assigned her. She leaned forward in her canvas director's chair, sweating under the makeup lights, and endured a range of banal interview questions. *Where have you been? What's it like being back? Which Contestant is the smartest?*

She acted as if the questions were meant for someone else – someone famous and empty. Her answers pat and her laughter forced. She spent most of her time wondering when the torture would end, and if Tommy would prove good on his word. She worried how Mom was doing. She worried about the Reunion.

The images were relentless. Riddle stations, falling in her path one after the other. Walls to climb and doors to unlock. Gillian hunched over some wooden puzzle box, her fingers clawed, her neck sore as she tried to solve the mechanism and release the secrets within. Sweating, gears locking, as the others passed her by. No tricks, no cheating, just Gillian not being good enough.

If she lost again, she'd be crushed. If she won, she was

back. She couldn't see beyond either outcome. Everything in the future, black.

The interviews wrapped and the fourth estate was left behind. Gillian changed clothes, PR-friendly fashion exchanged for workout wear. At one point Leah's laugh echoed down the hallway outside. Gillian stuck her head out but still didn't see Tommy.

Her publicist escorted her to the Bazaar, as far as the security perimeter. The evening was presented as festive. Paper lanterns lined the walk; piano music carried on the air and drinks were provided, for those who wanted them. But no cameras were allowed inside. No spouses, no glommers-on, only the original Contestants and the handful of staff working the event. A smattering of celebrities and industry players mingled on the grass, but protocol and chiseled security prevented them from advancing further. Two stone-faced guards bagged Gillian's wallet and phone, verified the woman on her California driver's license was indeed her. They studied her face as if they couldn't believe she was that original twelve year-old kid. To be honest, Gillian felt the same way.

She was guided into a small two-story foyer. The interior looked different than Gillian remembered. The same dark wallpaper and elaborate chandelier and antique console table, but the pieces rearranged. Like someone had assembled the room from a series of disjointed photographs. The others seemed equally uncomfortable.

The Contestants were all there. Lots of spandex. Lululemon. Gillian wore a baggy pair of leggings, a tight sports bra, and a tie-back tank she'd found on the discount rack at Forever 21. Her competitors stared. Leah saucy, throwing a wink. Ellsberg tipping finger to brow in mock salute. And standing apart from the others, Gillian's payday. The man who'd won this all before: Tommy.

He wore an athletic-cut polyester workout shirt and black nylon pants. He'd combed his hair and seemed relaxed, but he still had the look of a war-torn vet.

Gillian closed the distance. "I see you found the place."

He sized her up. His organic eye clear, the other seeming to watch her with suspicion. "You sound like Ellsberg," he said. "That didn't take long."

Their encounter in the street was still fresh, their dynamic strained. But Tommy was here, and the realization hit – she'd earned Sebastian's ten thousand. If he made good on their deal, she had an extension for Mom. Gillian felt a lift, like the one she'd experienced when that jet took off from LAX. But much like that experience, the exhilaration was fleeting. Ten thousand was a Band-Aid. A handful of aspirin.

"I asked your questions," she said. "Evelina. Leah. Ells. None of them seem to think there's any cheating going on."

His silence an accusation. Like he thought Gillian hadn't really tried.

Some guilt stirred. "Look," she said, "if you got me access to the qualifier footage–"

"You'll get your money, Gillian. After."

"I never said–"

"After I win." His back straight. His voice certain.

"You sound confident."

"I've been here before."

I'll beat your ass, she thought, the feeling quick and irrepressible. After only a week, all the competitive fire burned. If she stayed, this was how she'd feel, day in, day out.

She looked at Tommy. None of the good cheer she

remembered from the Contest, no offer of candy. She'd wanted this in so many ways – to earn her reward, to change the past – but this wasn't healthy, for her or for Tommy. She tried to make eye contact, but he avoided her gaze. Leah and Ellsberg the same, no pretense of socialization tonight, no friends. This evening was about challenging one another and themselves. Could they summon the thing that got them so far when they were young? Were they good enough to win?

For a moment Gillian was seized with the desire to talk everyone out of competing. Giving form to their worst demons. This was a bad idea. It would only hurt them.

Sebastian chose that moment to appear at the top of the stairs. He wore a raspberry three-piece suit and burgundy flat cap. He paused dramatically at the first step so they could all drink him in. He smiled down on them. She could almost read his mind. Here they were, gathered together again. All of Sebastian's children, ready for the challenge.

Again, her doubts vanished. She wanted to compete. Not just compete – she wanted to stomp them flat, every single one. Sebastian must have felt it. A crafty look came over his face, and for half a second Gillian expected him to slide down the banister. But the man was pushing sixty, and instead he slipped down the stairs with the grace of a tap dancer.

"I'm glad you all could make it," he said, when he reached bottom. "You're really going to enjoy tonight."

Sebastian charged toward the small door at the end of the hall. As in the first Contest, he produced a brass-plated skeleton key and rattled the teeth into the lock. The Contestants queued behind him, in the order dictated by their checkers performance.

The door opened. He stood aside and waved his arm. *After you.*

This was it. Little fanfare. No preparation. One open door and who knew what on the other side. Despite her reservations, goddamn, she was excited.

They passed over the threshold. Ellsberg first, Gillian right behind. They stopped in another small hallway, a curtain hanging at the end.

"You've all signed the waiver," Sebastian said. He didn't follow them through the door. "The releases are digital now, I'm afraid my lawyers can't maintain the paperwork. But just recall, every bit of fun in the universe is laced with the slightest bit of danger. Watch yourselves. Trust your wits. Trust what you've learned." He paused. "Or perhaps don't."

He smiled. Then firmly closed the door.

"Asshole," Leah muttered.

They laughed nervously. Then Ellsberg pushed through the curtain.

Across the threshold, a new world. The layout different than years before. Inside the room stood four lecterns, wyverns and sphinxes and other fantastical creatures carved into the giltwood. Each station had names engraved in the slanted tops, one for each of them. Also, a sheet of paper, a bottle of ink, and a quill pen. Four doors waited on the far wall – no knobs, only a paper-thin slot cut in each.

While nostalgia and history rooted Gillian to the spot, Leah surged to her post first. Ellsberg followed and, cursing, then Gillian. Tommy reached his lectern last. The room was initially quiet, but quickly filled with the sound of scratching pens. They all still held the fire. They all still wanted to win. Gillian's puzzle, maybe unique to her or maybe a carbon copy of those gracing every station, was a logic grid. A quick skim revealed the subject was meant to unnerve her, but after the last week, no way a puzzle broke her.

> *When arriving at her Toyota Corolla, Gillian discovers six notes tucked under her windshield wiper. Three of her past rideshare fares, Brad, Matt, and George, want to purchase one of Gillian's scarves. Of course, these past riders were all puzzle enthusiasts, and their notes require some deductive thinking to parse.*
> *Note 1: George does not like red.*
> *Note 2: The fare wanting a yellow scarf does not live in Pasadena.*
> *Note 3: One fare will pay $20 for the red scarf.*
> *Note 4: The fare wanting blue will pay more than George.*
> *Note 5: The Burbank fare has less than $30.*
> *Note 6: Inglewood will pay more than Brad.*

This was a warm-up. Logic puzzles simply required having the right mind to break things down. Gillian quickly sketched out the grid and walked through each note. Note 1 and Note 4 put George on the yellow scarf. Note 2 and Note 6 put Brad in Pasadena. The rest came together in short order, and Gillian grinned throughout the exercise. Christ, this felt good. This part right here. She'd wanted this rush for years, only she didn't know how to recreate it without navigating Sebastian and Miscellany. Maybe, after all this time, she'd found the path.

To her right, Tommy worked calmly on his challenge. She supposed she should find his composure encouraging. His presence and control a step in the right direction, a positive for him and for her bank account. But of all times, why did he have to pull his shit together now?

He didn't look over. And when he finished, he walked from the room and left the rest of them behind.

Quickly she completed her puzzle. Fed the answer into her door, which then swung open. She jogged down a long, poorly lit hallway that narrowed the farther she ran. At the end a revolving door with translucent glass, long shadows moving on the other side. She stepped in and pushed. The machine engaged and spun her around, but kept her trapped within. She rotated six times, fairly sure the enclosure lowered as it spun. When at last an opening appeared, she stepped through into a black-and-white checkerboard room. The room suggested levels and walls, but the uniform pattern made the contours difficult to grasp. No obvious exit presented itself.

A cold wave of panic rippled beneath Gillian's skin, but she took deep breaths. This was a puzzle. There was an answer. Not everyone could see the solution, and that fact gave her power. Her ability to persevere a measure of her worth. Sebastian valued the process and the answers.

She dropped to her hands and knees and crawled forward. The increased tactile contact grounded her. It also kept her from stepping through the hole near the far wall. There was a ladder painted the same black-and-white pattern as the room, which she carefully, with eyes closed to avoid confusion, descended. She found more checkerboard, but only near the ladder. Stepping away, she entered a massive library, floor to ceiling with books.

There was a single exit, a large weathered door crafted from solid teak. Gillian tried the handle, but the door proved locked. The Puzzlemasters had incongruously installed a card reader under the door handle, which meant there would be a card key or similar access token. It came down to the books in the room. There were hundreds.

In the middle of the room stood a long library table. One chair. One singular sheet of paper.

> *A good book is the key to your education in a number of ways, a fact we've known since ROMAN times. A good book can come to you at any time, even as you stand on the edge of the graveyard, nobody can deny. Find the correct book to unlock your future. Perhaps start with a biography of THE WARRIOR POPE.*

Then a scrambled array of words beneath.

She didn't bother searching for a book on The Warrior Pope, otherwise known as Pope Julius II. Instead, she married *Julius* to the capitalized ROMAN. Roman Julius. Julius Caesar. She'd need to apply a Caesar shift cipher to the scrambled letters. Of course, there'd be more to the riddle than clues to the cipher. The Contestants wouldn't be expected to brute-force the decryption; the riddle would provide the key. And sure enough, the first sentence screamed the answer. A good book is the key. The phrase "good book" mentioned twice, which was suspicious.

Gillian cycled through books she liked, figuring since Sebastian knew her favorite music, her favorite beer, he'd know her literary tastes. She turned those titles into numbers and fiddled with the decryption, but saw immediately she didn't have the right key. And none of her book titles felt right. The path cold.

A good book.

Number of ways. She thought of phrases with *ways. Six ways* for a six shift, or the craps dice roll *the hardways* for a shift of four, six, eight, or ten. And again, quickly, no dice, pun unintended. Frustrated, she banged the table. She could feel the others cracking their puzzles. Racing ahead to the end.

What would it mean if she finished worse than second place?

She studied the puzzle. In these kinds of riddles the answers had their own rhythm, and that rhythm differed from the main. She read the words aloud. Got caught on the phrase *nobody can deny*. An odd sing-song choice. "For He's a Jolly Good Fellow"? No, the phrasing would relate to the rest of the sentence.

When the answer came to her, she about slapped her forehead. She was an idiot.

Nobody and *Graveyard*. Nobody Owens, the main character of *The Graveyard Book*.

The Graveyard Book became a series of numbers, each representing the alphabetic position of the letters in the title. Those numbers were the shifts to use on the cipher text. Which in turn revealed the solution.

SECOND BOOK CRAVING CONTESTS DETECTING TERMINATE.

The second book of *The Hunger Games: Catching Fire*.

Gillian went to the wall of books, which were alphabetized by author. She found a leather-bound copy of *Catching Fire* and flipped through the book until a slim magnetic keycard fell out. She didn't know how much time had passed, but searching the entire library would have taken hours, if not days.

She pressed the card against the flat black pad on the door. The lock unsealed. She stepped through to confront the next puzzle.

***

And again, Gillian emerged in second place.

The subsequent puzzles had been brutal. More word scrambles and Vigenère ciphers. A game of chess. A climbing wall with one fastest way to the top, revealed in earlier clues. Antonyms and synonyms and anagrams, and placing flags with countries and knowledge and speed, and she was sweating and scratched and bruised and pushed to her limits. She loved it. Her doubts and fears shoved clear of her mind. She could win. She *would* win.

She knew Tommy was just ahead of her. They'd spotted each other in the casino-themed escape room. Gillian finally using her hardways clue to map the escape phrase from the many bets in play. Tommy parked at another table, extracting an answer from a blackjack dealer. He'd charged through the exit a minute, maybe a minute and a half, before she'd escaped.

Her confidence surged. This time she'd catch him. Ellsberg could swallow the Nile. This time she wouldn't be distracted by anyone else.

The hallway began to slope, turning to stairs, taking her down and down, into the subterranean depths below the Bazaar. A feeling of dread worked cold fingers along her spine. While there could be any number of mysteries waiting ahead in the darkness, Gillian knew how Sebastian worked. The puzzles to date had been fresh, the Bazaar reworked to feed the Contestants new challenges. But for all Sebastian's talk of forging the future from new materials, he loved to work in the past. And sure enough, the stairs leveled out. Blue neon light strips ran along the floor, stretching down to a dark, black point. A dull roar traveled the length of the passage, a familiar thundering. Gillian didn't dare slow. Although wrung out, she ran the entire tunnel, occasionally looking over her shoulder to ensure she wasn't pursued. But she knew the real danger was ahead.

And then it happened. The tunnel ended abruptly, the ragged lip gaping out over empty space. The concrete throat extruded into a giant cavern, LEDs hanging amid the stalactites like luminous webs. Water poured into the room from various pipes, dumping into a cloudy lake several dozen feet below. On the far side of the water, a sandy beach. Not an exact reproduction of the original, but close enough to underscore the point. And she could hear him, in her head. *You failed, remember? You couldn't do this.* Tough love. Scald her with truth, then apply the balm of challenge. *Or maybe you're not up for it?*

Gillian allowed herself only five seconds to be angry. Then she backed up, made her hands into fists, and charged into oblivion.

She fell. Time slowed enough she realized she could die, right here, right now. At no point had she searched for alternatives. A ladder. Another tunnel. Instead, she'd pulled a Gillian and ran off into thin air. What would her life be, if she'd returned to the site of her shame only to die in one of Sebastian's hamster wheels? She didn't have an answer.

The water erased all thought from her mind. The cold sliced through her. Air ran from her lungs as the frigid water squeezed her tight. She plummeted, losing up from down. Her limbs wanted to thrash, but she forced herself to think. Chanted the mantra over and over.

You will win, Gillian.

You will win.

She relaxed. Let her body right itself, the remaining air

in her lungs buoyant, eager to reach the surface. She tilted her head back and scooped the water aside and kicked ferociously. The black depths faded away, replaced with almost Caribbean blues. She broke the surface, sucking in the glorious air. This time there was no flailing Ellsberg to distract her. She heard only the angry rumble of falling water pouring into the lake. This cavern a labyrinth of water and trickery. Gillian watched the water sluice through the cavern's PVC capillaries and marveled at the lengths to which Sebastian would go.

And then she saw Tommy.

He was still wearing his workout clothes, although they were now plastered to his body. The pipe's intake suction had pulled him just above the waterline, the top half of his body visible, his legs concealed somewhere down below. He barely fit in the pipe – the clear polymer mashing his face flat. She felt the scream gather as she met his empty eyes, as she saw his tongue fat in his mouth, but all she allowed to escape was a low moan, a desperate wail as if she'd had her ankle raggedly snapped. Somehow, she tread water as she took in the lifeless stare of Tommy Kundojjala. He looked caught off guard. The man who had expected everything, even as a boy. The one time he'd been surprised. The last time.

Gillian screamed for help, even though she knew it was too late.

Twenty-Six

The police were everywhere. They'd invaded Miscellany with their cold faces and give-a-shit attitudes. Gillian was wary. She shouldn't talk to the police, but Tommy was dead. They were in her face, asking questions, studying her and turning over the idea in their minds. Probably his death was an accident. But if it wasn't an accident, could Gillian have killed him?

In the Contest days, Gillian told herself she'd do anything to win. Learn any language, follow any path in any maze. And after Ellsberg betrayed her and Tommy won, she told herself there were things she would not do. Or, at least, pretended such was true. Because when she thought back, she recalled the relentless critical voice in her head, the one that accompanied her throughout the lonely car ride home. The voice, her voice, preaching a different sermon. Gillian could have won, if only she'd done what it took. If only she'd left her friend to drown.

Tommy came to Gillian. Drawn by trust. A need for help. And what had Gillian done, but nothing?

They were still in the Bazaar, back on the first floor in a kind of study. She sat on a couch near a fake fireplace that didn't light. Her curls drooped in her face. A folded towel sat in her lap, but she'd been clear of the water long enough to dry. Sadness drowned her, her limbs waterlogged with a great ache.

A cup of coffee appeared at her shoulder, courtesy of Ellsberg. The years passed for him same as Gillian, but instead of thirty he looked a hard fifty. His skin was the waxy color of day-old cheese. She took the offered cup, freeing him to sit in the grandfather chair across from her.

"I want to see him," Gillian said.

Ellsberg placed his coffee on the end table. "You're upset. We all are." He didn't much react as she stone-faced him. His voice carried more Alabama than Germany, but still even-keeled. "They're not letting you near the body."

Her fingers rattled against the cup. Needing to do something, she drank.

"They found cocaine on him," Ellsberg said. "It's too early to say whether there was any in his bloodstream, but assumptions are being made." His eyes tracked the police moving through the Bazaar. "We have cameras all over this park, except here. The building has been shuttered since the original Contest. It was determined there was no need." He didn't sound like he believed the last part. "They think he tried to scale the intake. There's a suction cover on the pipe, but if he ignored the warning signs, or didn't see them, he could have kicked it loose." He scratched his cheek. She could hear his nails scrape against the stubble. "They're pursuing it as an accident."

"As opposed to?"

His eyes found hers. The pupils hollowed and dark. "Suicide."

"Suicide. That's ridiculous."

"I've been dealing with this longer than you. Think. You've been chasing him. How has he been, the last few days? How was he in Addison? Do his actions seem like those of a stable man to you?"

Every fiber in her being wanted to burst off the couch. To do something. She'd been pursuing Tommy, hounding him, riding him nonstop. It wasn't the way you treated someone with a crippling disease. She needed to fix this. Now. Today. How Ellsberg could sit so controlled, his pale fingers knotted in his lap, she didn't know.

"Sebastian's with Evelina," he said. "She's taking it hard. I'm hearing leave of absence. The Bazaar is closed again, obviously. There will be an internal investigation. The police, of course. Not that you have to stay." Like he was doing her some kindness.

"I am staying. I have questions."

"You're not a detective. You don't have any standing." Ellsberg retrieved his coffee, took a long drink. So cool, this one. "I can keep you on the premises. If it will help you make peace with things – the hotel can be managed. Leah will handle the police. But you're not questioning anyone. Anything beyond the actions of a concerned friend is outside your purview."

Gillian stood. She had absolutely no idea where she was going.

Concerned friend.

Ellsberg watched her like she might fall over.

"I convinced him to come," she managed.

He kept watching.

"Tommy was out. He wasn't coming back." All that time wary of any Sebastian attempt to lure her back to Miscellany. And she the one who'd played piper. "I keep thinking…"

She stopped. What she was thinking was too horrible.

Ellsberg set down his coffee. He knotted his fingers

together and leaned into his knees. "A few of us are getting together," he said. "The one bar on premises. We'll have drinks – maybe get stinking drunk. We'll remember the best of him."

Gillian imagined Evelina in her home, surrounded by pictures of her husband. The girlfriend in Addison, texting a number that would never text back. Tommy standing on the sidewalk back in LA, that easy grin still on his face after all these years, confident he could get her to break her number one rule simply because he asked.

Mom, waiting for Gillian to save the day.

A wave of failure swamped her.

"I'm sorry, Gillian," Ellsberg said. "I really am."

The words almost brought her to tears. Ellsberg the human being, who she'd missed so much.

She bowed her head.

Twenty-Seven

The next evening, they held a wake.

The bar known as The Hat was a monument to how Miscellany's success enslaved even the great Sebastian. He'd long been a Charles Dodgson fan, otherwise known as Lewis Carroll, the creator of *Alice's Adventures in Wonderland*. Although typically opposed to leaning on the creativity of others, Sebastian had always nursed a soft spot for the English intellectual. He admired him as an entertainer, not simply the author of a popular children's book. Young Charles had produced a magazine of riddles. He'd orchestrated games for his siblings. He grew up in poverty, fighting for every scrap. The man had developed multiple interests, pursuing photography, mathematics, and philosophy. There were obvious parallels. At one time, Sebastian had imagined an entire land within the park: MAD – Miscellany After Dark. But while Alice's literary adventures remained popular, shadow and suspicion tainted the author. Diary entries cast doubt over his relationships with children, and modern society struggled with a man so obviously close to young people. Sebastian's advisors made it clear Lewis Carroll comparisons would be lethal. MAD was scuttled before it ever began. The sole memorial to Sebastian's fandom remained this Victorian-themed speakeasy.

Gillian followed Ellsberg into the bar, the place packed shoulder to shoulder with black suits and somber faces. She hadn't come prepared with funeral attire, and instead wore the most conservative thing she'd packed, the black-and-white outfit she'd worn to breakfast with June. In a way the outfit worked. It wasn't her. It kept her numbed to her feelings.

Beside her, Ellsberg looked almost dapper in his suit of varying grays, the tie narrow, the pocket square sharp. He was somehow in his element, quickly trading hugs and handshakes. Gillian dispensed chin-lifts, more comfortable with distance. She was afraid human contact would break the spell. Stir her demons and send them running out of control.

If she'd never come, would Tommy have found help another way? The kind of help he needed?

When Ellsberg got tied up in conversation, they split. Gillian drifted in a sea of mournful faces, Tommy's closest all working at Miscellany. Strangers to her, although they recognized her face, and supposed they knew how she felt. She spotted Leah at the bar – the dress gone, tonight armored in black jeans and leather jacket. She talked on the phone, staring into space and chewing her thumbnail. No sign of Evelina, although that wasn't surprising. Gillian had called, but got only voicemail, the greeting pleasant, almost cheerful. She hung up without leaving a message.

Gillian found Sebastian in the back. He sat alone at a table near the window. He ignored the crowd, his gaze fixed on the star-shaped structure before him, one of those executive magnet sets. An iced tea melted at his elbow, wet with condensation. People came and went, laying a hand on his shoulder, offering condolences, but he said little.

There was another place at his two-man table, unoccupied and unoffered. He looked apart. Strangely defenseless and defeated.

After a moment's hesitation, Gillian threaded through the crowd and drew back the chair.

The top of the magnetic structure was narrow, a spire two metallic bricks high. The design underneath was essentially complete – everything Sebastian added since, ornamentation, making the structure increasingly unstable. Nevertheless, he crowned the structure with another magnetic brick, his brow furrowed in concentration. For a moment the spire wobbled, but it stayed intact. Sebastian barely noticed, only selected the next magnet.

Despite appearances, the man wasn't completely without protection. Behind him, sitting where the bar joined the wall, Jackie Alvarez drank a glass of water and scanned the room. A chin-lift when she spotted Gillian, a vague antagonism like maybe they should start Round Two. Gillian pointedly avoided her stare.

"I failed him." Sebastian said to her. He rubbed the magnetic brick between his gloved fingers. "All the resources at my disposal, and I failed him."

The magnetic structure teetered, the arrangement delicate. How easy to knock down what Sebastian had built. The impulse to wreck his creation so strong, Gillian squeezed her hands under the table.

"You don't disagree?" he asked.

"*We* failed him," she said. "The only people who knew how difficult the life was, the constant pressure, and we treated him like he was invincible. Like he was Superman."

The words left Sebastian at a loss. He glanced out the

window at his empty park. The grounds closed early. "Did I fail you?"

What she would have done with that question a week ago. Now, her emotions were a jumble. Anger at Sebastian dwarfed by the anger she directed at herself. "You pushed me."

"I don't regret that. I regret not reaching out. I could have pulled you back in. I could have offered words of encouragement. More than words – deeds. But I let you leave."

"You were never going to stop me."

"I could have tried. I'm not sure if you're aware, but I have a jet. I could have flown to LA. Even Gillian Charles can be found."

She had no defenses against this version of Sebastian. The man who mocked anything other than total confidence, embracing the uncertainty of regret. She found herself turning away. His vulnerability resonated. Made her uncomfortable.

"Regardless." Sebastian tapped the magnet against the table. "This is different. You did reach out to Tommy. I know you talked to him about his addiction, you and Evelina both. If anything, I treated him too delicately. A blunt conversation from me could have gone a long way, before it was too late."

She remembered the man outside Jessyca's townhouse. The Contestant reborn. Fired up and daring Miscellany to ignore him. "I don't buy it was suicide."

"No. An accident. I told them. I told them before any of you set foot in there to inspect the building. That was supposed to include the cavern and the water supply." He squeezed the metal brick like it was someone's throat. "He never should have been able to remove that cover. There will be consequences, Gillian. Rest assured." He looked over his shoulder at Jackie. She tapped her watch face. "Not least of all for me."

She watched him stand, his tabletop sculpture swaying but remaining upright. "I don't know what that means."

"It means I'll do what I should have done months ago. We will cancel Season Two."

Just when she thought she had Sebastian pegged. "That doesn't sound like you."

"I tasked Tommy with the Labors of Hercules. Him and a hundred others grinding themselves down against an impossible task, and for what? We have complaints. Lawsuits. This is not the world I pictured. We'll settle and take our lumps. The investors will come along once they see the landscape and realize this is the comfortable choice. *A reappraisal of expectations*. Evelina and Leah are already crafting the announcement."

Gillian tried to keep up. She felt slow, like again she was pushing through heavy curtains. "You're not just cancelling Season Two – you're settling with the Navarros?"

"Every moment we wait extends the magnitude of this tragedy. I won't have it."

He nodded at Jackie. She summoned the bartender and circled her finger. Wrap it up. Close it down.

"Can I do anything for you?" Sebastian asked.

Bring Tommy back, her brain offered. But she didn't say that. "I'm staying at the Leonardo for a few days. I want to check on Evelina. See how the others are doing."

Sebastian produced a wan smile. "I knew you were invested. We'll move you out of the hotel and into something long-term. Honestly, it should have already been done. I'll make the arrangements. Meanwhile you'll be a help for all of us, I'm sure." He flicked the last brick at the magnetic star and brought the whole structure tumbling down. "I wish Tommy had listened to you."

Gillian watched them leave, Jackie leading the way. It had been the most human conversation she'd ever had with Sebastian. The kind of conversation she'd always wanted.

Home again, Gillian's Miscellany dreams come true.

She didn't feel any better.

Twenty-Eight

Gillian was usually a beer girl, but the gimlet was quite good. She sipped the top off and stared across the table at the two sitting side by side like an old married couple. Ellsberg, with a tequila Manhattan, listing a bit to port. Leah, nursing a Balvenie, repeatedly folding and unfolding a napkin. As the night went on, they'd found themselves telling stories of Tommy. *Remember when he cut a hole in the corn maze? What's the deal with his handshake, that two-handed clasp?* Gillian faced gaps, the years she hadn't seen the others. She was able to shock them with the Jessyca revelation.

"His secretary?" Leah shook her head and ran her thumb along the latest napkin fold. "No wonder Evelina looks so pissed."

"I don't think she knows."

"She's a smart woman. She's got to suspect."

"Smart people tell themselves all kinds of lies."

Leah shook her head – disagreeing or disgusted, hard to say. The woman was a steely combination of lawyer and whisky.

As for Ellsberg, he kept quiet. Gillian watched as he took the barest sliver off his drink. Pen behind his ear, he could have been the beleaguered middle manager at any insurance company. Two different people run through the Miscellany machine, two different outcomes.

Alcohol thawed conversation. They filled in the blanks of their time apart. Leah lived almost exclusively in Manhattan, single and happy about it. Ellsberg resided in a downtown condo and his response to questions on a Mrs or Mr Ellsberg kept him cloaked in mystery. *I'm not a pond, you may quit your fishing.* The banter between the three was like riding a bike, requiring no more effort than the Wonderland puzzles hanging on the walls. Gillian knew them all by heart, as did Ellsberg and Leah. The Hatter's riddle. *Why is a raven like a writing desk?* Sometimes the questions like the people. Providing no answers.

Piano music tinkled in the background. Canned, some Victorian-themed Spotify list. Ellsberg placed his glass solidly on the table and stared at the wall where the riddle hung. Leah tipped her head back and closed her eyes, the Scotch hitting her. Suddenly Gillian didn't want to hate Ellsberg or Leah anymore. Tommy was gone. She'd wasted enough time.

Ellsberg broke the silence. "I left all this once."

"No shit?" Gillian said.

"No shit." Some of the Alabama accent slipped through. "I thought I was supposed to. You'd gone. Leah took a sabbatical."

"DA's office," Leah volunteered, without opening her eyes. "Two years."

Ellsberg gestured. *There you have it.* "You don't need a parking space to be part of the family. I felt it was time to leave the nest. Do something meaningful."

"What did you do?"

Leah answered. "He joined the FBI."

The look on Ellsberg's face was so serious. Gillian asked, "Did you pass the physical?"

The accent snapped back into place. "You may cordially go fuck yourself."

She toasted him, and he responded in kind. They drank, but Ellsberg remained pensive. "It wasn't what I thought it would be."

"What's that?"

"Working for the government. I thought I could make a difference."

Leah cracked an eyelid. "That's pretty bright-eyed of Marty Ellsberg."

The nickname conjured a frown. "Sebastian shaped us to use the talents we possess. I had ideas on counterterrorism. Hostage negotiation. They didn't want to hear any of it."

"Color me surprised they didn't reorganize based on the word of the FNG."

Ellsberg shrugged. "Here – I'm trusted. Sebastian listens. The Miscellany team, they recognize what I bring to the table. I enjoy the compensation, don't get me wrong, but at the end of the day, I'm lying in bed, asking myself, do I have influence? Do I make a difference?"

The conversation stirred all Gillian's latent ambitions. Flying coast to coast, on a jet decked out like a high-end automobile, a flight attendant bringing her croissants or stimulants. Her in meetings where people stopped talking when she opened her mouth. Kids tackling puzzles she'd designed with a combination of frustration and glee. She'd consult at Rice, Carnegie Mellon, MIT, Stanford. She'd solve problems that mattered.

Gillian picked her cuticles. Sebastian knew she'd be

tempted. The Miscellany promise a brightly colored web she'd plow directly toward.

Across from her, Ellsberg watched her fidget. "Tommy thought you'd make a difference."

She pulled her hands under the table. "Stop."

"He did." His gaze misty, like Tommy's ghost lingered. "Did he give you the answer?"

"Answer to what?"

"The first riddle. 2871."

"What? No."

Leah stirred and found her Scotch, interested. Ellsberg tread carefully.

"He wasn't positive you saw it. He said you were stuck, which should have been exactly to his design. But he felt bad. He didn't want you out of the Contest, not yet. So he mouthed the answer to you."

All the years fell away. Gillian saw the boy, the one she left behind in the very first room, the one who seemed nervous – concerned, even. Emotions she'd attributed to his own peril. Only now... Antifreeze plunged through her veins. "He gave me the answer."

"You already had the answer." Although contrary, Ellsberg's voice was soft.

"But he told me," Gillian said.

"Tomas said you were already walking away. He was being stupid. He was embarrassed, correctly. You never needed his help."

The last comment maybe Tommy's observation. Maybe Ellsberg's.

"He always wondered if you'd realized," he said. "And protected him by keeping quiet."

Stunned, Gillian only shook her head. She wrapped her

fingers around her drink and stared into the hazy yellow suspension.

Goddamnit, Tommy.

Leah had been watching with eyes brighter than her drink might indicate. She slammed her glass to the table, breaking the spell.

"When did you last do a puzzle?" she asked Gillian.

"Sorry?"

"Jigsaw? Sudoku? Hell, watched *Jeopardy*?"

Sluggish, Gillian didn't answer. Then Ellsberg chimed in. "It's a good question."

The two of them. Jesus. "Three days ago," Gillian said. "Helping your sorry ass."

Leah smirked. "It's all right if little Gilly's afraid."

The place seemed to get quieter.

"Leah," Gillian said, "you're an entertainment lawyer. You spend your days, what, reading Twitter?"

Ellsberg chuckled as Leah stared, nonplussed. Then Leah snatched the pen from behind Ellsberg's ear and unfolded her meticulously folded napkin. She began writing.

"2009. Beta Alpha Psi Alumni Mixer. I beat a field of fifty, with three picklebacks in me." She carved words into the paper, possessed. When she'd finished, she slapped the table and rotated the napkin so Gillian could read.

Ten stoned college bros stand in a dark tent. They've removed their ballcaps, a mix of red and blue. Each bro needs to grab a cap and leave the tent, dividing into the correct color group. They don't know how many caps are colored blue or red. They're too stoned to check the cap on their head. And once they leave the tent they can't speak, or it will be obvious they're blasted. If they get caught blasted, they're suspended from the lacrosse team. If they sort incorrectly, they're suspended. But these are University of Virginia Finance bros. How do they ensure they get away per the usual – unscathed?

Leah looked smug. "Place was packed with UVA grads – what can I say?"

Gillian knew a version of this riddle. Only it was horror-based, a hundred final girls escaping a slasher. Ellsberg pounced first. A slow grin spread across his long face.

"They exit one by one," he said. "Imagine the first bro is a red cap. Next bro, blue cap, he stands next to red cap. The third bro exits, he observes red cap bro and blue cap bro, he stands between them. The next bro does the same – stands between red and blue. In the end, all ten bros have self-sorted into the correct teams."

Hearing Ellsberg repeat *bros* over and over. Priceless. Even Leah seemed entertained. "The mall cop can solve puzzles," she said. "When there's no pressure."

Ellsberg let the challenge hang, for a moment. "I won a limerick competition."

Leah and Gillian exchanged a look. "The fuck you did," Gillian said.

"In the parking lot of a bar off Cedar Springs. February of my first year at Miscellany. Twelve degrees. Three gentlemen said something unkind, I challenged them to wordplay."

Leah snorted into her Scotch. Gillian shushed her. "A man from Nantucket? Not really a game."

"One person starts, the next finishes. Until someone cannot."

She could tell Ellsberg was dying to continue. "What was the limerick?"

Ellsberg raised his chin. *"There was a young sailor named Bates, Who danced the fandango on skates, But a fall on his cutlass, has rendered him nutless–"*

"And practically useless on dates." Leah finished, losing it. The two of them laughing their asses off as Gillian stared, incredulous. Then, slowly, giving in. Cracking up.

This. She'd missed this. When she'd run from Miscellany and Sebastian, she'd left her people behind. Her tribe.

Leah wagged a finger at Ellsberg, her eyes booze-lidded. *It's not over.* She turned and yanked down her collar to reveal her naked shoulder and a cherry-red bra strap. On her skin, tattooed lettering: Navajo script. "Guy who inked this, his dad was a code talker. Did it on a bet. He said he'd stop when I solved the riddle – without looking. I had to solve as he inked."

Respect for Leah – and no small amount of fear – had driven young Gillian to learn a little Navajo. She'd have been damned if she gave Leah an edge. She read the words.

> *If you tell a lie, we will hang you.*
> *If you tell the truth, we will shoot you.*

Gillian looked her in the eye. "You will hang me."

Pleased, Leah shrugged her top back into place. "What did the prisoner say to save himself? Technically I answered after *we will shoo*. I made him finish inking the line."

They all drank. Trading glances like they were the smartest people in the room, which maybe they were. A friendly warmth melted the marrow in Gillian's bones. She looked down so the others wouldn't see what she was feeling. Regret. Regret for the life she'd abdicated.

Ellsberg snuffled up his chest. English butler shaking off

generational dust, this German kid from Alabama. "I have you all beat. My first Miscellany challenge. Online, you submitted a riddle through the website. Many entered. Mine won. As a result, I'm responsible for the most important puzzle in Miscellany history."

They waited. Ellsberg deadly serious.

"*Exiguum corpus, sed cor mihi corpore maius,*" he said. "*Sum versuta dolis, arguto callida sensu.*"

The goddamn riddle mug. Gillian laughed, because what else was there? She joined in.

"*Et fera sum sapiens, sapiens fera si qua vocatur.*" Both of them with raised glasses. "*Vulpes!*"

Gillian and Ellsberg laughed like they'd cracked the Rosetta Stone of hilarity.

In her corner Leah also smiling, but melancholy. "Sebastian gave me that riddle for the interview. On the CD."

Ellsberg wasn't paying attention. He leaned back, a lazy grin on his face. "No one suffered more for that exercise than me."

Leah tilted her head, acknowledging, not agreeing.

"I was last," she said. "The recording team was tired, dealing with children all day. It was one of those Texas inferno summers, a thousand degrees in the shade, the AC never keeping up. Sebastian appeared – you could feel the tension in your skin. He bitched at some assistant, then sat beside me."

Ellsberg's smile flattened.

"He ignored me at first, talked to the techs," Leah said. "*Is the mix as bad as yesterday? I could have done better, it's not hard.* But eventually, we talked. *What do you want to be?* My response – *none of your business,* my signature line, me thinking I'm cute. Then he gave me the riddle. My Latin was always shit, it's a dead language, like who fucking cares? So of course, I stumbled through the translation, let alone the solution. He let me squirm. Five minutes. Ten. Seven pm came and went, the temperature still insane, ninety-eight degrees. Sebastian repeated the riddle, like I didn't hear him. *I don't know*, I said. *I'm sorry*. I cried. I told him I wanted to go home. You'd have thought I puked on his shoes. Four hours we recorded. The whole time Sebastian working. On his Sidekick, texting with those spongy keys. Writing puzzles. Making deals. Nobody could say he didn't work hard. He didn't even remove his jacket. Pewter buttons, wool suit. Four hours. He'd been in *Time* magazine, they'd shot the cover just that day."

Gillian couldn't move. Like she'd been harpooned to the seat.

"I had to pee, I had like three waters before we started. He looked at me as if he knew. Would she wet herself? Would she quit? And he didn't care either way. No, that's not right. He thought I couldn't hack it. And he wanted me to see. What would I do, if no one believed in me?"

Gillian felt invaded. Leah kept saying *I* and *me*, but all Gillian heard was *you*.

"Four hours. My face blotchy, in a room full of adults who didn't lift a finger. One of them, a woman, she brought me water – he let her do that. She made this noise when she got close and I realized – I'd peed my pants. I gave her this look, terrified she'd say something. That Sebastian would know. She left the water. You better believe I never touched it."

Gillian looked at Ellsberg. She'd never heard this story. She could tell by his face he hadn't either.

"Four hours. Four hours in and I finally noticed the pocket square. Spry little fox on it, frozen mid-jump. Why he picked foxes… There's Navajo stories where foxes are good or evil, but my uncle was a trapper. He said the truth was, foxes are vermin. Their fur worthless. I always said Sebastian embracing foxes was a sign he didn't know what the hell he was doing. I don't doubt he'd heard me. And, of course, he knew I was bad at Latin."

Leah drank her Scotch.

"I learned my Latin," she said. "Ovid. Virgil. I qualified for a minor, and I don't even practice Constitutional Law." She drank again. "He did me a favor. The Contest was every girl for herself. Same as life."

Leah looked across the table at Gillian. Another lesson successfully delivered.

"We win or we die."

Twenty-Nine

Later Gillian stood outside. Too much gin coursed through her bloodstream, and inside the bar had begun to feel stuffy and close. Although ultimately guilt flushed her from her seat.

Her mouth had betrayed her. A few minutes with Leah and Ellsberg and she was dishing on Tommy's affair. The man dead no more than a day, and she gossiped at his wake. Disgusting.

Worse, she'd started to enjoy herself. Had imagined herself staying.

She closed her eyes and let instinctive balance take over. Would her instincts keep her upright, or would she topple to the ground?

She wobbled. Waited. Wobbled again.

She felt so close to falling.

On the walk back to the hotel, Gillian spotted Evelina. She was dressed simply but still stylish. Black pants and high heels. A black linen vest that exposed strategic sections of pale skin. Even in mourning, the woman was runway ready.

The alcohol. The feeling of being apart. Whatever it was, Gillian chose to follow her.

With no crowds to navigate, the Head of PR moved direct and with purpose. She passed the Ballroom, the opening night party lost to the eons. Then she stopped and removed her high heels. Left the path to descend a hill. She tracked toward a familiar dark structure, and Gillian drifted along. She remembered this part of the park. She remembered the Maze.

The Maze was another longtime park fixture, although it had changed in the last eighteen years. In Gillian's memory it was a hedge maze, sturdy yews rising high above her head. Interlocked, solid, and grim. Now it was a corn maze, tall stalks rustling in the breeze, darkness thick between their swaying bodies. Less solid than the old hedges, but if you stood and listened, it sounded like the shifting corn was advancing. Coming for you. Back in the day, a typical journey through the Maze could last up to thirty minutes and end with a Miscellany team member escorting you free of the twists, turns, and dead ends – the park couldn't afford to have guests lost in the attraction for any longer. Contestants, of course, needed to finish in under five minutes, and the best in under two.

Fenceposts stood guard on either side of the entrance; a sign strung on a chain between: *Closed.*

Evelina knew she'd been followed. High heels hung over her fingers, she stopped at the chain, snuck a look over her shoulder. "I've never been here at night." Her eyes glowed. "I'll bet exploring would be fun."

Despite everything – the death of her husband, the grind of working at Miscellany and seeing, daily, how the sausage was made – Evelina retained a sense of childish wonder. Gillian desperately wanted to find the twelve year-old version of herself, ridiculous braids and all.

"He's changed it, since my time."

"They're not hard to solve, right? You just keep one hand on the wall and follow all the way to the end?"

"Nine times out of ten. But Sebastian's mazes don't play fair. He throws pits at you. Tunnels, bridges, walls of thorns. Fire."

Evelina smiled knowingly. "Last Thanksgiving, we had a company party, a fall festival. I mean, nothing pagan, although that would have been a blast." Her unexpected laugh carried across the lawn. "It was an Olympics. No potato sack races, very Miscellany. Sudoku, acrostics, although fairly pedestrian stuff, as not every employee is Contest-worthy, if you know what I'm saying. But the finals took place in the Maze. It was all hollow concrete then, before we brought in the corn. Once all the contestants were in, we sealed the entrance. The winner didn't emerge for three hours." She cupped her hand over her mouth and whispered, telling tales out of school. "We moved the walls. We had to hire a hundred temps."

Instinctively, Gillian wanted to roll her eyes. But she also found herself imagining how she'd tackle the problem. "That sounds like Sebastian."

"No. The walls were Tommy's idea, actually." Evelina fell silent. Stared into the behemoth of swaying nature. "He always had grand ideas."

Gillian didn't know what to say. She'd seen Tommy with his mistress. What could she say to the man's wife, who missed him so badly she'd trekked out to a cornfield in the middle of the night, just to connect with his memory? Gillian liked Evelina; she really did. Evelina was an interesting combination of glamorous and down-to-earth. She was disarming and wasn't cowed by any of the former child geniuses. Tommy hadn't deserved her.

An objection, that voice in Gillian's head, powered by the kid who'd never given up on her.

She knows about Target Practice.

Gillian drifted forward to stand at Evelina's side. "Do the police know what happened?"

"The police?" The disdain reanimated her. "They don't have answers, they have stories. *You knew he was abusing drugs, ma'am? Did you know he was using the night of the Reunion?* Like I can't connect dots." She let the shoes hooked over her fingers swing. "My grandmother – Moscow born and bred – she'd tell you. The police don't find people. They explain why they're not missing."

"Preach." Gillian waited for what seemed a respectful beat. "You don't think he–"

"Accident." Her voice firm. "Brought on by his disease."

They stood in silence.

"Before he…" Evelina's eyes scanned the corn stalks for answers. "Did you talk to Tommy?"

The question not unusual. A grieving widow gathering mementos.

"Not really. There wasn't much time."

"What about your fellow Contestants?" Evelina asked. "Leah and Captain Curious?"

Gillian chuckled. "I'm going to call Ellsberg that to his face." She considered what to reveal. "You know, Tommy did mention something. It didn't mean a lot to me, but maybe to you. Target Practice?"

"Oh." Evelina's eyebrows arched, then quickly smoothed. "Target Practice was one of the qualifiers. Guns on one side, targets on the other, letters in between. All props. The guns plastic, the letters hanging on string from the ceiling.

You traced the path of an imaginary bullet to the correct target." She placed her hand in the air, touching imaginary guideposts. "The letters in the path spelled out the answers." Her mouth compressed into a thin line. "There are phrases that you don't think about, not really, or at least never used to. And of course you can't use them, of course you can't. But people are human. They make mistakes. So, we used an answer we shouldn't have. *One red cent*. It's debated that maybe it simply refers to the copper penny, but it reads very much as an insult to American Indians. It was a historical quote. Robert Goodloe Harper. *Millions for defense*? It's not as if Miscellany traveled back in time and endorsed the sentiment. At any rate, that was the question. *Millions for defense. Dot, dot, dot*. The answer was *not one red cent*."

"I don't understand."

"We never asked the question. It wasn't part of the qualifier."

Gillian stared.

"The Harper question was pulled, last minute. The morning of. Someone in Operations with half a brain. I mean, we wouldn't have liked it either. Legal. My people in Social. In an era of representation, and we go with *one red cent*? So the people on the ground pulled the question. They didn't have time to change the letters. They didn't even have time to inform Sebastian. Which is fine and everyone is fat and happy, except my husband. Because one of the children used *one red cent* as the answer."

Gillian frowned. "Did the puzzle even make sense?"

"They used a replacement question. *Put in your*, and the answer, *two cents*. Very quick, not very challenging, but they were able to reuse some of the letters, and they had to do something. Under the gun, so to speak." She tried to find a smile. "At any rate, it's easy enough to understand the confusion."

"But Tommy thought someone used *one red cent* because they had the answer already?"

"Right? Does that even sound logical? As if we wouldn't know. Every single qualifier is recorded. The inputs on every object transmitted wirelessly and captured by our analytics. We print the results and courier them to our accountants, Ernst and Young. Someone could check, if they wanted. The integrity of the games is paramount."

"But Tommy–"

"He went to the family – the *one red cent* family, the poor dears. They called the police. It was incredibly messy. We called in favors to keep that out of the media." Emotion warped her voice. "I've been mourning Tommy for ages. He was gone long before yesterday. And he was so unpredictable at the end. Reckless. Like he wanted to burn it all down, with him inside. I…"

She dropped her head.

It was hard to read Evelina. It was dark. She was good at presenting emotions. But the truth of it was that Tommy had been a very public wreck. One only had to look at Evelina, at the Navarros, at Tommy himself, to see the damage. And here Gillian was trying to solve the woman. Trick her into revealing what, exactly? She'd broken into Evelina's family home. Rewarded her warmth and friendship with the third degree. Gillian liked Evelina. Why was she trying so hard to see through honest enjoyment of another person's company?

Lost in her head, Gillian missed Evelina studying her. "Should you still be here?"

"Excuse me?"

"I feel responsible," Evelina explained. "I may not be a Contestant, but I believe in Miscellany. And we've used you. My husband. Sebastian. Who's thinking of Gillian Charles in all this? What I mean to say is, if you're staying out of some loyalty to Tommy, or a promised financial windfall, it's wrong for us to take advantage."

Nearby, the corn rustled.

"I can take care of myself, Evelina."

"But you wouldn't be here unless you felt you had to be."

Mom, maybe safe for a few months, but then what? "Some of us have to make choices."

"What if I could help?" Evelina held up a hand before Gillian objected. "I haven't forgotten what it's like. I wasn't born in couture and heels. Believe it or not – Little Havana, Miami. Six of us living in one house. My two brothers. My grandmother. We didn't have a car, we rode bikes everywhere. And forget airplanes. We might as well travel to Mars." She swung the shoes over her finger, weighing options, coming to some decision. "If the money is unappealing, I could put you on the jet. I could have you home tomorrow." The woman seemed to think she still had some fortune. And too cavalier about it by half.

"You and Ellsberg. Throwing jets around like confetti."

"People badmouth the jets – we fought hard to get here. I won't apologize for protecting what we earned." Evelina frowned, a small crease between her sharp eyes. She was irritated the jets were even a topic. "But imagine you stayed. I don't know what Sebastian said – he's sometimes as bad as Tommy – but to spell it out, we need you. It's a new age. People expect digital. Online, open world, endless opportunity. We need more puzzle content than we can generate. Engaging puzzle content."

"I don't do that anymore."

Evelina laughed, her face the only star in the sky. "What a liar. You competed at the party. In the Reunion. How did it feel?"

Great. It had felt fucking great. Running from puzzle to puzzle. Solving challenges on the fly, riddles no one else could crack, not as quickly. That voice still loud in her head. *I could have won. I could have won the whole thing.*

"Come work for me," Evelina said. "The men have been running this place too long. You and I, together? Nobody could stop us."

Somewhere out in the night, a loud whoop. People leaving the wake, moving on, embracing what the future had to offer. Endless opportunity, like Evelina said. When had Gillian ever experienced endless opportunity, truly? She was Black. From South Dallas. One parent an addict, the other crippled with sickness and bills. She shook her head. What choices had she ever had?

Then her old anger returned. A fire that ignited in her belly and burned out to her fingertips. *No.* Few choices, sure, but she'd be damned if she apologized for them. She'd made a difference. She'd helped people. Bria's ex – that fucker would pay, because of Gillian. Her scarves – somewhere out there was a woman looking in the mirror, thinking she looked damn sexy with the silky melange around her neck. Gillian had nothing to be ashamed of. If she was a hustler, fine, she was a first-rate hustler. And Evelina should recognize her skills.

Gillian turned to her companion, unsteady. "Let's get drunk."

The remark caught Evelina off guard. She shattered the silence with another abrupt laugh, dropping her fancy shoes into the grass. "Have I mentioned you're a delight?"

"You could say it again. I won't mind."

Gillian wasn't going anywhere tonight. And tomorrow was another day. The pair of them walked back across the grass and up the hill. Gillian left her doubts and Evelina left her shoes, the two of them in cahoots. They'd take what they needed, and steal the rest.

Thirty

Morning came early. Last night's decisions stuck Gillian's lids to her eyeballs, not hungover but in the same zip code. She forced herself out of bed, loaded the ice bucket and drank two entire glasses of frigid water. She threw back the curtains and undid the NASA-class polarization keeping the glass dark. She dropped to the ground and did sit-ups and pushups until she was bathed in sweat. Then she rolled onto her back and stared at the ceiling.

It had been a long time since she'd cut loose like that. Evelina was fun, a lot of fun. That Tommy had to die for Gillian to learn that fact, a tragedy. That Tommy was cheating on Evelina, heartbreaking.

Judgement came easy. But Gillian couldn't forget – Tommy had always looked out for her, despite his demons. Trying to give her the answer in the Contest only one of many such times. So, sure, he'd been unfaithful. But she remembered the peace on his face when he'd been with Jessyca. The woman – the girl – brought him a serenity when no one else could. And now she was probably texting Tommy from her expensive townhouse, wondering why he didn't answer. Given the clandestine nature of their relationship, nobody would have told Jessyca the news.

Gillian sat up.

Shit.

She tried to talk herself out of the idea. She didn't know the woman. If anything, Gillian was friends with Evelina, not Jessyca. But she'd conned the EA's phone number along with her address. She'd seen them together. Gillian could make the call no one else could. Gillian could call and tell Jessyca her lover was dead.

But Jessyca already knew. And she was furious.

"You killed him," she spat.

Gillian stood and went to the window. As if Jessyca was in the room, angry and raw, and Gillian needed the distance.

"Look, I'm sorry. We're all upset about Tommy. The accident–"

"Bullshit. He said you were following him. He knew you'd try something. It's too late."

"Hang on. Slow down. He said I'd try something?"

"They'll go to the police with what he gave them. Don't think you can buy them off. Or scare them."

"Wait a minute. What are you talking about?"

"You know he was going to get out? We were going to get away. He'd found this great place in St John, in Upper Peter Bay. Just blue water and white clouds and none of the fantasyland poison you people have been pumping into his veins."

They'll go to the police with what he gave them.

The peanut butter sandwiches. The cross nailed to the wall. The look in that little girl's eyes, the freight train desire to win.

What did Tommy give the Navarros?

Gillian backed away from the window. She grabbed her string bag. "I'm coming to see you."

"Don't you dare show up here. Don't you dare."

But Gillian was already hanging up the phone.

One of the valets drove her to Addison, where Jessyca waited, braced in the open doorway. Her face eerily calm, although a shine around her eyes suggested she'd been crying. She gripped her phone in one hand. "I already called the cops. You've got like two minutes."

In Gillian's neighborhood it would take hours for the police to show. In this tony Addison location, the police might indeed be only minutes away. "I don't work for Miscellany. I worked for Tommy. I was his friend."

"None of you were his friends."

Gillian's worst fears and accusations, given voice.

"Please," she managed.

Despite her anger, Jessyca let Gillian slip around her and into the apartment. The place was an aesthetic potpourri. Dirty clothes on the floor, a lava lamp on the bookshelf. Pictures from rock concerts and national parks, Tommy smiling in many of the photos. There was amateur art on the walls and a few pictures of Jessyca at a microphone.

"He brought me all the way from Los Angeles," Gillian said. "He told me something was wrong with Season Two. Something about kids getting answers?"

The woman worked her jaw. Ready to fight, if given something to attack.

"I never saw any proof," Gillian said.

"He had proof."

"All he said was Target Practice. One red cent. The answer to a redacted question."

Jessyca breathed through her nose. Her eyes slid between Gillian and the door. Eventually she pushed the door closed, although she didn't get any closer to Gillian.

"There's evidence," she said. "Emails. Answers sent to parents, and not only that – the bosses knew. He said they knew exactly what was happening all along, and now he had the smoking gun, and it was going to cost them. Millions, once that family knew."

Three days ago, out in the street, Tommy's whistleblower claims felt like bravado. The boy of old playing swashbuckler, bolstering himself as much as anything. But emails? Emails changed everything. Cold hard words, absent the mania of the man.

The Navarros and others like them cheated out of their future, and Tommy begging for anyone to give a shit. Gillian desperately wanted to tear at her cuticles.

She hadn't done a damn thing.

"Did you see any emails? Does he have copies? In the cloud? On a drive?"

Jessyca remembered who she was talking to. She pointed the phone like a gun. "No, no, no. You almost had me. Thirty seconds. Good luck finding anything before they arrest your ass."

"You're worried about the wrong person. It's not me he was scared of."

The hope must have carried in her voice. Jessyca was silent for a few seconds.

"He was afraid all the time," she said quietly. "He said they must have been in my place. He was going to keep the data somewhere they wouldn't think to look."

"You have to tell me. No one else is asking questions, they'll let it stay buried." Uncertainty on Jessyca's face. "Tommy always said I had a big mouth. I won't drop this."

A car pulled up outside – Gillian couldn't see the vehicle.

Across from her, Jessyca stared, her eyes watery. She was catching only a glimpse of how contests operated at this level – when the stakes were high and nobody waited on your feelings. The poor woman simply wanted to mourn. Let someone else carry Tommy's burden.

Jessyca swallowed, then turned and slipped into the back bedroom, where Gillian could hear her rustling. She emerged with a folded piece of paper. Handed it over as if it represented her life savings.

"He gave the girl a gift," she said.

Only once Gillian was ensconced in the valet's back seat did she unfold the sheet. Yellow legal paper, creased into quarters, each quadrant awash with ballpoint dots. Scanning the page, Gillian calculated about three hundred dots per quadrant. Numbers adjacent to the majority, but not only numbers. About a third instead neighbored by handwritten phrases:

> How many cuckoos missed the nest
> Beethoven's Morse Code
> Dolly has to go to work

Connect the dots. With some of the numbers replaced with clues. Likely the resultant images were clues themselves, although Gillian wouldn't know until her pen lanced through the points in sequence. Safe to assume, then, that the paper related to an object in the Navarro household. Hoops within hoops, the kind of tragically elaborate puzzle only a paranoid like Tommy would create. Or a former puzzle kid with something to hide.

What are you hiding, Tommy?

Gillian focused on the first pane. She pulled back, a combatant seeking the high ground. Rules applied to all games – and connect-the-dots' strictures were obvious – but puzzlers learned to examine those rules from all angles. She wanted to see if the dot clusters suggested an answer. Parse the answers without investing all the time in a solve. But already she could shape the unconnected dots into multiple objects – a dog or an ice cream cone or a budding flower. A quick scan of the other three panes revealed similar complexity. There was no avoiding it – she'd have to do the work.

Out came Gillian's pen and pad. The pen to trace a path, the pad to provide a solid backing. Gillian guided the ballpoint from dot to dot, converting movie and book references into numbers as she traversed. One *Flew Over the Cuckoo's Nest. Beethoven's* Fifth. Dolly Parton sang "*Nine to Five*". Number sewn to number until the outline of a chair surfaced. The chair ornate. Could be a specific kind of chair. A throne. The word choice would be important. With puzzles, with Tommy and Sebastian and all of them, words were important.

The next pane presented as an amorphous blob. A mushroom cloud. The fleur-de-lis. Again, Gillian ground through the clues. She popped her neck side to side. Rolled her shoulders.

Shades of Grey
Phileas Fogg out of office

Anyone could count, and most *Jeopardy* watchers could sleuth film and literature answers. These questions were easy. The puzzle assembled under duress and bounded by time. That, or money and drugs had made Tommy soft. An uncharitable thought, Gillian told herself. She owed Tommy more kindness than that. Or, in death, did she sell him short? Did she instead owe Tommy absolute ruthlessness in pursuit of the answers?

Gillian solved the second quadrant and revealed the outline of a pacifier. She strung the words together. *Chair* and *pacifier*? She decided *throne* and *pacifier* were better. Instructions to appease the king – a message about Sebastian? Possibly, but this process bothered her. Hiding information about Sebastian behind connect-the-dots was akin to plugging a Glock with Juicy Fruit. Not a serious obstacle. But Tommy knew that fact, so no way the message was simply about Sebastian.

Nena's Luftballons
Disney Dalmatians

The third image proved to be an old-style landline. Or phone, or handset. *Throne* and *pacifier* and *phone*? No, the alliteration would drive Tommy insane. *Throne* and *pacifier* and *landline*? Call Sebastian? But why?

Time ticked away as the valet drove. Gillian wondered if this excursion and the subsequent puzzle was worth her time. Was she chasing answers or running from problems? She stared out the window, saw the passengers in the adjacent car laughing. A joke on the radio, or an entertaining phone call? The jealousy surged. She wondered what it would take to get her to laugh again.

Back to the puzzle. The fourth and last panel. She must have been on a roll, as she immediately knew the answer was either a fishing pole or a rifle, and fishing pole quickly removed itself as a possibility. The rifle snapped into place after only a hundred connections. The last word in a message she couldn't understand.

Throne. Pacifier. Landline. Rifle.

Call someone to kill Sebastian? Jesus, who didn't dream of that?

Gillian let her head settle back. She stretched out her legs. She knew there was more to the puzzle than she'd grokked.

"You get the answer?" the valet asked.

"Puzzles don't always give up the answer right away," Gillian responded. "They take patience."

Now she wanted to laugh. Listen to her. As if she'd ever followed that advice.

The houses around the Navarros were quiet, Dallas-area heat having driven fragile humanity indoors. But the Navarro doormat still said *Welcome*, and a soft TV murmur leaked through the front door. Gillian knocked rather than ringing the bell, afraid of disturbing the home's delicate balance.

She shouldn't be here. Fresh off manipulating Jessyca, ready to exploit a damaged child. She pictured herself as the Navarros would. Standing on their front stoop, disheveled and manic. Waving scribbled paper in their faces. The crazed messenger. Tommy reborn.

"Tommy," Gillian said, his name slipping from her lips.

Had she listened, would he still be alive? Could they have avoided all the arguments and that terrible accident at the Reunion?

If it was an accident.

Eddie answered the door, clad in sweatpants and a New York Giants T-shirt. When he saw her, he was at a loss.

"Can I come in?" Gillian asked.

"I already dealt with your lawyer," he said. "Unless this is about the money, I've got nothing else to say."

"I just want to talk."

"All you people do is talk. We've had enough. Leave us alone."

Over his shoulder, Vanesa sat on the couch. Watching some tween show about a rich kid summer camp, her face slack. TV had been Gillian's escape of choice, too, after the Contest loss. She had drunk in the faraway images – no books, no riddles, nothing she had to solve.

"Hold on. Miscellany already settled?"

"Your lawyer was here, yeah. I signed the papers. You're not taking the money back."

"I'm not with them." The words hollow, even to Gillian. "What lawyer?"

"The woman. She looked more like a biker. Wore black leather. But I guess you guys enjoy dressing stuff up. Making it look like it isn't."

Gillian frowned, thinking of Leah at the wake. Leah the lawyer. Leah the Contestant. "Did she take anything?"

Over on the couch, Vanesa started to cry. Katie appeared and noticed Gillian at the door.

"You people took everything," Eddie said.

Then he closed the door.

Gillian stood on the doorstep, listening to the muffled shouts and screams. The connect-the-dots still in her back pocket. It struck her how quiet the house had been when she arrived. What had the home been like, before Miscellany touched it?

***

The valet returned her to the park. Gillian made the call from the back seat. Leah answered after the fourth ring, plenty of time to consider her words.

"Hey, Gillian." *Damn shame* vibes. "You hanging in there?"

"I don't know." Gillian was careful. She envisioned the moves Leah had planned. "I keep wondering what else we could have done."

"You can't fall into that trap. We gave him every chance. Tommy made his choices."

Gillian stared out the window. Behemoths of concrete and steel whizzed by, dwarfing the people at their feet. "I went to the Navarros'."

A pause. "That's maybe not the best idea."

"They say you settled?"

"I mean, we haven't announced, but yes. Of course, our position remains there was no fault here, but in the interest of all involved we thought it best to move on. For Miscellany and the family."

Gillian tried to summon a memory of young Leah, squirming under Sebastian's relentless attack. She couldn't imagine this Leah squirming at all.

"That's good to hear. You know, it's actually why I called. I wanted to thank you."

A stunned silence. Gillian felt a flush of satisfaction, catching Leah off guard.

"They think I'm part of Miscellany," Gillian continued. "I was worried they might come after me. If we're being honest, by settling, you might have saved me from a lawsuit."

Leah recovered quickly. "You're welcome, you're

welcome. No worries at all. We'd certainly protect you. You're part of the family, Gilly."

How far would Leah go to make Gillian believe those words? She took a breath. "Listen, I left something at the house, last time. A book on space. Considering everything that's happened, maybe that's a thing I should take back."

The pause was slight. "We did recover some of Tommy's personal items. He kept giving the girl gifts, you know, totally inappropriate. Gift shop crap mostly. I gave it to Sebastian. I don't remember a book, but we'll check it out."

Gillian pictured Leah on the other end of the line, anticipating. Two kids playing Battleship. But instead of plastic ships, lives.

"Thanks." Gillian forced a laugh. "They wouldn't let me in."

"Honestly? I'm surprised they didn't shoot you."

"No winners this time, huh?"

"There's always next time, Gilly."

Gilly meant Leah was comfortable. And why wouldn't she be? Tommy gone. The case settled. Any evidence of wrongdoing safely under Miscellany protection.

"Next time," Gillian said.

Thirty-One

"You have a sickness," Ellsberg said.

It was late but Ellsberg, like all the Contestants, kept late hours. He worked in a cube no different than the hundred other dark cubes surrounding them. An empty microwaveable tin left next to his monitor. A stack of notepads. Tape. Stapler. A crayon drawing of the Hulk, signed with a child's scrawl. Two paperback books – *The Westing Game*, *Slow Horses*. Ellsberg sat in his chair with his back to it all, staring at Gillian like she had lost her goddamn mind.

"This need to seek cheap thrills," he continued. "Did you not just see what it did to Tomas?"

Despite everything that had happened, she felt on secure ground. The goal, for once, was clear. All she had to do was work her way to it.

"You have questions about how he died," she said. "I know you do."

"That's a long way from letting you into Sebastian's office. No one goes up there."

"*Au contraire*. I've been."

Ellsberg's frustrated response caught in his teeth. He rubbed the side of his head, stopping short of the birthmark.

"Leah took something from the Navarros," she said. "I just need to see what it is."

"Why not ask her?"

"Tommy wasn't dead twenty-four hours and she was out there tying off loose ends. What kind of answers do you think she's going to give me?"

Ellsberg wavered. He stared as if he could crack open her skull and divine her intent.

"They don't have to know it was you," she said.

"Outstanding. An intruder worms her way into Sebastian's office and they'll only think I'm incompetent."

He was working his way to no. She didn't have time to steer him over the course of days or weeks. "Was it you in Addison?"

He frowned. "I don't understand."

"Did you follow Tommy to Addison? Or did you know about Jessyca all along? What else did you know? Is Jackie still working for you?"

A look of anger and disappointment slowly pinched his face. He shook his head and turned his chair about. He began typing.

"I would have let you in," he said, his face lit by the screen's glow, "without the manipulation."

A part of her wanted to apologize. She was using him. The way she'd used the Navarros and Jessyca. But she was afraid he would stop typing and she wouldn't be able to access Sebastian's office.

Leah had said it herself.

Win or die.

Sebastian's office looked different in the dark. The furniture nefarious. Mirrored reflections became writhing demons. The high windows let in spotted moonlight but not enough illumination to surface detail. Gillian navigated by the light of her phone.

Ahead of her, Sebastian's Lilliputian chair. She couldn't deny there was a certain thrill. Attacking him in his home, the most impenetrable riddle of all.

She let her eyes roam. His office not unlike her last visit, carefully eclectic but otherwise devoid of information. But that didn't mean the evidence wasn't there. And sure enough – a cardboard box on the ground near Sebastian's perch, the flaps angled open. She squatted over the box and swept light across the contents. All gifts from Tommy to Vanesa. High-end sneakers, uncreased. A Cowboys jersey. A CD-ROM game adaptation of Christopher Manson's *Maze*. Gift cards for local restaurants, for online shopping, for a private VIP tour of Miscellany. Gillian dug through all the tokens of Tommy's good intent. She found no clues. No secret data on Season Two.

Gillian left the box on the floor. She sat in the chair. A keyboard tap woke the computer, revealing a shuffling puzzle screensaver. The Dunes of San Cosme, a beautiful image of rippled sand and slate sky pressed together in a hard line, a snapshot from years back before tourism and the elements took their toll. A password locked the screen, but Gillian hadn't the foggiest. She typed in *Sebastian*. The screen remained stubbornly locked.

The papers were many and revealed nothing. Half-scribbled puzzles. The beginning of his memoirs. *My mother died bringing me into a world of Asunción table scraps.* Gillian had read one of the existing unauthorized biographies.

She wasn't convinced the tale would be any purer having been written by the man who lived it.

She flicked up her light. Caught sight of something unexpected – the goddamn photo. Mister No Looking Back had allowed himself an exception to the rule. She stared at the specters of their past, frozen forever, trapped in a shadow box and marred, in this case, by Sebastian's florid scrawl. Gillian reached but stopped short of touching. All those dopey children, smiling like their dreams were about to come true. Tommy front and center, all confidence, the kid too clever by half. A sad smile tugged at Gillian's lips. She wanted to pull him from the photo, this dreamer who'd handed Gillian a fistful of sticky, smeared M&Ms. Capture him untouched, before the finish, before his family swarmed him and they rocketed away from their old life. Before the tragedy of what came after.

Her own goofball face drew her, and she thought about Mom. What would all this quixotic tilting change, in the end? Expose some wrongdoing inside Miscellany, proving culpability in Target Practice and Season Two? Did she believe Tommy was murdered for what he knew? Money polluted the question, impacted every outcome. Mom's health, Tommy's accusations. With so much at risk, with so many unknowns, why was she here?

The Puzzle Master offered no answers, his face inscrutable, even in the photo. She recalled his words at the Proscenium. *Everything we do at Miscellany is possible only because of the children.*

Ellsberg the actor's shredded dreams. Can't-be-broken Leah, broken and repurposed. Vanesa Navarro, all sixty pounds of her, carved down to the rind.

Gillian abruptly pushed herself from Sebastian's chair.

She searched the bookshelves. Leafed through volumes on Cicero, Leonardo da Vinci, Nikola Tesla, William Shakespeare, José Rizal, Ibn Rushd, Thomas Edison, Jagadish Chandra Bose, Helen Keller, and Walt Disney. An impressive collection of polymaths and otherwise willful humans. All dead now, and exactly what she expected to find. None of the books a smoking gun.

Up close, the ornate pendulum clock ticked as normal. Gillian stuck her finger in the housing's dusty swirls, but failed to uncover any hidden messages or notes tucked in the scrollwork. She stood over the table of odd devices – the plumb bob and the others. So deliberate, this arrangement. *Look at the unusual way my mind works.* Gillian had taken pains to keep her apartment simple, her only allowance to form beyond function her beloved cactus. A real plant, not a plastic monstrosity. Something that reflected who she was now.

More words from Sebastian, standing on that stage. *We don't like to live in the past.*

Earlier, when she'd scaled the stairs to find the old bastard preening – not one single photo in the place. The man's credo more powerful when he demonstrated the concrete truth of it. He wouldn't deliberately crack that facade, the famed snapshot not part of his permanent aesthetic. The photo was a new arrival.

Gillian returned to the desk, and the autographed snapshot of their smiling faces. Quietly she set her phone on the desk, the flashlight aimed up. She pulled down the shadow box and rotated the frame in the glow of her phone. The light revealed no hidden messages, no communiques finger-smeared on the glass. She flipped the picture over and found only the plywood backing and a price tag. She shook it. Heard a knocking. Using her blunt nails, she pried open the metal tongues. The backing separated, revealing a gap between plywood and spongeboard. A USB drive dangled from the backing, held in place by one slender bit of tape. Gillian pulled the tape free and the drive came with it.

The drive was cold between her fingers. Inert. Yet it teemed with secrets.

After unslinging her string bag, she withdrew her sticker-encrusted laptop. She booted up, the lid low, her body shielding the screen as she glanced nervously around the room. Once the beast came to life, she inserted the drive. And promptly ran into a password prompt.

The yellow legal paper. Had Tommy expected Gillian to follow his trail? Another of the Contestants? Or was Tommy's life riddled with enciphered grocery and to-do lists, a paranoid cancer? Nobody needed to tell Gillian the risks of the road not taken.

thronepacifierlandlinerifle

No.

thronepacifierhandsetrifle

Jackpot.

The USB decrypted, Gillian went through the contents. Emails. Screenshots and saved text contents. From someone in Legal, Leah on the CC.

Unauthorized access to Mr Kundojjala's email...

Answers provided to many Season Two qualifying families...

Under the cover of donations to Sebastian's Circle ranging from $50,000 to $100,000...

Terms of your separation and settlement are considered proprietary...

Prohibited from discussing any aspect...

All the messages sent to one address: Evelina Kundojjala.

Gillian grew as cold and hard as the data in front of her.

My wife, Tommy had said. *Under the same covers.*

Email perms – EK.

The blood in her veins turning to ice.

She needed to get out.

She reassembled the shadow box. Placed the photo back over Sebastian's desk, where he could be tortured by the memory. She pushed the USB drive into her bra, slipped the laptop into her bag, and hurried down the stairs.

"Stop right there." The words hard, with a frayed edge. "Do not move."

Lights flashed in her eyes. Gillian had the impression of two large shapes, brutes looming in the darkness. She hoped the men were Ellsberg's, jumpy after Tommy's death and the prolonged police presence. But she knew better. Instinctively, remembering what her father taught her about dealing with cops, she raised her hands. *Don't act out. Do as you're told.*

"It's OK," she said. "I'm allowed to be here."

"You're allowed where we say you're allowed." The voice bedsheet white. "Come out. Slowly."

She took the smallest steps she could without looking smart. Playing somewhere just above a third-grade education, to keep them at ease. Out of the stairwell and past the green door.

"Bring your hands down real slow." This voice came from behind her. Probably a Black man, although the thought was no more comforting. "Put your backpack on the ground."

She unslung her bag and set it down. Put her hands behind her back when instructed and tried not to flinch when cold steel bit into her wrists. Not security. Police.

The white cop lowered his flashlight only once his

partner had her completely restrained. As Gillian's eyes readjusted, she could make out his uniform and badge and gun.

She played it cool as they escorted her from the building and into their squad car. Inside, she wanted to scream.

Thirty-Two

The cell was bigger than Gillian's closet, but not by much. She sat head-down on her bunk, occasionally looking to the window embedded in the sliding steel door. This suburban jail was sleepy, haunted by a minimum of detainees. When they'd paraded Gillian in, only a pair of prisoners – a Black man at one of the communal tables, his eyes on the ground, and a sweaty white man in a ragged muscle shirt who watched her quietly from the cell catty-corner. They'd taken her bag, laptop, wristband, and phone. Executed a cursory pat-down that hadn't turned up guns, drugs, or the USB in her underwear. Afterwards they'd left Gillian alone, her sole company her thoughts and the occasional officer who strolled through, dead-eyed. The place was an advertisement for living in the suburbs. *See, we don't even have criminals.* Gillian imagined she'd been detained in the public relations cell. They probably kept the chain link and shackles in the basement, along with the Tasers.

Who set her up, that was the question. Ellsberg knew where she'd be; he could have fed her the rope, then called the police. But why do that, when his name wasn't on the USB stick, just Evelina's over and over. *I've been mourning Tommy for ages.* Evelina, the shattered widow. Evelina the kindred spirit. Evelina, Gillian's friend.

The image wouldn't leave her, of Jackie lurking outside Evelina's home, and Gillian never questioning why. Tommy had espoused Gillian as the best and brightest, but she was an idiot. A fucking child, still to this day. Trusting the wrong people didn't mean second place anymore, but Tommy dead in the morgue. When was she going to wake up?

Heels clacked against polished concrete. A female cop appeared in the window, Martin Ellsberg visible over her shoulder. The cop unlocked the door and slid it open, then stepped aside and jerked her head. Gillian exited, warily. Ellsberg turned and marched back the way he'd come. Like Gillian could stay and rot for all he cared. She followed from a distance.

"They have my bag," she said.

Ellsberg walked with a head of steam, maybe intending to burst through the front door. She repeated herself.

"I have your bag," he managed, through clenched teeth. "I threw it in the trunk, along with my career." He shoved open the door but didn't hold it, leaving Gillian to sidestep as it closed. "Do you know how fucked I am? Everyone knows how you got into Sebastian's office. I spent years building relationships out here. Plano. Allen. Frisco. McKinney. These are suspicious departments with long memories. You know how they regard people like me? As moneyed assholes who buy their way free of justice." He glared at her over his shoulder. "As if Sebastian didn't have enough on his plate. He'll have to kiss ass with the city council. The mayor. He can't stand that man. He's a Trumper." He stopped outside a bland silver Accord. "When will it be enough? When everyone you blame is destroyed?"

He seemed genuinely pissed off. But everyone at Miscellany seemed to be something.

"It's not good," she said. "I understand that."

"You understand? That would be a first."

"This is not how it looks. I was set up."

Ellsberg rolled his eyes. "The Great Gillian Charles. Too good to simply be arrested."

"How did they know I was there?"

He frowned – Gillian a headache he couldn't kick. "What?"

"Why not Security? Why not your people? How did the police know I was there?"

"I assume you were spotted."

"Sure. By who?"

"It's an enormous glass building in the middle of a popular amusement. Anyone with two eyes and a cell phone."

"Someone caught me walking while Black, is that it?"

He grimaced, but otherwise offered no response. He dug for his keys and went to the trunk. "Get in the car."

She watched him fumble with the remote locks, as if he couldn't manage a single button click. The image took her back to Ellsberg at twelve years old. His chin barely lifted above the water, seemingly only moments from drowning. Of course, history proved he could navigate turbulent waters just fine.

She wanted to tell him about the USB drive. But she didn't know which Ellsberg stood across from her.

She approached the car but didn't open the door. "Maybe it was one of your people who called it in. The ones following me around the park."

"This again?" He popped the trunk, grabbed her bag. "I let you in, only to sic my people on you, is that it?"

"You tell me. Everything was fine when I was here for show and tell. I start asking real questions, looking in uncomfortable places, suddenly I'm fitted for prison orange."

Ellsberg looked at her as if he'd never seen her before. So good at pretending.

"Did you know about Evelina?" she asked.

"What about her?"

"She had access to Tommy's email. Those emails Sebastian wasn't supposed to send? Evelina saw puzzles. She sold answers to the qualifying families, bribes masquerading as bullshit donations. You said the truth was hard to see with her, but you let me cozy up next to her anyway. Probably got a good laugh out of it."

Ellsberg didn't say anything.

"Am I close? How much did you know? I can't imagine your Security nazis aren't watching everything, right? It must have been hard to keep the truth on the down low. Imagine if the Navarros had found out. That could have cost Miscellany millions. And forget the settlement – how cute, to just pay that out. There's the PR damage. Talking about Evelina like you didn't understand her – this was your language all along, Mr FBI. How much is Sebastian paying you? How much does it cost to keep Ellsberg quiet?" She shook her head. "Tommy would be disgusted."

Across from her, Ellsberg huffed like a cornered bull. At first silent, only pointing his long bony finger at her. And then he said, "Fuck you." He sounded genuinely hurt. "I needed to win the Contest as much as you did. You don't know what it was like to grow up in that house. Looking like I did. Wanting the things I..." He turned his head away, staring into the street. Early morning traffic blazed past, the drivers blissfully indifferent. When Ellsberg faced her again, he was composed. "Get in the car," he repeated. "You'll go to the hotel. You'll pack. You'll wait, patiently, while I arrange transportation, and then you'll be taken directly to the airport. Don't worry about your money. I'm sure you can be paid for your time."

He got in the car. Frustrated, Gillian shut her mouth and got in alongside him. The drive back was a quiet hell, and when they reached the hotel, she took her bag and watched Ellsberg drive off without a word. Angry he dared be so righteous.

I needed to win the Contest as much as you did.

Imagine if Ellsberg was right, and Gillian was still settling scores? The anger in Ellsberg's voice real, his flushed skin real. And Gillian the petulant child stomping on lives until everyone felt her misery. Hadn't Ellsberg protected from the start? Paid for her hotel. Helped her track Tommy's band. Bailed her silly ass out of jail.

Miscellany turned you around and upside down and emptied your pockets. She'd known from the start.

She slung her bag over her shoulder. Reclaimed cell phone and wristband from the outside pocket. She couldn't take back the words, or change the past. All she could do was act smarter from here on out. Try harder. Be better.

Gillian headed toward Miscellany HQ and Sebastian.

Thirty-Three

Sun, cheer, and paying customers had returned to Miscellany, but the flags flew at half-mast. Gillian walked with the crowds, but felt alien and apart. She kept her head on a swivel. Every few minutes she checked to ensure the USB drive was still in her bra.

Sebastian would see. Once he saw the proof, he'd have to act. At the wake, she'd noticed the pain in his voice. *I failed him.* Toying with his magnetic structure as if he could rebuild Tommy. Big money would tempt him to shove the whole Season Two affair under the table, but Sebastian's life was a testimony to singular vision. The investment only fuel for the cause. If the cause had been co-opted, subverted, he'd act. She'd seen it, as a child – no lack of purity tolerated in his utopia. Especially if that corruption led to the death of his favored son.

The headquarters building was abuzz. Men and women flocking from one end to the other with blazers shucked and shirtsleeves rolled. Interns ran schooners of coffee and boxed meals. Amid all the chaos Security almost passed her through, pausing only when a note appeared on screen.

"Sebastian is looking for you." The security guard, a woman with a killer mohawk, raised her eyebrows. "The big man asked for you by name."

That suited Gillian fine. "Where is he?"

Through the security barricade and up to the PR Pit on two, toxic bra data in hand only once she'd cleared. She found Sebastian surrounded by highly animated types in ballcaps and Chucks. He sat with his back to her at a table in a large cubicle. The others fidgeted in chairs, some paced, all wielded high-end cell phones. A pack of hyenas, none white, most in their twenties, apart from Leah. She wore a shirt that read *Geek* and did most of the talking.

"The optics on this are bad. You need to be seen."

"I never worry about being seen," Sebastian said. "I'm not one of those people. It's always about what's best for Miscellany."

"You've never had a company executive die on the property. There's already speculation his death was drug related. They're saying methamphetamine and cocaine. You don't want an Amy Winehouse – people wondering why you didn't step in. You want Philip Seymour Hoffman. A tragedy. Who knew?" One of the young people shared her phone with Leah, who ingested the information quickly. "No, we don't talk to him. He called Sebastian a loon in *Vanity Fair*. Find me someone else. The one from the *Journal*."

Sebastian's flat cap sat on the table. He pulled it close and kneaded the headband between his fingers. "This is our business. No one else's."

Leah's eyes found Gillian. She shifted her body, as if ready to stop a bullet for her boss. "Speaking of our business."

Pickleback Leah a thing of the past. Gillian wondered if she knew about last night's escapade. If she'd been the one to call the cops.

Sebastian looked over his shoulder. "You're late."

"I can't be late," Gillian said. "I'm looking for you."

"Tommy is dead, the police are still on property, and we've got the announcement. I needed you eight hours ago. Believe me, you're late."

Gillian came around the table so she could see Sebastian's face. Like Leah, he was intent, all business. But maybe that was better. What Gillian carried threatened the business.

One of the immortal young vacated a chair, and she sat. She had the USB stick clenched in her fist. "I need to talk to you."

"Team, I'd like you to meet the famous Gillian Charles. You'll be seeing a lot more of her."

An uncertainty become de facto. For their part, the team didn't seem thrilled at the prospect. Low grumbles eddied around the group. A muttered, "Not if I can help it," which drew knowing chuckles. The kind of cliquishness Gillian once believed would die in high school. Reality often enjoyed proving her wrong.

"People." Sebastian raised his gloved hands. "This is supposed to be my group of problem-solvers. Let's be civil, please, and thank you."

The sniping died down. Still, Gillian could read the room. This group didn't give two shits if she was a Contestant. Ordinarily she'd have rejoiced, but today she needed their respect. The USB data demanded their respect.

"Gillian needs to be brought up to speed," Sebastian said. "We're going to lead with the memorial. The foundation in Tommy's name, the work Evelina is doing."

"Where is she?" Gillian asked.

Sebastian looked annoyed. "Who?"

"Evelina."

"She's working the Season Two announcement. This group covers everything else. Where have you been? The most crucial time in our history and you went, where? Dealey Plaza? Southfork? I know you can make a difference here, but you have to prove it to everyone else. This is not how you start."

He kept talking like Gillian at Miscellany was a done deal. She couldn't find the words to correct him.

Leah, like most in her circle, kept one eye on her phone. "They say it's $150k. If we rebrand the Inglewood project."

Sebastian waved his cap like he was shooing away flies. "I would write that check right now. Tell them to figure the numbers out. We're announcing within the hour."

The USB bombshell lay in Gillian's hand, and the longer she sat there, the harder it became to drop it. "My Inglewood?"

"Los Angeles is the biggest market in the United States without a Bazaar," Leah said. "We're acquiring an existing property. Doing a refresh – some light demo, new coat of paint. You Californians get bored unless your entertainment changes every fifteen minutes–"

But Sebastian was already talking over Leah. "This will be significantly more than a new coat of paint. The Kundojjala School will be the first of its kind. Courses in history, dramatic arts. A culinary school. Chemistry. Botany. Small classes. Intense focus. Fully funded scholarships. And just outside Los Angeles." He pointed at Gillian. "Right in your backyard."

He never stopped. He just never stopped.

"Sebastian." The volume of her voice plowed everyone else under. "I never said I was working for you."

Reality finally provided Sebastian's army with something more interesting than their cell phones. Heads lifted, eyes darted back and forth. Sebastian and Leah exchanged a look – volumes transferred in seconds. Then Sebastian said, "Let's regroup in fifteen, everyone. Gillian and I need a moment."

The group scattered, disappearing into the maze of cubicles. Only Leah lingered, in case Sebastian needed protection. Yet another glimpse into a different future. Had Gillian let Ellsberg thrash in the water all those years ago, would she be here, defending Sebastian's turf? Sitting here, she was positive the answer was yes. And still could be. The realization scared the shit out of her.

Sebastian changed chairs so he sat at her elbow. "I took care of your mother."

Gillian's face went numb.

"It's a facility with a private room," he said. "We'll carry the cost, for now. Call it an advance on your benefits. But you'll take over the payments after six months. The rate we're going to pay you, you should find the cost achievable. The place is here, near UT Southwestern – I assumed Stephanie wanted to stay local. I don't know what you're doing – if you're going to move, fly back and forth. We can work that out. But you need to sign the employment papers. I've got numbers people and they don't like it when I pay someone who doesn't work for us."

What should have been amazing news felt like a handcuff clapping around her wrist again. The wrist attached to the hand holding the USB drive. Gillian set her closed fist on the table. "There could be a problem."

"Could be? Why do you think Evelina is killing herself less than seventy-two hours after her husband died? The press release on the rather abrupt end of the Contest franchise goes out today. That experiment is an anchor, and if we don't cut it loose, we're going to drown."

"I don't mean just the Reunion. What if Tommy found something at Miscellany? And Evelina is involved, covering something up? Maybe there's reason for those families to be upset."

Sebastian looked at her as if she was a couple of time zones behind. "Covering something up? She's in public relations – of course she's covering something up. Tommy nearly exposed our backsides for the world to see, and despite the fact the man is her husband, her deceased husband, she's burning the candle at both ends trying to pull up our pants. How do you think this place works? No one is on our side. Not our competition. Not the government. They want our good name and our success and, failing that, they'll accept our demise. They don't like us. Every time we build a new Bazaar, we upset some entrenched conservative power. We're too liberal, too intellectual, too diverse. We disrupt economic imbalances that have existed for decades. I'm surprised you don't understand. Since when did you care what *the Man* thought?"

She told herself anger blinded him to the truth.

"There could be bad faith efforts. If there are people on your team breaking the rules–"

"We're building the dream." He spread his arms to take in the whole of the building, and beyond. "Do you think I built this place without breaking rules? Stepping on some toes? We have enemies throughout the halls of power. When we educate, we create future leaders, leaders with different views and different skin tones. That's the mission. But you know how quick these things fall apart, if there's a whiff of impropriety – the idea the kids are in danger? Everyone has cell phones. I loved Tommy, and we're trying to keep a lid on his problems, but he put us in a terrible spot. No parent will bring their kid to a Bazaar where the face of the institution is involved in drugs and infidelity. The Bazaars will close. Our entire mission will fall apart, and this will all be for nothing. The millions – the *billions* – we're raising, the good we're doing... all that will go away. I cannot have that. No more Contests, no more Seasons. We'll suffer some grief, but we will do it for the kids. Look at the lives we've changed, the lives we intend to change. New Bazaars in India, the Middle East, in disadvantaged locations all over the world. We'll invest in places no one else is looking. No one. This is the future we're building and I'm not going to slow down because Tommy couldn't keep his nose clean, and his dick in his pants."

Sebastian going for shock value, Gillian figured. His profanity calculated, designed to throw her off balance and further the impression he was just a human being, impacted by loss like anyone else. His strategy was working. She was off balance.

He beckoned with a gloved hand and Leah came in from the edge of the cubicle. "I want you on Inglewood, immediately. We need you, frankly. But I can't play games with another Contestant."

Leah hovered at Gillian's elbow. She stared down at Gillian as if she'd been caught skipping school. "There's certain protections we enjoy, but only if you're an employee," Leah said. "This isn't a consulting arrangement. I've emailed you the forms – you can sign digitally. I don't know what he's told you, but it will look better if you don't report directly to Sebastian, so starting tomorrow, you work for me."

"For now," Sebastian interrupted. "Until this all settles down."

Gillian retrieved her phone, the USB drive still clutched in her other hand. Leah's forms were already in her email, along with a formal offer of employment, and a compensation package unlike any she'd seen in her entire life. Her throat closed up tight.

"I'm on the fence about this," Leah said. "So you should sign before I change my mind. Or his."

Gillian had been so sure. The *right thing* burning bright in her mind. But now she sat at this table with everything she'd ever wanted and a way for her mother to be free. She couldn't let go of the USB drive.

Sebastian stood and cast an inquiring eye at Leah. "Where are we doing this? The Proscenium?"

Like all of Miscellany's faithful, Leah switched gears quickly. "Evelina doesn't want it there. That's the last place Tommy was seen in an official capacity. We're setting up downstairs. Keep business in the place of business."

Sebastian pulled on his flat cap. His gaze settled on Gillian, but she couldn't tear her eyes away from the dollars blazing inside her phone. The dollars, and what they represented.

"The facility can take Stephanie today," he said. "If you sign."

Gillian wasn't sure how long Sebastian and Leah were gone when she finally looked up. She was sure only that she'd never handed over the data.

Thirty-Four

Gillian kept her hands below the table so her mother couldn't see them shake. She called from her room at the Leonardo, a brand-new Miscellany laptop open on the desk and a cold beer sweating within reach. No reason not to use their equipment. No reason not to drink their beer.

Was she celebrating? Mourning? She wasn't sure.

A woman with limp gray hair answered the video call, angling the camera so Mom could converse from her wheelchair. Behind them, the wide expanse of an eggshell-white room with a comfy bed and an end table and a pair of pictures hanging on the wall. One picture of Gillian, another of Mom, Dad, and June.

"Are you sure this thing is working?" Mom looked at the nurse, not at Gillian. "I don't like these things."

"Mom, I'm right here." Her mother seemed good. Her makeup on. The muscles around her eyes tight and her skin healthy. There was pluck in her voice as she groused at the nurse.

"Oh." Her mother's chin swelled on screen. "There you are. Where are you?"

"I'm at work, Mom." Gillian set her hand around her beer but didn't pull it close. "How are they treating you?"

"I don't know. This place is very nice. Sebastian must be spending a fortune. Did you win another contest?"

The question made her think about the cavern. About the pounding water and Ellsberg's theatrical splashing and Tommy with his arms raised in victory. Then Tommy with his slack face mashed against the inside of a glass tube.

"It's a busy time," she said, her voice low. "I don't know when I'm going to get out there. I wanted to make sure they were taking care of you."

"Well, first of all, they say we're going for a walk. It's six-thirty at night and we're going for walks? I take my walks in the morning, you know that. This is Texas. It gets too hot."

"Exercise is part of the treatment. You need to stay strong."

"And these drugs. I can't even pronounce all the names. What's wrong with Tylenol?" Behind her, the nurse was laying out clothes and a pair of her mother's walking shoes. "Are you sure you can't come out here?"

Gillian turned the beer bottle between her fingers. "The medication is specific for lupus. We've never been able to…" The words not what her mother wanted to hear. Gillian produced a tight smile. "I'll try to visit soon."

"Tomorrow would be good. June is driving out. I think she's going to be very impressed with this place. This is the kind of fancy that impresses your sister."

The nurse spoke to Mom from off screen. Her mother grew flustered.

"The colonel says we need to get our walk in before dark. What did you sign me up for? It's like boot camp."

"It's a good place, Mom."

"Oh, I know. And thank you. Although I still wish your father could stay. He doesn't know what to do with himself at your sister's. You have to check on him. He'll be living on bologna and toast and sitting in that recliner in his underwear."

Her mother was always worried about people. Perpetual concern, her cross to bear. It would be nice when she didn't have to worry about Gillian. When her daughter could provide for her.

They'd admitted Mom because Gillian had signed the agreements. Twenty-some-odd pages of legalese binding Gillian Charles to Miscellany. At least if she expected to be paid. If she expected her mother to be taken care of.

"This really is a nice place, Gilly," Mom loud-whispered. "But don't tell the colonel I said so."

The USB drive sat behind the beer. So long as Gillian didn't move the bottle, she couldn't see it.

"Go for your walk." Gillian touched the screen. "I love you."

"I love you too, dear."

The screen went dark. Gillian returned her hand to the beer bottle and pushed it to one side, then used the back of her hand to push it back, the glass sliding against the wet wood, revealing and hiding the USB drive.

In theory, Gillian had everything she would have secured had she won eighteen years ago. But it was funny. She'd run the race twice now and never finished first.

Tapping the space bar brought up the time. It wasn't quite seven. Room service would be nice – call it a night, rest, let her body process what she'd lost, what she'd gained. She'd barely slept in the last twenty-four hours. The smart play was to grab some shut-eye.

The USB drive remained on the desk. Too heavy to move. Too heavy to hide.

All right, Tommy. Let's find out. Let's find out what would have happened.

Gillian closed the laptop and went to change clothes. What she had planned – she'd need room to move.

Thirty-Five

Gillian wore the same ragged athletic gear she'd worn to the Contest. A flashlight, a pen, her wallet and cell phone, a pocketknife, and the rubber-banded notebook went into her string bag. The damn drive she slipped into her sports bra.

After a tepid cup of hotel coffee, she ventured into the park. Guests still milled about, eager to take in the evening rides, to tackle the nighttime-themed puzzles. Gillian felt that familiar prickling, excitement and imminent discovery. And again, she sensed someone on the periphery – maybe a familiar brunette ponytail and the hint of a scar. But she didn't spot Jackie, not conclusively, and tonight she wouldn't feed those demons. Those were Tommy's demons, and look where they'd led him.

She forced herself to stop checking blind spots, to walk like one of the crowd. She made her way to the Bazaar and found the gates closed, which she'd expected. She followed the fence behind a line of food trucks, chucked her bag over the fence, and climbed up after it. The defenses were not Jurassic Park – she wasn't fried to a crisp. No one even shouted her name.

Darkness cloaked her as she approached the Bazaar. The paper lanterns still lined the path and a plastic champagne flute lay in the grass. Only three days prior, they'd all gathered to recreate the moment that made them family. Sebastian pressuring her to attend, and Gillian in turn hounding Tommy. Thinking about her role was problematic. Either she'd experience a crippling amount of guilt, or worse, she wouldn't feel any guilt at all.

She kept walking, her eyes boring into the Bazaar. If she looked down the path to her right she'd find the split leading to the Ballroom, and the Maze. The Maze where she'd talked with Evelina like maybe they were friends. Evelina, who'd rigged the qualifiers. Who knew the Navarros were right, and wanted them plowed under anyway. A USB drive full of her crimes.

How far would Evelina go? *He is charming, isn't he.* So polished. Even her anguish composed. What would Evelina have done to Tommy to survive? What would Miscellany? Those questions didn't matter now. Gillian had chosen herself, and in so doing she'd sided with Miscellany. What choice did she have?

What choice did she ever have?

A warning sticker sealed the Bazaar doors, but otherwise the building was unlocked. Gillian slit the sticker with her knife and the door yawned wide. Once inside, she pulled the door shut and flicked on her flashlight. The foyer was empty, the chandelier dark. At the end of the hall the small door gaped open. As she retraced her steps, she imagined the complete lack of pomp and circumstance as Sebastian opened the Bazaar for the police. The great man pontificating, the cops tempted to put a bullet in him, only to shut him up.

On the far side of the doorway, she found the room empty, the giltwood lecterns and their puzzles hibiscus flowers, blooming bright for only the one day. There was no need to feed an answer sheet into the door, all the exits open. Into the checkerboard room, the path no longer daunting – Gillian's flashlight beam revealed arrows drawn on the walls, markers so law enforcement didn't have to burn brain cells quicker than absolutely necessary. The arrows led to a hidden door Gillian had never seen. She stepped through and into a passageway.

The passage was unfinished, all metal and drywall. No magic fairy dust carried on the air. Gillian's blood warmed; the spot on her neck blazed hot. She smirked. Of course Sebastian hid passages behind the walls – ways to adjust the game at any time and leapfrog the Contestants. But as she turned and took in the breadth of the place, her grin faded. If Tommy's death wasn't accidental, someone could have used the passageways to move unseen. To drown Tommy, before he drowned Miscellany.

Quietly she walked down the path. Doors appeared in her flashlight beam, and she investigated each one, finding rooms she recognized from the Reunion. The library. The casino. She stuck to the tunnel, and eventually exited onto the beach through a door hidden in the rock wall. She cast her light around. The man-made lake was drained, the area near the intake tube marked off, plastic numbers and tape visible from across the distance. Gillian only stared. Didn't approach. Any number of things she might claim to be, but police wasn't one of them. Besides, the answer to Tommy's death didn't reside in a fingerprint smudge hidden near the scene of the crime.

Gillian sat on the beach and pulled off her shoes and socks. Dropped her string bag and walked barefoot through the sand. There was no sprawling cat's cradle of rope this time. A wheelchair ramp zigzagged along the rock wall, and then entered the cave. She padded into the dark mouth and, sure enough, her flashlight beam found the object of her search. Four large boxes stretched across the path, all untouched, symbols stamped into their sealed lids. Gillian's box marked with a squid-like creature, the tentacles stubby. The cuttlefish.

Her lips wrinkled. She still hated the term.

Opening the cuttlefish box revealed another object inside – a wooden mechanical puzzle. Sebastian at his most predictable when he thought he'd found a teachable moment.

Gillian sat on the ground, cross-legged. She positioned the flashlight's beam. Fuck Sebastian. She could do this.

Between her hands she held the unpainted wooden rectangle. It was slim, more cell phone dimensions than cube. Horizontal slots divided the dark walnut covers, vertical blond wood pins visible underneath. Metal sliders were housed within each slot, the sliders obstructed or freed depending on the position of the vertical pins. At the top of the device, a handle, or shackle. The goal to move the sliders and the pins in such a way the shackle came free. The thing one giant sliding lock. A puzzle box, one of famed German designer Jean Claude Constantin's, or a Sebastian-modified version. Ellsberg would have been in heaven. Not only a puzzle box but one designed by a German – Constantin, no less? She found herself smiling. She honestly couldn't wait to tell him.

There was no key. No instructions. This is exactly what Gillian wanted.

She began to move the sliders. No real idea how to open the box at first, just adjusting the components enough to understand the mechanism. The first few minutes designed to clear her mind. Put everything else – Tommy, Sebastian, Evelina, Ellsberg, Mom, the money – out of her mind. Her breathing deep. Her muscles relaxed.

The box was an n-ary puzzle – a six-ary puzzle to be exact. Puzzle solving required intuition and native smarts, but also study and a grasp of numbers. Four sliders, one that moved freely and three with limitations imposed by the interior wooden pins, allowing six positions, including the start. Five moves per slider. Two hundred fifty moves minimum.

Understanding the mechanism was key. The puzzle box initially confusing, but not difficult. She worked from the bottom, moving the slider, which in turn shifted the interior pin and released the slider in the slot above. She forced herself to be methodical. The bottom sliders having to work left to right and right to left multiple times to ultimately release the top row. She knew this wasn't her best work. She moved a slider in the wrong direction and had to backtrack and repeat a series of moves. She questioned her approach and paused more than once, assuring herself she was on the right path. While well assembled, the box was still a creation of wood and glue and screws. Several times she had to knock it against the ground to fix the alignment and work the sliders. But she fed on the frustration. Scoured herself clean pushing through obstacles. And finally, after about ten minutes, she had the solution. All the sliders moved to the right. The shackle came free and a key-shaped wooden slat came with it. This piece of wood was lighter than the rest, and hollow. A scrap of paper was stuffed inside, something gold and shiny cut from a larger sheet. Gillian withdrew the paper and held it between her fingers. The message fragment still bright, even after eighteen years.

Winner of the Contest Extraordinaire
Gillian Charles

She flipped the paper over. A fresh handwritten note, written in black ink.

I knew you could do it.
–S

Underneath, a pattern of dots and numbers in cells six-by-six. It was a Slitherlink.

This wasn't the answer to Sebastian's game, to the life she'd lost. This was yet another puzzle.

Gillian stood, leaving the puzzle box on the ground. She stared at the twin dark passageways leading deeper into the cave. In her head, a few seconds was all she'd needed. A few seconds to run down the correct tunnel and secure first place. But the game wouldn't have ended; it would have only changed, Sebastian progressing her to the next set of puzzles, the next step in her evolution.

She looked at the note gripped in her hands. She went back down the sand and stared at the plastic tube where she'd found Tommy's body. His last moments were right there – the boy with the charming smile. All those years ago Gillian had rescued a drowning Ellsberg, but she'd swum to the aid of the wrong Contestant. Tommy had been the one drowning, and she'd failed him.

Her eyes followed the tube up until it disappeared in the walls along with a twisting host of others. She no longer had any desire to find out where they went.

She crumpled the paper in her hand. With Sebastian, there would always be more puzzles to solve.

She returned to the passageway.

As Gillian approached the front door, she realized she'd forgotten her shoes. Left them on the beach, along with her socks and string bag and everything inside. Items too valuable to leave behind. She swung her flashlight beam back and forth, uncertain which way to head.

She smelled the smoke, but only seconds before she saw the flames.

The inferno roared like a monster. The fire raced up the south wall of the Bazaar, chewing through the old timber hungrily. The heat knocked Gillian back, sent her tumbling down the front steps and her flashlight rolling off into the night. She fell smack on her ass. Scrambled backward, crab-walking. She spied a figure sprinting away from the conflagration and shouted, but the intruder didn't break stride. She staggered to her feet and the fire seemed to chase her, lancing from the back of the house to the front as if it smelled her. Flame licked at her skin. A heavy fuel stink hung in the air. Gillian backpedaled, the fire driving her toward the security fence. She blinked away tears and tried to spot the shadowy figure, but all she could see was flames. The reality of her situation became inescapable. She spun around and ran the last few yards to the fence and climbed the chain link. She threw herself over the top, intent on slow-scaling to the ground, but she fumbled and went down the hard way. She landed on her back, her lungs compressed, the breath knocked clean out of her.

The fire drew closer. It would not respect the fence.

Suddenly there were people. A crowd gathered, the prospect of someone else's tragedy overriding their instinct for self-preservation. The bystanders hauled Gillian to her feet and pulled her away from the flames. The sirens of Miscellany's private fire department split the air. This far from fuel the fire's leading edge had slowed, but in the rear the beast continued to chew at Sebastian's pride and joy. The Bazaar had gone up quickly. So very quickly.

Gillian coughed until she bent double. Someone backslapped her until she waved them off. Her eyes continued to water. She realized how naked she was, standing among strangers with no bag and no identification, nothing other than the clothes on her back. Spooked, she twisted around. She felt hot and itchy; nervous spiders crawled her skin. Every instinctive alarm she'd suppressed, wailing. Someone had followed her from the hotel. She'd seen a figure run away from the Bazaar. Maybe a black ponytail. Could a telltale scar be far behind?

Someone had set that fire. Someone who knew she'd be inside.

More people arrived. Faces she didn't know. Strangers with cell phones and questions, maybe with things worse. She was a Black woman with no shoes near the scene of a crime. They'd gravitate toward her with their suspicions and their biases. And eventually Jackie would find her.

Backing away slowly, Gillian melted into the crowd.

Thirty-Six

Gillian spent the lonely haul from the park thinking about who to call. Walking in the dark in the tall weeds along the roadside, cringing as oncoming headlights washed over her at sixty miles an hour and she cut her feet on rocks and broken glass. Someone had honked and pulled over just behind her. Gillian had never run so fast.

The first building she came upon – the first she considered far enough from Miscellany – was a Whataburger. Too many black SUVs in the parking lot and too many people inside. She stood on the edge where gravel met grass. Her gaze darted from vehicle to door, from face to face.

She put her hands to her mouth like she was praying. Her skin was hot. The smell clung to her. Smoke and sweat, and underneath, the whiff of fear. In her ears, the cries as she scaled that fence, then fell. The fire hunting her, hungry, with not the slightest concern for her so-called smarts.

A guy in the drive-thru lane watched her, his face all long planes and hard angles. Gillian moved into the shadows. She threw the Miscellany band into the dumpster. *There's no GPS*, Ellsberg said. Sure, but Sebastian knew about Tommy's phone call with Gillian. Maybe even Ellsberg wasn't aware of what the bands could do.

Sheer animal terror had propelled Gillian this far. But

adrenaline had ebbed, and she needed a plan. No way June would leave her kids. Mom couldn't drive. She couldn't trust anyone associated with Miscellany, she didn't think. Her fear – even if she landed on a name, all her nearest and dearest were likely monitored. She needed someone who was neither.

When the name hit, her knees buckled. But being in exile put him off the radar, a place Gillian desperately needed to stay. At least until she plotted her next move.

Her phone was back in her bag, food for the Bazaar fire. And no place would feel any safer than here.

Inside the restaurant Gillian caught a break – no one at the counter. The girl manning the register – Black, sixteen if a day – lent Gillian her phone. She didn't ask a single question, only shot furtive looks at her coworkers before producing the cell from her back pocket. Gillian dialed the number from memory, wondering what that meant.

Within forty-five minutes, the Dreamcatcher Saturn pulled up outside. Gillian finished the coffee the girl had generously provided and quickly went to the car. She yanked open the door and dropped herself into the Saturn's passenger seat. The car smelled like him. The goddamn Brut and something else. His skin and sweat. The literal decay of the man, as he ground his way through life.

He'd come right away. A handful of questions, but nothing a father might not ask.

"You eat?" he said.

Gillian kept her eyes directed out the window. Shook her head no.

"Fire's all over the news." In the automobile's confines the smoke smell intensified. "They say you're missing."

She squirmed. The USB drive pressed into her skin,

like a brand. "Can we go? This is a little close for me."

The engine idled but the car didn't move. "Thank you," he said.

She looked at him. For a moment, it was as if he was never gone from her life.

"Thank you," he repeated, his voice gravelly.

She nodded.

They drove away.

Thirty-Seven

Café Brazil provided a window table where Gillian could see the parking lot. She wore jeans and a Rolling Stones T-shirt. The jeans bought from a warehouse store with borrowed money. The T-shirt was Dad's. He sat across from her, drinking coffee, humming. Behind him, over the coffee bar, a TV tuned to Channel 5. The network already had video. The dark-skinned female anchor appropriately somber.

"Another down day for the entertainment empire Miscellany and its CEO Sebastian Luna, shown here throwing out the first pitch at Globe Life Field." A picture of the man throwing a baseball overhand, like some ace reliever. "Only three days after the passing of Tomas Kundojjala, the company's COO and Winner of the Contest Extraordinaire, a fire broke out at the storied Miscellany Bazaar, site of that same competition and the first of what would become many such entertainment centers around the United States. The damage to the structure is said to be total, and although the building was closed, there are unconfirmed reports that another Contestant, Gillian Charles, was inside when the fire broke out. Many had expected to hear news today of Season Two, a rebooted Contest featuring a new set of child wonders. Instead, Miscellany finds itself struggling with more tragedy. We take you live to–"

Dad had snuck out of the booth. He leaned across the bar and stabbed off the TV. "News ain't nothing but misery," he said.

She watched him settle into his seat. He seemed small, her father. His life occupying only the barest footprint. The spare room at June's. His crappy car and pointless job. But he'd come when she called. He knew what was important, to him. When he'd paid for the jeans, she'd seen inside his wallet. Credit card, cash, and a picture of her and June. She'd stared at the picture: she and her sister too cute, looking like a pair of dolls. Dad had lost everything, hit bottom. Somewhere in there he'd found a way to go on. For the family he'd lost and never quite regained.

His eyes flicked up and she looked away. It was too much to look at him, to meet that battered stare with every regret blooming on her face. The fire had burned away her protections. He'd see into her heart and know she should have forgiven him years ago.

Gillian told him everything. Hiding from herself these past eighteen years. Tommy lighting the fuse to bring her back and blow up her life. Her stress over Mom's treatment, the money involved. And how puzzles made everything simpler and more complex at the time. Puzzles asked everything of her, and Gillian embraced that focus, the rest of the world melting away. And yet she couldn't help but think – she'd assigned the wrong value to the solutions. The puzzle answers weren't life answers.

With no small amount of shame, Gillian circled her relationship with Evelina. Recounting the trust she'd invested, and how, like before, that trust had been misplaced. Her father didn't say much. He rolled an empty sugar packet between his dry fingers, listening to the crackle as much as Gillian's tale. The habit reminded her of Sebastian, his tendency to use silence as a lure. Counting on others to fill the quiet with their secrets.

"What do you think?" she said.

Dad was slow to disgorge the words. "I never trusted the man."

Her old anger surged, not gone that quickly. Dad sat there in his booth. One car ride and a cup of coffee making him ruler of the roost. "Easy for you to say. Where were you then?"

"You didn't need him. You still don't."

Only a thread of common sense kept her in her seat. The devil on her shoulder whispered, *Leave him here*. Storm out into the night; fuck Dad right along with Sebastian.

"What about Mom? Where will the money for her treatment come from, exactly? You?"

The look on his face said he held no answers, not for any of it. And suddenly being there with him, in that moment, seemed a terrible idea. Nothing had changed, Gillian was circling old ground, and they'd resort to bone-deep habits.

She stared at him. At his younger man's hair, more of it laced with gray than she'd realized. At the loose clothes, like he was a scarecrow come off the stake. He was no rock; he could fall off the wagon tomorrow – the man himself would admit it. Wallace Charles had chased money, when he wasn't chasing liquor. Like June said, he'd imagined slights and slings and all kinds of obstacles to his dreams. His own electrician business. Running a restaurant. A thousand and one carefully constructed ambitions of which he'd been architect and destroyer. Gillian wondered – if he'd ever hit the jackpot, made enough money, would he have walked away from the booze?

What would it take for Gillian to walk away from Sebastian?

Dad tried to kickstart the conversation. "The German fella could help," he said. "You always liked him."

Thinking about Ellsberg only confused Gillian. She shrugged.

"He probably feels guilty," Dad said.

"You think he shouldn't?"

Dad pursed his lips and shook his head. "Guilt's good. Nothing better for calibration. Every day a reminder how you can..." He paused. "Foul things up."

She could see Dad struggling with himself. He picked at the skin on his flaking thumb.

"You don't owe him a second chance," he said. "But if you reach out for help, might answer his question."

"What's that?"

He kept picking at that dry skin. "Am I good enough?"

The question she'd posed to herself at the start of the Contest, and the Reunion. It made her uncomfortable. The desperation and uncertainty so close to her own.

Ellsberg's words outside the police station. *I needed to win the Contest as much as you did.*

Gillian excused herself and trekked to the bathroom. Light-headed and numb, she stood over the sink and stared at herself in the mirror, pulling her cheeks long. She looked older, she thought. Not much different than Ellsberg. Aged so quickly by the Miscellany machine, like all the other cogs. A weird impulse surged – the urge to rip off her clothes. Stand under a cold shower until everything was rinsed clean, the smoke and the ash and the fingerprints, the touch of people steering her since she'd arrived.

Jackie may have run from the fire, but the woman only

jumped when someone said boo. Someone like Evelina, although she wasn't half as smart as she thought. The emails proved that the powers-that-be at Miscellany had unearthed her misdeeds. And if the machine knew, didn't it stand to reason the man at the controls knew also?

What would they do, to protect Sebastian's mission? Sue a family, certainly. Wage war in the press, bristle and close ranks. Then if things got too hot, settle, take some low-publicity lumps. In such a world they'd certainly have no problem buying off a scarf salesman from Los Angeles. But what if she didn't get the message, and wouldn't quit poking? *Well, old buildings have fires all the time*. What was the cost of a building, next to a dream?

Evelina's words, the instinctive response to attack outside the Maze. *I won't apologize for protecting what we earned.*

Which *we* did she mean?

Were they prepared to kill because they'd done it before?

Gillian pulled the USB from her bra. Set the drive on the edge of the sink. She considered flushing the evidence down the toilet. What was she going to do – defy Miscellany and Sebastian? At best, that kind of crazy ended with Gillian returning to a life spent hustling scarves. Broke. At worst... Well, at worst still smoldered in her wake. Sebastian's behemoth would bulldoze her like an old neighborhood. The house always won.

One winner, Evelina had said. The games designed so most of the participants lost. The Contest. The Reunion. Every event fashioned to isolate. To pit the Contestants against one another.

Gillian left the bathroom. She took the USB drive with her.

Thirty-Eight

Even when Evelina relaxed, she was perfectly composed. Miscellany-stylish in a spotless navy suit, complete with waistcoat. Gillian watched from inside the house as Evelina dropped her purse and keys and phone on the marble slab kitchen island. She slipped off her heels and leafed through some mail that she then spilled into a wicker basket.

"Stephen?" She shouted for her personal assistant, who Gillian had convinced to let her into the house before taking an evening for himself. "I've got that call with Singapore at eight. Can you have dinner ready after? It shouldn't be more than an hour."

Silence. The woman of the house noticed, and was disturbed. Something was out of place. She padded deeper into the home, calling Stephen's name. She halted when she found Gillian in her living room, again.

"I gave Stephen the night off." Gillian had taken the corner of the white couch, nestled in with her legs tucked under her. A pair of cheap sandals sat on the floor. More money borrowed from Dad. "It's been a busy few days."

For a second, Evelina's mouth gaped. Then she pulled in her jaw and turned the shock into a smile. "Gillian. Everyone is looking for you. We thought you were in the Bazaar when–"

"When your people started the fire?" Her face still felt tight. Residual heat simmered under her skin. Her accusation froze the smile on Evelina's face, enough to show the fear behind the mask. "I wanted to believe you didn't know I was inside when you gave the order, but you had Jackie following me. She wasn't just destroying the scene of the crime. She set the fire because I was inside."

Evelina wore a perplexed expression. "I don't understand. Are you suggesting Miscellany was involved in the destruction of the Bazaar? A treasured piece of our history?"

"I'm saying it was you or Miscellany, or both. I can't always tell where one ends and the other begins. And don't give me that crap about treasured history. You and I both know Sebastian only looks ahead. The past is entirely disposable." She set the USB drive on the glass coffee table. "*Almost* entirely."

Revealing the drive produced a Lauren Bacall eyebrow arch from Evelina. "What is that supposed to be?"

"Pain in the ass, isn't it? In the old days you'd just burn the paper. Now this shit is like glitter. The data gets on everything. You can never delete it all."

Evelina's pointed little tongue pressed against her cheek. "I'm sorry to say this, but I think you should leave. I didn't invite you into my home. If you don't go, I'll have to call the authorities."

"And ordinarily that would be great for you. A white woman calling the cops on a Black intruder. Only, I've got this drive." She flicked the USB and the drive spun lazily across the glass. "They'll have to take it. Even if the arresting officers don't understand what they have, someone else will. Only a matter of time until the press gets a hold of the contents, and they'll ask the real questions. Did you break into Tommy's email by yourself, or did you have help? The money the families sent, for Sebastian's Circle – where did those donations go? What does this mean for the Navarro settlement? What *really* happened to Tommy?"

"This is nonsensical." Evelina's breath-of-fresh-air attitude vanished, replaced with hard edges. "To come in here, and to fabricate some wrongdoing in the shadow of a very difficult company decision to cancel Season Two, to disappoint all those children. And to imply my husband was somehow involved. My poor Tommy." She turned away and marched toward the kitchen. "I'm not staying here for this. I'll have you removed from the property. To hell with whatever you meant to Sebastian."

Gillian rose to follow her. "You're going to Sebastian? Oh, it's too late for that. Once you burned down the Bazaar, you made it difficult for him. There's scrutiny now. Outside eyes – his least favorite thing. He's going to need separation. A fall guy... or gal."

Evelina slowed.

"What's funny – you didn't have to kill me to shut me up. You could have gone to him in the first place. He'd already bought me. I'm one of Sebastian's kids, I do whatever he tells me – didn't you know that? Or were you too busy having your husband killed?"

When Evelina turned, she'd aged a dozen years. Skin pulled tight against an angry skull. "What do you want from me?"

"I don't want to be one of Sebastian's kids anymore. I want out. And you can make that happen."

Gillian could see her weighing the options. Calculating the angles as the PR beast within gathered strength. "This is about money?"

"Jesus, you people. As if it was ever about anything else." She stepped closer. "Yes, it's about money. I agreed to come back to keep my mother off the street, but I didn't have any real leverage then. Today is a new day. I don't want to come back, I want to go away. I want my family taken care of, and I want enough so I can stop driving drunk hipsters to their bungalows. And I want to make it so I never have to solve another of Sebastian's fucking puzzles ever again."

Evelina's eyes sought the edges of the room. Maybe she considered a dash for her phone. Only who would she call?

"I don't want to be Sebastian's anymore," Gillian said. "You give me what I want, you can go on being his right-hand man." She glanced at the suit. "Or be him, for all I care. But I want to forget all this. Tommy, the Contest – all of it."

The house wasn't as perfectly quiet as it appeared. Overhead the ducting ticked. Expensive recovered barn woods groaned. The perfect house was made of imperfect things, and they responded to air and water and time.

Evelina's face went mannequin smooth. "We could come to some arrangement."

"Some arrangement? No. I need more than that."

"Money. We could get you money."

"This conversation is getting real crowded. We who? I want cash, from you, today."

She frowned. "I don't know that I have that kind of liquidity."

Gillian turned sideways, so Evelina's view of the USB drive was unhindered. "I hear Publishers Clearing House botched a contest and settled a $30 million class action. And they're not even all that large a company. Imagine being ten times as big."

Evelina bit her lip. "That's the only drive?"

"It can be."

The woman was coiled tight as a rattlesnake. "Fine. I can get you $250,000. It will take a bit–"

Two quick steps and Gillian was in Evelina's face. "My dad taught me Hold 'Em when I was five. I've been reading people since I was knee-high, and you offer me two-fifty? Higher."

The words drew a flinch. "Five hundred?"

"My mother has lupus. Most of the time she can't walk. She needs constant care, and I don't mean some ground round, best effort care at Parkland. Sirloin, OK? Kobe steak. I want one."

Recognition flickered in the depths of Evelina's brown eyes. She'd known the number from the beginning. "I don't know–"

"You want me gone? You want to make sure I destroy every copy and don't hit you up for seconds? You want me to forget your husband's shocked expression as he was crushed against the glass of that tube? You promise me right now."

"Fine." Evelina's voice cracked like a whip. "One million dollars. But you destroy every copy of those emails."

And there it was. The value of a person. The worth of Tommy's life and Gillian's soul. Enough money to buy the future Gillian always felt was stolen from her.

She walked across the tile back toward the front door and left the USB drive on the table.

"I win," she said.

The slap of Evelina's feet followed her. "Excuse me?"

But Gillian didn't stop moving.

"The idea that you could have competed. That you would

have stood a chance against me." She pivoted, bringing Evelina to an abrupt halt. "I finished second in the Contest Extraordinaire." She made sure the disgust was written on her face. "You didn't even *qualify*."

Horror slowly dawned on Evelina's face. "You're not taking the money."

Gillian opened the front door. Ellsberg stood framed there, along with a number of serious people in conservative suits. The suits spilled into the home as if pulled by gravity.

"Who are you people?" Evelina mustered some indignity, but the words were laced with nervous tremors. "Get out of my house."

The intruders streamed past Gillian with quiet deliberation. They took Evelina by the arm and steered her away from the exit. The woman was trapped, defanged. Gillian expected a flush of satisfaction, but any joy she found was similar to the Contest's end, when she'd separated the fox keys. Victory that wasn't victory.

What would Sebastian do now? Sebastian in his flat cap and shiny buttons. His pointed shoes and tiny little teeth. Foxes were opportunistic hunters. They'd eat whatever it took to survive.

Gillian went to the front door. Ellsberg caught her at the threshold. "They heard everything."

Her chuckle was forced. "Irony is, she doesn't even have a million dollars."

"You're not happy?"

Gillian shrugged. She looked coldly at the many marked and unmarked cars outside. "Feds aren't going to do anything. They'll chase her for years."

"You did the right thing."

"Sure. But did we get the right person?"

She glanced at Ellsberg. He looked uncomfortable.

Behind him, agents read Evelina her rights and moved throughout the house, looking for answers.

They wouldn't find any. Not here.

Thirty-Nine

The Aerie was unchanged. The mirror, the old clock, the nautical paraphernalia. The books spine-out, the computer monitor, and even Sebastian with his back to the door. Dust motes hung suspended in the air. The office crafted to withstand the tide of outside events, and serve only its creator's whims.

Sebastian pecked at the keys. Momentarily stirred by inspiration, he'd set to typing, then the fount dried up and he'd return to staring at the screen, rubbing the nub of his thumb. He never did explain what happened to the tip. Stories abounded. Devoured by a tiger. Lopped off by a jigsaw. Severed with a paring knife. All the rumors suited him. Unresolved misfortune contributed to his air of mystery.

He knew she was there. She knew he knew she was there.

"Writing your resignation letter?" she asked.

"Quite the contrary." He typed three characters, squinting at the screen. "I'll be taking a more active role. It appears Miscellany languished in the care of my children. Recent events suggest everything I taught was forgotten."

"*Your* children?" Slowly she stepped into the room. "I already have a mother. And a father."

"And I wish you nothing but happiness with them. I hope

you find a place that can competently treat Stephanie's disability."

Sebastian's ten thousand had appeared in Gillian's account. Payment, but also a warning. The calls and texts flooding her phone only moments later. The clinic administrator. Some flunky in Miscellany Legal. Mom was to be evicted from the new facility in days, if not hours. Gillian had to believe she'd find a way to stop it, although she had no idea how.

"We'll manage," she said. "I'll take care of it."

"I'm sure you will."

The picture of the Contestants still sat above his head. It had been disturbed, Gillian was sure, just a touch. There had been nothing to discover, Gillian having removed the USB.

Sebastian's finger repeatedly tapped the delete key. The man unhappy with what he had produced.

"I heard the news," she said. "Season Two is officially canceled."

"That was a non-event. You can't cancel what was never announced."

"What I didn't hear was anything about the Kundojjala School. The first of its kind, you said."

"And it will be. When the time is right." Finally, her words pulled him away from his keyboard. He spun his chair. His face was glacial but there were cracks. Irritation leaking through. He sat there on his throne and dared be irritated Tommy had died. That families like the Navarros had been wrecked. Irritated because concern for human life slowed the delivery of his vision.

Gillian asked, "What was the point?"

The question caught him off guard. He fish-mouthed

until he could summon an answer. "For the children, of course."

He'd recited the folklore so many times, it was possible he even believed it. Gillian herself had been willing to believe again, after so many years.

She drew closer. She could smell his shower soap, something clean and reminiscent of mountain air. But underneath, the stench of sweat. The byproduct of exertion. He worked hard to keep the hustle going.

"We're you," she said. "We're just like you."

"What does that mean?"

"You have these molds. You say you're breaking paradigms. Crossing boundaries and creating new people. But that's a complete lie. You take these kids, these innocent malleable kids, and you shove them into Sebastian-shaped molds. And if they don't fit? If they break? You throw them away and start over."

She wanted him to object. To stand, to pontificate, to offer her a better version of how the pieces fit. The vision was his, after all. No one evangelized the mission like Sebastian. Instead, he dropped his hands loosely into his lap. He stared down at them, as if they had failed. He shook his head. "I never could get through to you."

On the beach, when she'd solved the puzzle and found Sebastian's message, something fundamental inside her had cracked. It had surprised her how much it hurt, after everything. She'd expected to be angry. Expected to hate him. She hadn't expected to miss Sebastian. He'd been there, the version she'd built, for a very long time.

The clock caught her eye. The plumb bob and other assorted props. Performance art, all of it. Theater. But dangerous, to a captive audience.

"They won't let you hurt children," she said. "They'll stop you."

"They?" He laughed an angry laugh. "They who? Miscellany isn't going anywhere. I built an empire from nothing. I've constructed puzzles and games and riddles and mazes and rhymes to entertain millions of children. No gender bias. No racial or economic bias. Any and all welcome to exercise their mind and excel. Released from the shackles of their environment and a society that starts children in a hole. We teach them ABC and 123 and rosey-posey and expect them to grow into anything other than drones? The mind..." He mashed a finger against his skull. "This is the escape. This is the mission. I am sorry you feel used, but I don't need you to thank me. You exist. That's my reward."

For a moment, he had her again. Tugging the bonds of her insecurity. Perhaps he was innocent of what had happened to Tommy. Maybe Evelina concocted the whole plan, and maybe Leah hid the details. But Sebastian's complicity in this plot didn't matter because he was complicit to the bone in all the others. Miscellany the longest con of all.

Worst of all, she knew she'd sign up again. Stand in line to be swindled. At the word of a man who'd appeared onstage and stared at an audience of hundreds and made Gillian believe she was the most important. That he talked only to her.

She couldn't let him into her life. Not even a little bit.

"Miscellany is you," she said. "And it will die with you."

Sebastian's face remained a mask, but around the eyes, he flinched. Gillian had hurt him, as he'd hurt her. For the first time, the pair truly equals.

When she left, she wondered if his people would be waiting, like all those years ago. Security ready to escort her from the grounds. But no one touched her. They let her walk loose and unfettered into the world.

Forty

The car had been arranged by Ellsberg and waited in the same spot where she'd been dropped off. The driver was a gravel-voiced man who resembled Santa Claus, should he drop a hundred pounds and take up a beard-yellowing pack-a-day habit. Santa seemed content for her to sling her bag in the trunk without any fussing. Gillian appreciated that.

Ellsberg waited by the car. He clutched another daily puzzle challenge in his hands and scratched away madly. Gillian came to his shoulder and watched him work.

"20 across is Brian Eno."

"Thank you. I'm aware of that."

"You haven't filled it in."

"It's not a competition. I'll get to it in a moment."

"It's always a competition." But Gillian chased the comment with a smile, and this time she meant it.

Gillian had hoped Tommy would pull a fast one. Pop out of the car, grinning, yanking off his corpse mask with a *ta-da*, having once again beaten her to the punch. Unfortunately, the back seat remained empty. It was only her and Ellsberg.

"I'm truly going to miss this part," she said.

"Busting my balls?"

She laughed. "Yes, exactly that."

He slipped the pen behind his ear. "What's next for you?"

"Not driving cars again." She watched Santa hawk a yellow glob of mucus onto the ground, then shake loose a cigarette. "At least, not without a better plan."

"The great Gillian Charles planning and scheming?" Ellsberg seemed loose. Funning with her as if he was two decades younger. "The world should watch itself."

She wanted to believe him. But she had no plan for Mom, let alone herself. "That's the kind of confidence boost I need."

Ellsberg pursed his lips. Studied her like she was a new crossword to solve. "Might I make a suggestion?"

The old wariness returned, but Ellsberg's face was smooth and open. And Gillian was too raw to consider new betrayals. "Have at it."

"The Big Idea Competition."

Gillian was familiar. An entrepreneurial competition for alumni and students of UT Dallas. "I didn't attend UTD."

"You, of all people, should realize exceptions can be made. But influence aside, the event is most important as a circulator for money. More venture capital running around than clowns at a circus. Mark Cuban was a judge last year."

The sun cast Miscellany-shaped shadows over the parking lot. Gillian turned and took in the great wall and towering spires. From here, thank Christ, she couldn't see Sebastian's face. He'd be watching, though.

She'd come here to make things better for Mom. With Miscellany against her, things would certainly be worse. But Gillian had faced long odds before. She and her family fighters long before the Contest, and since. If Ellsberg's Big Idea wasn't the path to victory, then others would follow. Inroads she could make without Sebastian. MacArthur

Genius Grant. Her LA contacts. The hotel valets who ferried Dallas money hither and yon. Anyone who didn't live in a tower and speak in riddles. Like Tommy had said, her relationships would open doors. Her mouth could do the rest.

A glance again up high. Walking out had established the nature of Gillian's relationship with Sebastian, but she hadn't cut the ties that bind. That would take more work, and it might never happen. She'd be damned if she wouldn't try.

She needn't try alone.

"Come work with me," she said.

Ellsberg dropped his pamphlet. "What?"

Her heart skipped a beat. Yes. Yes to this.

"Come work with me."

The offer sent him a tad cross-eyed. "Selling scarves?"

"What are you afraid of? Sebastian? Why does he get to be the gatekeeper? He doesn't own our dreams, not even close. We competed in the Contest. One kid in a million got there, and not even half did as well as you and I. Together, without him in the way..." Had she been walking, she'd have strut. "Not a soul on this planet could stop us."

He let out a gust of air. "That sounds risky."

"You're not wrong. It's risky as hell."

He worked his jaw like he was chewing walnuts. "What would we do?"

"The better question is what *won't* we do."

He liked her answer. A devilish grin tickled the corner of his mouth. "And the money?"

Her smile froze. She wouldn't Sebastian him. Honesty, first and foremost. "Ellsberg, I have no idea."

The truth sobered him. He straightened. Nodded. He

looked up at the blue sky and the white fluffy clouds. There was a darker cloud on the horizon. Where it was headed, difficult to tell.

He said, "I know how to find you."

It was hard not to be disappointed. She'd very quickly seized on the image of the two of them, driving off into the sunset to accomplish great things. But he had to come of his own accord. Otherwise, what she said meant nothing. She stuck out her hand. "You can try."

He smiled. Gave her hand a firm shake. Then he scooped his puzzle off the ground and strolled back to Miscellany as if he had all the time in the world.

Gillian got in the car. Nicotine Santa stubbed out his cigarette and heaved himself into the front seat. A Christmas tree air freshener swung to and fro on the rearview mirror. She half expected a tipsy reindeer to fall across the hood.

"You work at that puzzle place?" His Deep South accent was deceptively comforting. The kind of lulling cadence that might convince you to set aside your better judgment, ultimately trapping you in some swindle.

She decided she liked hick Santa Claus. "Nope. Just here for a visit."

He put the car in Drive. "Business or pleasure?"

She considered. "Little of both. Kind of a… reunion."

"Oh, the contest thing. I heard about that on NPR."

She loved that he listened to NPR.

"So the contest," he said. "Did you win?"

All those years ago Sebastian denied Gillian victory, or so she'd always told herself. But she'd invested him with that power. She'd taken every missed opportunity – every bicycle they couldn't afford, every school she couldn't attend, every job she didn't land – and bound up those failures into the one moment when she hadn't danced fast enough for Sebastian Luna. She was never going to dance fast enough. But maybe she didn't have to.

Did she win?

Gillian smiled, and gave the man his answer.

Acknowledgments

More people go into the process of making a book than I can say. I'll try anyway.

To my wife Karen, who endured much, including go-nowhere stories about writing. I swear the process is more interesting than it sounds.

To my kids Rachel, Riley and Sean. You didn't contribute to this book, but I love you anyway.

To my mom, who repeatedly asked when this book was coming out in hardback. No, Mom, you can't "just pay them to do it".

To my writing pals from Viable Paradise, the Cord, or wherever. Most especially Stephen Blackmoore and Hector Acosta, who graciously read early versions of this book. I'd bury bodies for you guys. Metaphorically…

To Lisa Rodgers, my agent. This book doesn't exist without you. I wish I could say the next time will be easier, but we know better.

To Gemma Creffield and everyone at Datura. You believed in me and this book. At least before you read the burying bodies bit.

And to everyone else who helped make this book possible. What did you do? Maybe you just stayed out of the way. For that, I thank you.

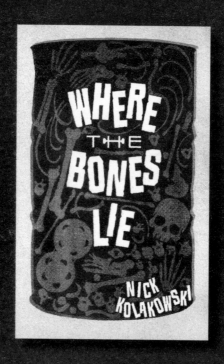

Manny found me after my set on the *Giggle Lounge*'s second stage, the smaller one where they dump the newbies and terminally unfunny. I was working on new material but nobody in the audience laughed until I made jokes about traffic. When all else fails, you can always joke about traffic and Angelenos will at least give you a chuckle, even the hipsters from Silver Lake who work from home and travel around on electric scooters.

"You really bombed," Manny said. He had followed me from the stage to the far end of the bar, where he cornered me against the wall – one of his classic moves, allowing him to use his massive girth to its most intimidating effect. "They pay you for that?"

"They pay me in alcohol," I said, shoving a free drink ticket at the bartender, who retaliated with a watered-down rum and Coke. "Why are you here, Manny? You finally develop a sense of humor?"

"I got a sense of humor. I hired you, remember?" He jabbed a finger at my neon-orange Hawaiian shirt. "I also remember when you, the great Dash Fuller, the terror of paparazzi everywhere, used to wear lovely suits instead of that abomination."

"Helps me blend with this crowd," I said, noting how Manny's two-piece Tom Ford suit was impeccable as usual, but his dress shirt was wrinkled around the collar. Given his intense dedication to always looking faultless – *my image is the job*, he liked to say – it was a startling flaw. Something big was distracting him.

"Maybe it's time for you to unleash the bespoke," he said. "I have an urgent quest for you."

"I quit, remember? I'd rather dunk my head in a barrel of fire ants."

"Oh, stop being dramatic. We need someone who's not on the payroll. The scumbags are all over this one."

"Not interested," I said, draining the drink. Onstage, a shaggy dude in a Scooby-Doo t-shirt launched into his first joke of the night, about the ghost of Marlon Brando watching a Marvel movie. He was unfunny enough to make me feel better about my own performance.

"Yeah, like your standup career is going so well," Manny snorted. "Come on, we both know you could use the cash. And you won't have to hurt anyone this time. Promise."

I considered it. It was five days until the end of the month, and I was down to a couple hundred dollars in my bank account. I had originally planned to re-download the usual gig apps and spend fifteen hours a day delivering food and driving people around until I could cover my rent. I preferred gigging for ZoomFood, a local app that paid a great rate but forced its drivers to wear a purple vest and baseball cap stamped with its yellow 'Z' logo, a humiliating costume I kept wadded in the corner of my car trunk. A job with Manny could spare me that exhausting fate.

I didn't want to dip a toe back into his swamp.

But I didn't want to end up on Skid Row, either.

"Half in advance," I said, already hating myself. "And if I don't like where the job is going, I'm keeping the cash and walking away. Can you live with that?"

Manny nodded. "It'll have to do. I'm not explaining the job here. Come outside with me."

"Why? It's a hundred degrees out."

"More like eighty. Don't tell me you've gone soft like all these twits in here."

"Careful," I said, gesturing for him to lead the way to the doors. "They're very sensitive."

We exited the *Giggle Lounge*. The air smelled faintly of smoke and the night sky had an orange tint. There was a fire in the rolling hills near the Getty Center, three hundred acres burned and counting, powered by the Santa Ana winds. As we stepped beyond the club's bubble of air conditioning, the heat was like a feverish hand over my face.

Manny's blue Mercedes SUV sat at the far end of the parking lot. He unlocked it to disable the alarm before leaning against the driver's side door and pulling a vape from his suit pocket and sucking on it. "I get the comedy thing. It's the girls, right?" he said, blowing a cloud of apple-scented vapor. "You're still relatively young. You can score those hipster chicks, they're fit from all that Pilates, they'll do anything to show they're marriage material. It's got to be that. It's sure as hell not the money. How much does the average comedian make? A buck-ninety?"

"Instead of exposing me to your grodiest fantasies," I said, "how about you tell me what the wonderful world of Hollywood PR needs tonight?"

"Okay." He blew a cloud of apple-scented vapor. "You follow Karl Quaid on social media?"

"I don't do social media, remember?"

"Oh yeah, you're one of the few smart people on that front, I forget. But even in your precious bubble, you know about the Karl Quaid situation, right?"

I nodded. How could I not? Karl Quaid was the front-page story on every tabloid website from here to Karachi. The studio had structured a superhero franchise around his performance as Doppler, a heroic vampire with the powers of eco-location and flight, and the first two movies had racked up almost two billion dollars at the box office. Of course, that was before Quaid went nuts.

"As of now, Karl's officially crossed the line from weirdo to dangerous," Manny said, taking another hit of nicotine. "Filming on the next movie starts in three weeks, and nobody can find the guy. One of the biggest stars in the world, and he disappears, poof. What makes it even worse is–"

"News said he's got that actress with him, right?" I said. "The parents are upset?"

"Amber Rodney, yeah, and the shooting on her new show kicks off in a month. Thank everything holy she's a couple years too old to be jailbait, but her parents are threatening to sue the studio, and so's the streamer producing her show. That's not even the worst of it. Karl's posting about crazy Jonestown stuff – demons run the world, everyone needs to commit suicide at the same time, one big adios to save the environment. Police are getting a little too interested."

"And you can't find him?" I grinned, enjoying Manny's discomfort. "Even with all his posting?"

"No. He's smart enough to never post a photo of a place we recognize. It's not a criminal investigation, technically, so we can't get a court order for the location metadata. I got people sitting outside his houses – he's got three, if you're wondering. We're watching his mom in Utah, his sister in Colorado, anyone else he usually hangs out with. Nothing."

"And you think I can do something."

The front doors of the *Giggle Lounge* crashed open, ejecting a crowd of drunken twentysomethings into the parking lot. Manny quieted until they stumbled past. "You were my best guy," he said, not quite meeting my eyes. "Look, I'm sorry how it ended. I shouldn't have asked you to do certain things. But I appreciated it, and I know the studios did, as well. This situation with Karl, it won't be like the old days. We need fresh eyes on it."

"Ten thousand," I said.

"You don't come cheap," he said.

"You're well aware of what I can do."

"Sure, but I can't do that amount. How about four?" He nodded at my ancient Nissan Altima in the far corner of the lot, beyond the flickering edge of the *Giggle Lounge*'s neon lights, where I'd parked it in the forlorn hope that the shadows would cloak its rusted panels, the dented driver's door, the sky-blue paint bleached in odd patterns by years of fierce sun.

"I can't believe you're driving that," he said, "instead of that beautiful Benz you used to have."

"I couldn't deal with the Benz," I said.

"Then upgrade to something that doesn't burn as much oil as gas, mother of God. Please tell me it's got more power than a Prius," he said, and winked.

"Ten grand," I said again, before dropping into a passable Liam Neeson imitation: "You need my very particular set of skills."

We regarded each other. Manny's gaze was like a laser heating flesh, and the longer I stayed within its focus, the harder it was to keep my face stony and my eyes neutral. Except I was tough enough to win this round. He notched his head to the left, his laser drifting to the front of the club, and said, "Fine."

"Half in advance."

He patted his jacket. "Got it right here. Figured you'd drive a hard bargain."

"Plus expenses." Maybe I couldn't tell a joke that brought down the house, but I could leverage a desperate soul.

He raised a hand. "Just a couple hundred bucks at most. I won't give you more leash than that. You know what you'd do with it."

Yes, something unbearably stupid. Deep in the tailspin of my former life, I'd tried to expense a bad weekend in Vegas. Studio accounting is a wiggly game, and its high priests ensure even the biggest blockbuster never earns a profit on paper, and yet they'd objected to my attempt to pass on several thousand dollars in liquor and gambling expenses. Nor had Manny appreciated my joke about itemizing Krystal (the champagne) and Krystal (the stripper).

"Fine," I said. "But I'm not signing anything. No NDAs, no non-disparage agreements. I'll never talk."

"Yes, yes, okay. I love how you get more annoying with age."

"Making sure we're clear."

Manny puffed again, tilting his head to follow the roaring lights of a 747 descending toward LAX. I wondered if he regretted his choice of profession. I could have told him that quitting feels liberating at first, but the memories never leave. I had cracked the heads of hangers-on who'd leaked to the press, stolen phones and laptops from expensive villas, rescued kidnapped dogs, and escorted pregnant girlfriends onto buses bound for Omaha, all so the studios could keep their stars untarnished and the money rolling in. How do you ever scrub clean of that?

And now they wanted me back in.

I hated how that idea made my stomach tingle, but I couldn't deny a part of me had always loved the hunt.

Manny prodded my elbow with a thick envelope. "Here's the first payment," he said. "You know the drill: absolute discretion. You find Karl, you call me immediately, and only me. You got it? Silence, cunning, and deceit."

DATURA BOOKS
catering to the armchair detective,
budding codebreakers, the repeat
offender and an emerging younger
readership.

Check out our website at
www.daturabooks.com to see our entire
catalogue.

Follow us on social media:
Twitter @daturabooks
Instagram @daturabooks
TikTok @daturabooks